Praise for *Swann's*

"From Manhattan to Coney Island to the steamy shores of Alabama, Charles Salzberg delivers a top-flight mystery with his latest Henry Swann outing. Highly recommended."
—Tom Straw, *New York Times* bestselling author as Richard Castle

"Psychics, double-crosses, missing persons—Charles Salzberg's latest Henry Swann book has it all. Whether this is your first Swann adventure or the latest, you won't want to miss the brass-knuckle punch that is *Swann's Down*."
—Alex Segura, author of *Blackout* and *Dangerous Ends*

"Swann's wry wit, quotes from authors and philosophers, genius for questioning suspects, and dark past make him a character readers will follow anywhere as he seeks his quarry. This is another thrilling addition to this excellent series."
—Rich Zahradnik, Shamus Award-winning author of *Lights Out Summer*

"Fast. Funny. And smart. This time out, Swann crosses paths with a psycho hitman, a phony psychic and Swann's mysterious partner, a disbarred lawyer. Who could ask for more? I hope we'll see a lot more of Swann in the future and that this isn't Swann's swan song."
—Paul D. Marks, Shamus Award-winning author of *White Heat* and *Broken Windows*

SWANN'S DOWN

CHARLES SALZBERG

SWANN'S DOWN

A Henry Swann Mystery

Down & Out Books
3959 Van Dyke Road, Suite 265
Lutz, FL 33558
DownAndOutBooks.com

The characters and events in this book are fictitious. Any similarity to real persons, living or dead, is coincidental and not intended by the author.

Cover design by JT Lindroos

ISBN: 1-64396-011-3
ISBN-13: 978-1-64396-011-1

"The fault, dear Brutus, is not in our stars,
But in ourselves, that we are underlings."
—William Shakespeare, *Julius Caesar*

"There are more things in heaven and earth, Horatio,
Than are dreamt of in your philosophy."
—William Shakespeare, *Hamlet*

"Corruption, embezzlement, fraud, these are all characteristics
which exist everywhere. It is regrettably the way
human nature functions, whether we like it or not."
—Alan Greenspan

"A psychic reading is not just about career opportunities,
good fortune or meeting tall, dark strangers. It is
a sacred portal to manifesting your true destiny."
—Anthon St. Maarten

1
THE AGE OF AQUARIUS

"We're partners, right?"

Nothing good can come from that question when it comes from the mouth of Goldblatt.

"I mean, all for one and one for all, am I right?" he quickly added in an attempt, I was sure, to seal the deal.

"I think you're confusing us with the three musketeers. May I point out there are only two of us, and I'm afraid that's not the only fallacy in your declaration. But you might as well finish what you've started."

We were having our weekly Friday lunchtime sit-down to discuss what Goldblatt likes to refer to as "business." I have another name for it: waste of time.

Our venue changes from week to week but the concept is always pretty much the same: a cheap diner-slash-coffee shop somewhere on the island of Manhattan. Today's eatery of choice (Goldblatt's choice, my destiny) is the Utopia Diner, on Amsterdam, near Seventy-second Street. And as for the business we'd just finished discussing, well, to be honest, there never is much actual business to discuss and today was no exception.

At this particular moment, we were going through a bit of a dry spell, which always makes me a little nervous because no matter how much I banish it from my mind, the rent is due the first of every month and at least three times a day I seem to develop a hunger that must be quenched. Still, a good fifteen, twenty years away from Social Security, and with precious little dough in the bank—okay, let's be honest, no dough in the bank—and no 401(k) to fall back on, I need to keep working. And, as much as I don't like to admit it, lately it's been my "partner," as he likes to refer to himself, as opposed to my preferred "albatross," who's brought in the bulk of our clients.

We'd already finished eating—though technically, Goldblatt never actually finishes eating which means a meal can easily turn into an all-day affair if I don't apply the brakes—and we were just waiting for the check to arrive. This is a crucial point of any meal with Goldblatt because it is the opening gambit in what has become our weekly routine of watching the check sit there in no-man's land somewhere between us until I inevitably give in, pick it up, and pay. Otherwise, I risk one of two things: either we'd be there all afternoon or, worst-case scenario, Goldblatt will decide he's still hungry and threaten to order something else. Neither of these options is the least bit appealing.

"I'll get right to the point," he said.

Just then, out of the corner of my eye, I spotted the waiter, like a white knight, approaching with our check in hand. If I acted quick enough I might be able to get out of there before being sucked into something I don't want to have anything to do with.

"That would be nice," I said, reaching for my wallet. "What is your point?"

"I need to hire you."

I was stopped in my tracks before I got my wallet halfway out of my back pocket.

"Really? To do what?"

"I want you to find someone for me. Well, to be more precise, it's not really for me. It's for my ex-wife."

Wait a minute! Goldblatt married? Goldblatt with a wife? Goldblatt a husband? This was a new one on me, something I'd never even considered.

"You...you've been married?" I stammered.

Truth is, I never pictured Goldblatt being in any relationship other than with, yes, as irritating as it might be, me. I mean the guy isn't exactly anyone's idea of Don Juan, although I suppose in theory there are women who might find him if not attractive in the conventional way, at least interesting in a specimen-under-glass way. Or maybe as a project. Women love a project. They love a challenge. They love the idea that they have the opportunity to remake a man in their image. Maybe that was it. But whatever it was, my world was shaken to the core. And what would shake it even more would be to find that he was a father, too. But one shock per meal is more than enough, so there was no chance I was going to pursue that line of questioning.

"Unfortunately, the answer is yes. More than once, in fact."

"Holy cow," I blurted out, channeling the Scooter. "You're kidding me?"

At this point the same bald, squat waiter who seemed to serve us in every diner we patronized, reached our table and dropped the check right in front of me.

"This is not something a man usually kids about."

"How many times?"

He held up three fingers.

"Three times! You've been married three times?"

"Yeah."

I gulped.

"Are you married now?"

He shook his head. "Nah. I'm kinda between wives. Giving it a rest, if you know what I mean. But chances are I'll be back in the saddle again soon enough."

"Okay, so let me get this straight. You've been married three times and now you're single but you would consider getting married again?"

"Man is not meant to be alone, Swannie. You might consider the possibility that your life would be enriched if you found your soul mate."

You're fortunate if you find one soul mate in life and I'd

already had mine. She was yanked from my life as a result of a freak accident, a matter of being in the wrong place at the wrong time. I didn't know if Goldblatt knew the circumstances of her bizarre accidental death, but I wouldn't have been surprised because he seemed to know a lot of things he had no business knowing.

"Some men are meant to be alone, Goldblatt. I'm one of them and after three failed marriages, maybe you should consider the possibility you are, too."

He smiled and puffed out his chest. "What can I say, Swann? I'm a friggin' babe magnet."

I would have laughed, should have laughed, but I was still processing the scary fact that he'd been married three times. That meant there were three women in the world who not only were willing to marry him but *did* marry him. I wanted to know more. Much more. Everything, in fact. But this was not the time and certainly not the place to delve into Goldblatt's mysterious, sordid past. Nevertheless, I promised myself I would revisit this topic in the not too distant future.

Still in shock, I avoided our weekly "who's paying for this meal" tango, grabbed the check and reached for my wallet... again.

"So, wanna know the story?" he asked.

"Which story would that be?"

"The story of why I want to hire you?"

"Desperately."

"It's for Rachel. She was my second wife. The best of the lot, actually. Sweet kid. We had our problems, that's for sure, and maybe I should've stuck with it. You know, like given it more of a chance."

"It's a little late for regrets, isn't it?" I said, but Goldblatt wasn't listening. His head was cocked to one side and his eyes rolled up in their sockets. It was obvious his mind was off in the ether somewhere, strolling down Memory Lane, I assumed.

"How long were you married?"

"Let's see." He closed his eyes and started counting on his fingers. His eyes snapped open. "Technically, I guess it was a little more than six months."

"Six months? You call that a marriage?"

"It was legal, if that's what you mean."

"And exactly what do you mean by 'technically'?"

"I mean we were together for a few months before we actually got hitched, and then we were legally married for maybe three months before the annulment…"

"You got an annulment?"

"Not me. Her. I woulda stuck it out a while longer. You know, I'm really a traditional kind of guy. But she needed an annulment. Something to do with the church. It woulda looked bad on her record if she got a divorce. I guess Jesus don't much like the idea of divorce. Mumbo jumbo, as far as I'm concerned. But I went along with the annulment thing. What'd I care? Remember, I'm a lawyer. I know all about legal fictions."

"Why?"

"Why what?"

"Why'd she dump you?"

"I'm really not fond of the word 'dump.' I prefer, parting of the ways. Or, better yet, we had different priorities. It's complicated and kind of personal."

"Of course, it's personal. That's why I want to know."

"Yeah, well, maybe some other time."

"Man, this is a little too much to digest all at once, so we might as well skip to the part where you need to hire me."

"Yeah, right. None of the rest is important. Anyway, Rachel, that's her name. Did I already say that?"

I nodded.

"She's a real sweet kid, but she's always been kinda, shall we say, naïve…you know, trusting. Too trusting, if you ask me. And she's also a bit woo-woo, you know, out there." He waved his hands and rolled his eyes, aiming them up toward the ceiling that was blocking the way to heaven, which I presume was what he was shooting for.

"What's that supposed to mean?"

"You know, like what do they call it?" He snapped his fingers. "New Agey. That's it. She believes in all that bullshit like astrology, tarot cards, tea leaves, all that spiritual garbage. She wouldn't marry me while Mercury was in retrograde. I don't even know what the hell that means but hey, it wasn't like I was in a hurry to tie the knot."

"I thought you were a traditionalist?"

"That doesn't mean I was stupid. You gotta get to really know a person before you take a step like that."

"You took it three times."

"No one's perfect, Swann."

I'm sure we could have gone on like this all afternoon, but I had better things to do, which meant just about anything else.

"Let's get on with it," I said, tossing my credit card on top of the check. It's always a crapshoot as to whether or not I've reached my credit limit, but since I'd uncharacteristically paid it off a couple weeks earlier after a minor payday, I figured I was in the clear. Goldblatt had been making noises for several weeks about getting a "company" card, "for tax purposes," he explained. But I didn't see him making a move to apply for one and I sure as hell wasn't going to sign on for a card where I'd be on the hook for any expenses he chalked up.

"So," he continued, "not long ago, she goes off on this trip to San Francisco. You know, one of those things where she's gonna find herself. Anyway, she's hanging out in that old hippie district..."

"Haight-Ashbury."

"Yeah, that's it. She meets this guy. Nice guy, she says. Turns out he's into the same shit she is and he's even from back here. He's out there for the same reason she is: to find himself. I guess there are lots of lost people out there, right? Anyway, she likes him a lot and he likes her well enough so when they get back here to the city, they start to go out. After a couple dates she falls for him. Hard. According to her, he falls hard, too. One night they have this date to go dancing downtown only he doesn't show. She gets worried, 'cause she says that's not like him. She keeps calling, but he doesn't answer. She leaves messages. He doesn't call back. What can she do? She figures he skipped out on her. She's heartbroken, of course, but what can she do? A week or so later she gets a call from some woman. Says she's his sister. Kate something or other. Tells Rachel her brother died."

"Died?"

"Yeah."

"Murdered?"

"Nah. She says natural causes. Heart attack or something sudden like that. She tells Rachel he went just..." Goldblatt snapped his fingers, "like that. Poor kid. She can't even go to the funeral because it's already over. They cremated the body, so she doesn't even have a grave she can visit."

"Sad story, but would you please get to the point where you tell me why you need to hire me."

"Keep your shirt on. I'm getting there. So, he croaks and she's heartbroken, I mean really torn up. Bad. She's an emotional chick anyway but I've never seen her that bad. She loses weight 'cause she's not eating. She can't get out of bed and when she does she barely makes it to the couch. She sleeps most of the day. You know the drill. She's so depressed she goes to a shrink. He gives her a prescription for one of those antidepressants. Doesn't work. She don't know what to do with herself so she winds up wandering the streets. Day, night, it don't matter. She's out there looking for something but she doesn't know what it is."

"There's an end to this story, right?"

"Yeah. I'm getting there. Anyway, she figures the only way to snap out of this is to maybe reconnect with him in some way, so she calls his sister. She talks to her and it seems to help a little 'cause Rachel starts to feel connected to the dead guy. They call back and forth a couple, few times. You know, like they become telephone pals. One day, when she tells his sister she's still feeling really down about the whole thing, the sister mentions this fortune teller named Madame Sofia. She tells Rachel how she went to her when their father died and how she really helped by giving her closure. Don't you fucking hate that word? Like it's some kind of real estate deal. Anyway, Rachel, who believes in this kind of crap, decides she's gonna try it too."

"You mean going to this fortune teller?"

"Yeah, that's right. Like I told you, Rachel's not only a little spacey but by this point she's pretty desperate. I mean, when better living through chemistry doesn't work, what else is there? She's willing to try anything to get rid of the pain, right? Even something like this. So, she goes to this fortune teller and this chick tells Rachel she can make contact with the guy."

"The dead guy?"

"Yeah. Right. The dead guy. Now you gotta understand this about Rachel. She believes we don't really die when we leave this mortal coil. She believes in an afterlife. Like, we don't really die we just move on to 'another room.'"

"Another room?"

"Yeah. Like another dimension, maybe. You don't really die, according to Rachel, you just move to another place. It can be a better place or it can be a worse place. But it's a different place. So, this fortune teller supposedly finds the 'room' this guy has moved on to and she supposedly makes contact with him."

"Makes contact?"

"Yeah."

"And Rachel believes this?"

He nods. "She believes, all right. Now Rachel may be woo-woo, but she's not stupid. She had to be convinced, but she was. Evidently, according to Rachel, this Madame Sofia knows stuff about the dude and about her and him that she couldn't possibly know."

"Like what?"

"You'll have to ask Rachel. But evidently it was enough to convince her that the chick really has made contact. At the end of that first session she tells Rachel she can only continue if Rachel can come up with some dough."

"Big surprise."

"Yeah."

"How much?"

"Like twenty-five grand."

"You're kidding?"

"I wish I was."

"For what?"

Goldblatt, the man of a thousand faces, made one of them. "You're gonna love this one. It's for a fucking 'time machine.'"

I couldn't help myself. I laughed. But Goldblatt, dead serious and not too happy about the situation, wasn't laughing with me.

"You're serious, aren't you?"

"Like a heart attack. You and I know it was for that trip around the world and a Rolex watch and maybe a diamond pendant but Rachel, by this time she's under some kind of spell. She's bought everything this gypsy woman told her, hook, line, and sinker."

"Didn't she question the money thing?"

"Nope. She rationalizes. Tells herself, 'everyone has to make a living.' Me, I look at it as a killing, not a living."

"And Rachel was able to come up with the dough?"

"She was. And a lot more. Because you know the drill. Once you're on the line, they're not about to let you off the hook."

"Where was she getting the money?"

"Inheritance from her father. He was some kind of big-shot lawyer. He died before I met her. That's probably why she married me. You know, what with me being a lawyer and all. Maybe she connected me with her dead father."

The idea that Goldblatt could remind anyone of their father struck me as odd at best, but women are a strange lot. As Freud said, "women, what do they want?" In this case, at least for a few months, I guess it was Goldblatt."

"What was this so-called time machine supposed to do?"

"It wasn't an actual time machine. You know, one of those H.G. Wells thingies that's supposed to send you back in time. It was some kind of otherworldly apparatus that was supposed to make a clear connection between them while he's in this other 'room.' I'm sure you know what comes next."

"The time machine isn't quite enough, right?"

"Bingo. She asks Rachel for another twenty-five grand."

"For?"

"Now that she's made contact, she needs to build what she calls a 'golden bridge' across the dimensions, so Rachel can 'visit' the 'room' where this guy is parked, probably for eternity."

"Give me a break."

"Yeah, real *Twilight Zone* stuff. But Rachel bought it. She believed she could actually communicate with the dead guy."

"So, she came up with the dough?"

"Yeah. But now when she sees nothing's happening, she starts getting a little suspicious."

"About time."

"You're telling me. So, she tells me the whole story and wants to know if I think maybe something's fishy. I practically have a fucking heart attack...I mean, that's a shitload of dough."

"And here I would've bet it was food that was gonna get you."

"Very funny. Anyway, she starts crying, because in her heart she knew all this was just a load of bullshit. But the poor kid was lonely and she wasn't thinking straight. She feels worse now that she was taken for such a sucker so she makes me promise to get her money back."

"Which is where I come in."

"Right. I could probably do it myself but if I found this quack I'd probably kill her."

"What do you mean, 'find her'?"

"You don't think after taking Rachel for all that dough she's gonna stick around, do you? Rachel goes back to the storefront to confront her to try to get her money back and abracadabra," he snapped his fingers, "she's gone."

"Storefront?"

"Yeah. She worked out of one over on First Avenue, near the Fifty-ninth Street Bridge, or whatever they're calling it now. Only it's not there anymore."

"What do you mean it's not there anymore?"

"It's a Subway sandwich shop now. So, partner, you gotta help me out by helping Rachel out."

My gut response was to say no. I didn't want to get involved in Goldblatt's life any more than I had to. Besides, this sounded like a no-win situation. The chances of finding this woman were pretty slim, the chances of getting the dough back even slimmer. But I knew I couldn't say no to Goldblatt. It wasn't just that we were partners, even though the idea of that turned my stomach, it was that he'd helped me out in the past and although I would never admit it to him, I did owe him something. And it might give me a unique opportunity to find out more about Goldblatt, My Man of Mystery.

But if I took this on, I had to set firm ground rules because if I didn't, he'd be hovering over me like a helicopter mom, second-guessing my every move. Getting all up in my face.

"When can I meet with Rachel?"

"I'll give her a call and set it up."

"Just give me her number and I'll take care of it."

"And you'll let me know so I can be there, right?"

"You'll just get in the way."

"She'll be much more comfortable with me in the room. Otherwise, she'll clam up and you won't get anything from her."

"I wouldn't worry about that. I'm pretty good at getting people to give me what I need."

"She don't know you, Swann. She's skittish."

"Look, Goldblatt, this is nonnegotiable. Either I meet Rachel alone or you can find someone else to help her."

"You're threatening me?"

"It's not a threat. It's how I conduct business. You want me to do my best, don't you?"

"And your best means I don't tag along?"

"Exactly."

He was thinking it over. I knew this because he grabbed for the last roll in the basket, split it in half, buttered it generously, and took a couple bites. This is what he does when he thinks. Eat.

"Okay. I get it. I don't like it but I get it. But let me talk to her first so she doesn't get spooked."

"Fine by me," I said, trying to remain calm as I imagined the fun that might be in store for me in meeting the former Mrs. Goldblatt.

2
EASY COME, EASY GO

She had a gentle, breathless little girl voice that reminded me of a cross between Jennifer Tilley and Marilyn Monroe singing "Happy Birthday, Mr. President" to JFK in Madison Square Garden. There was a slight hesitation in her speech, like she was a recent stroke victim searching for the right word, when answering simple questions like, "When would you like to meet?" "Uh, anytime is, uh, fine, with, uh, me." "Where would you like to meet?" "Uh, anywhere is fine, uh, fine with, uh, me."

Fine so long as it was in a public place. So, after way too long negotiating, I wound up agreeing to her suggestion we meet on a park bench on the path that led to the zoo, near the Fifty-ninth street entrance to Central Park, at three o'clock the next afternoon. She was happy with this choice because she said she "loved being around nature." Me, not so much. Nature and me don't always get along. To be honest, I think nature has it in for me. Give me the big city anytime, where the aggression is always in your face, as opposed to sneaking up on you when you least expect it.

Before we met, I spent way too much time constructing a picture in my mind of what this former wife of Goldblatt's would look like. It was a toss-up between mousy and eminently forgettable and tall, blonde, blue-eyed, full-figured, dressed in some outlandishly stylish, baby-doll outfit. As it turned out, it was somewhere in between.

I arrived at the agreed upon bench fifteen minutes early and spent the time watching people pass, trying to guess which one was Rachel. Finally, a few minutes past three, I was pretty sure I spotted her. She was a petite, dark-haired woman wearing blue jeans and a blue hoodie sweatshirt. As she got closer, I could see she was very pretty in that cute, wholesome, Karen Allen way. I'm pretty good at reading faces but even if I weren't, hers was surprisingly easy. Honest. Sad. Confused. Embarrassed. Vulnerable. All adding up to a woman on the edge. I know the species all too well. In fact, over the years I seemed to attract them, both professionally and personally. Now, it appeared as if I had one more to add to my list.

She moved so slow that it seemed as if she were in a trance, completely unaware of what was going on around her. Or maybe she was just preoccupied, thinking of all that dough she gave away. Like a frightened animal, her eyes darted from left to right, then right to left, as if she didn't quite know where to let them settle. And yet it appeared as if she wasn't quite focusing on what she saw. I thought she'd walk right past me, but I was wrong. Instead, she smiled and headed in my direction. When she was a few feet away, I surprised myself by standing and bowing slightly at the waist. It seemed like the right thing to do, but I honestly don't quite know where that came from. I mean, it's not as if I was a graduate of the Emily Post School of Proper Etiquette. Me, who keeps confusing which side of the plate the fork goes on.

"You must be Mr. Henry Swann," she said, extending her hand.

"And you must be Rachel." I took her tiny hand in mine, not knowing if I was going to shake it or kiss it. I chose the former. Even though it was an unusually warm day for late May, her hand was surprisingly cool to the touch.

"That's me. Have a seat. And you can drop the mister stuff."

She nodded and offered a half smile. "Would you mind terribly if we walk a bit? It's such a beautiful day and..." She never finished her sentence, or at least I didn't hear her finish it. Instead, she swiveled her head right then left, as if to see if someone was watching us.

"Sure. Got any particular direction in mind?"

She hesitated a moment. This was a woman who didn't make decisions easily. "Let's walk into the zoo. I loved visiting the animals when I first moved here. They had such a calming effect on me."

"Seeing animals in cages calms you?"

Her face turned red. She got all fluttery. Like Diane Keaton in *Annie Hall*.

"No. No. That's not what I meant. Seeing the animals, realizing I'm not the center of the universe, that's what calms me. I see the animals in their cages then close my eyes and imagine them in their natural habitat."

"I was just kidding, Rachel."

"Oh, sometimes I can't tell when someone's kidding. I think maybe I'm a little too serious. Do you think I'm too serious? I'm afraid I'm always the one who doesn't get the joke. May I tell you something a little crazy?"

"The crazier the better."

"I used to fantasize about breaking in here at night and setting all the animals free."

"I imagine that would create quite a stir."

What I didn't add is that it's always people like me who wind up cleaning the stirs left by people like her.

She smiled. "I know you're kidding, but you know I wouldn't really do it, right?" She stopped and turned toward me. "You do know that, don't you?"

"I do have a sense of humor, Rachel, so the answer is yes. I know you're kidding." I said that but the truth was I didn't know anything of the kind. I was tempted to ask if she talked to the animals, but I was afraid the answer might be yes and then where could we possibly go from there?

"You know, I really appreciate your taking the time to meet with me, Mr. Swann..." I gave her a look. "I mean, Henry. I'm so embarrassed about this whole thing." She buried her head in her hands.

"You're not the first person to be..."

"Suckered?"

"That's not the word I was going to use," I lied. In fact, it was the first word that came to mind.

We started to walk again.

"What word were you going to use, if I may ask?"

"Taken advantage of in a time of deep emotional stress."

"You sound like you've been in therapy."

I shook my head.

"Then you do have a heart."

"Was there a doubt?"

"My husband said you weren't, and these are his words, 'all touchy-feely.'"

"He's right about that. I'm probably the least touchy-feely person you'll ever meet. You still call Goldblatt your husband?"

Her face reddened. "Oh, my, I suppose sometimes I do. I'm sorry about that. I'd say it's force of habit except we were married less than six months and that was over six years ago. I suppose it's because that's pretty much the only context I know him in. We didn't know each other very long before we got married. But he still kind of watches out for me. He's very loyal, you know. His putting you in touch with me is exhibit one of that loyalty. It wasn't his money that was...lost...but he took this very personally. I think he would have gone after the money himself except..."

"Except what?"

"He knew he couldn't be objective. I think he's afraid he'll do something...harsh."

So, was that what all this stuff about the Israeli martial art was about?

"Besides, he thinks the world of you."

That last part hung in the air for an awkward moment. She probably wanted me to return the compliment but for some reason my lips were sealed shut. What I really wanted to do is ask questions to find out more about their relationship. How they met. What attracted her to him. Why they married so quick. But that's not what I was there for, so I restrained myself.

"Look, Rachel, the quicker we get through this, the quicker I can get started. I know this must be uncomfortable for you, and Goldblatt did fill me in on most of it, but I'd rather get the facts straight from you. So, tell me all about it. From the beginning."

And so, as we approached the entrance to the zoo, her voice so low I often had to lean forward to catch what she was saying, she began.

"Last fall I was in a terrible state. My life was falling apart. I'd just lost my job as a translator at the UN and I'd recently broken up with my boyfriend. We'd been together almost a year—well, together and apart and then together again, to be more precise. I finally realized it wasn't going anywhere, but that didn't make it any easier. In fact, it probably made it worse because he was only one more in a long string of..." She stopped and looked up. Her eyes shrunk to pinholes. "Losers." She shook her head. "I hate that word, but that's what they were."

I smiled.

"I don't mean to put my husband in that category..."

I shook my head. "Didn't even cross my mind," though it most certainly did.

She began to walk again, her gaze straight ahead, as if she were walking alone.

"I guess in your line of work, you know what I'm talking about."

"I've come across more than my fair share of them, if that's what you mean. I've learned not to judge too quickly. We all do things we aren't proud of. But I'd be out of business if they weren't plenty of 'losers' out there."

"I had no idea how I was going to put my life back together, or even if I was ever going to be able to put it back together. I wasn't sleeping. I wasn't eating. Basically, I was hardly functioning. I tried just about everything. Therapy. Medication. Meditation. Holistic cures. Yoga. Nothing was working, so I decided I needed to get away. You know, so I could get some perspective and figure out what I was going to do with the rest of my life. So, I went to San Francisco." She stopped and looked at me. "I know what you're thinking."

"What's that?"

"That you can't run away from what's in your own head. All I can say is that when you're in the state I was in, you'll try anything."

I knew what she was talking about. For many, the West Coast is the last stop. A fellow I knew from my days at Columbia, a guy who turned out to be a pretty fair writer, threw himself off the Golden Gate Bridge several years ago. They found his shoes, his wallet, and his eyeglasses set neatly in a pile at the spot where he jumped. No note. No indication as to why he did it. They never found the body. Just like those guys who escaped from Alcatraz back in the early sixties. I indulged in the usual kind of self-examination stuff after something like that happens. Trying to make sense out of something that appears to be a senseless act, a waste of human life. You ask around, and I did, and all you get is, "He seemed so happy." Or, "He didn't seem like the type." But I guess that's the point. There is no type and none of us knows what's really going on in someone else's head. Believe me, I've tried. It's part of my job. Sometimes, if I'm lucky, I get close. But I don't kid myself. Close is about as good as it can get and if I'm lucky, close is enough to get me where I need to be. The truth is, most times I don't even know what's going on in my own head and why I do the things I do. That's what really scares me.

"Goldblatt claims you went there to join some kind of cult."

She made a face, and started walking again.

"That's not true. That was just his interpretation. He's really a very sympathetic and empathetic man, but sometimes he just doesn't get it. The truth is, I went out there to check out something called the Second Lives Institute. Have you heard of it?"

I shook my head.

"It's a relatively new movement that focuses on second chances. So many people get into a rut they can't climb out of. Or they feel they're moving in the wrong direction and don't know how to shift gears. I read about it online and it seemed to make a lot of sense. Once I was out there, I wound up taking a class called 'What comes next?' It was focused on dealing with grief and then moving on, reinventing oneself if necessary."

"Did it help?"

She shook her head. "I was in no condition to sit in a classroom for hours and hours listening to advice I knew wouldn't work. If anything, it was making things worse. I guess life is so much about timing and for me, the timing wasn't right. I was ready to walk away from the whole thing and then I met Michael."

"That's the guy?"

"Yes."

"How'd you meet?"

"At the end of what I thought was going to be my last day in the program, he approached me and asked if I'd like to get coffee. I'd seen him hanging around the institute. I think he may have sat in on the class a couple times. But I hadn't paid much attention to him. I was too much in my own head. Besides, I wasn't in any condition to connect with someone when I couldn't even connect with myself. I'm not even sure why, but I said yes. There was something about him. I don't know what it was. An energy, maybe? We connected immediately. Turns out we had a lot in common. He was in pretty much the same state I was in. His business had recently gone bankrupt. He'd split with his wife. His kids wouldn't talk to him because they blamed him for the marriage breaking up. The way he put it, he was drowning and it really frightened him when he started to think that wouldn't be such a bad thing."

"What do you mean?"

She stopped and turned to face me.

"I mean, drowning. Literally."

"You mean he considered committing suicide?"

"Yes. He said he thought about it and once he started he couldn't stop. But after a while he came to his senses. He realized he couldn't do that to his kids. In the end, he decided it was a selfish act. It might solve *his* immediate problem but it would cause so many other problems for so many other people. I knew exactly what he was feeling because there were times when I was feeling the same way. It's not that I would have actually ended my life. I really wouldn't have gone that far. But I have to admit the idea of going to sleep for a very, very long time, shutting down all the voices in my head, was very appealing."

She paused a moment and faced me again. I could see teardrops beginning to form at the corner of her eyes. She swept them away with the back of her hand, took a deep breath, and continued.

"I hope you don't think I'm crazy."

"I've met plenty of crazy people in my line of work, Rachel, and you're not even in the top hundred."

"That's good to hear. Anyway, we bonded very quickly. He was so smart. And he was very sensitive...but not in that touchy-feely way." She stopped again, turned to me, and smiled. "Like I am, or at least the way I'm accused of being by some people who know me. I fell for him almost immediately. I know what you're thinking. I was vulnerable and that's why. But you'll have to take my word for it that it wasn't that at all. It was real. It would have happened no matter what state I was in. You know how it is, right?"

I nodded as if I did.

"It's a once-in-a-lifetime thing, right?"

"So they say. What about him?"

"He felt the same, at least that's what he said. We had a couple more dates in San Francisco and then when we got back here we began to see each other on a regular basis."

"What'd you do?"

"I don't understand your question."

"What kinds of things did you do together?"

"Oh, you know, regular things. Movies. Dinner. Dancing. Walks in the park. The things people do when they're getting to know each other. The same things you probably did."

She had no idea the kinds of things I did and I wasn't about to tell her. Suffice it to say, my courtship was nothing like those romantic, Hollywood movies.

"Tell me all you can about him. What did he look like? How old was he? What did he do for a living?"

"Why do you need to know all this? I mean, how is this going to help me get my money back?"

"I ask a lot of questions, Rachel, because it helps get me where I have to go. It's the way I work. I need to piece together a whole picture in my head. It's how I make sense of things that otherwise make no sense at all. It's like what novelists do for the characters they write, and actors do for the characters they play. They build them from scratch. They have to know everything about them, much more than they put on the page or on stage. They need to know how they'll act and react in any situation. So, they're continually constructing them, layer upon layer, until they breathe on their own, until they become real. The more I know about everything in your life during this period, the easier it's going to be for me to figure things out, which means the closer I'll get to finding Madame Sofia and possibly getting your money back."

"Do you really think you can?"

I shrugged.

"Have you ever been married?" she asked.

I nodded.

"Do you have children?"

I had to stop her there. Not only because I wasn't there to talk about me—I never like to talk about me—but because it was not a subject I wanted to talk about period. If I did, I'd have to think about my son and my missed connections with him and about what a rotten father I was and what a rotten human being that made me. No good could come from that. For either of us. Especially me.

"Listen, Rachel, we're getting way off track, so let's just get this done, okay?"

"Oh, of course. I'm so sorry. I guess I was starting to forget why we were here. I mean, you're so easy to talk to it was almost as if we're on..." She stopped herself before she could say the word "date." I was glad she did. It only would have embarrassed both of us.

"You wanted to know more about Michael, didn't you?"

"That's right."

"His name was Michael Stephenson and he was a few years older than I am. He was about six feet tall, a little on the chunky side. Not fat, you understand, but he could have stood to lose a few pounds, I guess. I used to kid him about it, though I like a man with a little heft on him."

I smiled. That might explain Goldblatt.

"He wasn't classically handsome. You know, one of those pretty-boy types. But there was something very appealing to me about his face. I guess that made him handsome to me. He resembled that actor, what's his name? Oh, yes, Oliver Platt."

I knew who that was and I wouldn't consider him handsome. But women's idea of handsome and men's idea of handsome rarely coincide. You ask a woman and they'll tell you it's a reflection of a man's insides. Men aren't that evolved . We rarely consider that when we think about appearances. It's that "inner glow" thing we just don't get. In the end, it's always that "a pretty girl who naked is/is worth a million statues" thing.

"Michael had a daughter and a son. She's eight or nine and he's a couple years younger. Michael worked in the family business. They owned several of those mailbox-package storefronts. You know the ones I mean, right?"

I nodded.

"But once the internet took hold there wasn't much need for them anymore. People were ordering things off the web and having them delivered straight to their homes or offices and so one by one they had to close the stores. That was devastating for Michael, not only because he lost his livelihood but because his father did, too. And when his father couldn't find a job, he fell into a deep depression. Michael told me he became suicidal and eventually, they had to institutionalize him. I think that's why he was so frightened of those self-destructive impulses he was feeling. He thought it might be genetic."

"The depression?"

"Yes. And the suicidal tendencies."

"Did he say how he'd do it?"

"Excuse me?"

"How he'd commit suicide."

"That's a very odd question. Why do you ask?"

"Just popped into my head, I suppose."

This was a lie. Nothing just pops into my head. I make it a point to think before I speak. I asked because if and when I did find this fortune teller, the more I knew about Michael, the better prepared I'd be. Besides, curiosity is one of the hallmarks of what passes for my personality and it's what makes me good at what I do.

"I never thought of asking. I didn't want to let him to linger on that subject too long."

"How long between the time you met him and the time he..." I searched for the right word, a word that wouldn't be as harsh as was the reality.

"You can say the word, Henry. Died. I know it might seem like it sometimes, but I promise you I don't live in a fantasy world. I know he's dead, so it's not like I can't talk about it."

"How long's it been now?"

"Just over three months."

I could see her mind wandering. Her eyes became unfocused.

She was thinking about him. About them. This was fine. I wanted her back in that space. She would remember more and I could share that space with her.

Suddenly, she snapped back. I could see it in her eyes, which became more focused.

"Things were moving along so quickly. We were already talking about moving in together."

By this time, we'd made it through the zoo and were headed out of it, back toward the Fifty-Ninth Street exit out of the park. But before we made it to the edge of the park, she stopped in front of a park bench that faced an art installation of several bronze figures in typical city poses, like hailing a cab and rushing down the street with a newspaper tucked under an arm.

"Do you mind if we sit down a while? I do get a little emotional when I think about Michael."

"Be my guest."

We sat and I made sure to leave at least a foot between us. I don't know why. Maybe I didn't want to let anyone get the wrong idea.

She continued.

"I like to think I knew him well but I guess the truth is, I really didn't. I believe you can see into a person's soul after knowing them a relatively short time, but you can't really know them, can you?"

I wasn't sure if she wanted an answer from me and since I don't believe you can see into anyone's soul, if there even is such a thing, I wasn't about to get into the kind of touchy discussion that almost always ends in hurt feelings.

"That's not very long, Rachel."

"Maybe not. But evidently it was more than enough time for me to fall in love with him."

"That ever happen before?"

She smiled. She knew who I was alluding to, but she wasn't about to fall into my trap.

"Maybe. I don't remember. How about you?"

I shook my head. "I don't believe in love at first sight."

"Why not?"

"Because love isn't the same thing as passion. 'Love is friendship set on fire.'"

She looked at me as if she'd suddenly discovered I had a depth she'd not expected.

"Did you just make that up?"

I could have lied and said yes, but then I would have ultimately become a victim of someone else's expectations.

"No. It was an English clergyman named Jeremy Taylor. Disappointed?"

"No. Just the opposite."

I needed to get us back on track. "How did you learn about his death?"

"We had a date to go dancing, downtown, this club in Tribeca. The day before I gave him a call, just to say hello and confirm, but it went straight to voice mail. I left a message, but he didn't call back. That wasn't like him, but I figured he was busy, or maybe he'd missed the call. So, I called again. Left another message. Still nothing. I started to worry, but I didn't know what to do."

"Was there anyone else you could call?"

"No. I never met any of his friends. I certainly didn't know where to get in touch with his ex-wife."

"Didn't you find it a little odd, having no contact with people close to him?"

"Not really. Remember, we were both in no condition to interact with other people. We could hardly interact with ourselves. He spoke about friends, but we never hung out with any of them."

"Did he meet any of your friends?"

"No. It seems a little odd coming out of my mouth now, but the truth is, it was just the two of us."

"Did he know about Goldblatt?"

Her face turned grim. "You're making me a little uncomfortable, Henry. It's like you're accusing me of doing something wrong. Like cheating on my ex-husband."

"I didn't mean to do that, Rachel. Remember, I ask a lot of questions. Some of them might not make sense to you, but they do to me. You'll have to trust me. If you don't, then it's probably a good idea to find someone else.

"No. No. I trust you. I don't want anyone else."

"Fine. But maybe it's a good time to tell you something about me. I'm not so good at respecting other people's feelings, or about respecting boundaries. When I have a job to do, I do it by getting information the fastest, most efficient way I can. I can't worry about people's feelings. I'm not interested in winning any popularity contests. Understand?"

She nodded, but I wasn't sure she did.

"When you couldn't reach him, did you go to his apartment?"

"I know this is going to sound strange, but I'd never been to his apartment, so I didn't know where it was. I knew he lived way out in Brooklyn, but I don't actually know where. It was always easier to meet here in Manhattan. Sometimes, if it was too late to go back to Brooklyn, he'd stay with me."

"How did you find out he," I tried not to hesitate but I failed, "...died?" It wasn't that I didn't want to hurt her feelings. It was that I didn't want her to get sidetracked by grief.

"I received a call from his sister, Kate. I'd never met her. In fact, I'm not even sure he ever mentioned he had a sister. She said she had some bad news for me. Michael was dead."

"Just like that? Dead? No explanation?"

"It's a bit hazy. I mean, I don't know her exact words. At first, I thought it was some kind of joke Michael was playing on me."

"A joke?"

"I know. I know. But I wasn't thinking straight. He'd never do anything like that."

"She didn't give you any details?"

"Not at that point, and I guess I was too much in shock to ask."

"How did she know to call you?"

"She said that a day or two after the funeral, when she went to his apartment to clean it out, she came across my name and phone number on a piece of paper taped to the refrigerator door. It was the same piece of paper he'd written it on when we met in San Francisco. He'd spoken to her about me and when she saw the name and number, she realized who I was and called to tell me what happened."

"How long after he died did you get the call?"

"A little over a week, maybe. She apologized, not that she had to. She said she didn't think about me what with all that was going on. I can understand that. And even if she had, she wouldn't have known how to contact me until she found that paper."

Her head sank.

"I'm so, so sorry I missed the funeral."

I could see tears starting to form again at the corners of her eyes. I thought about putting my arm around her shoulder, but I didn't. I don't know why. If it were someone else, I might have. But not her. Was it because of her connection to Goldblatt?

She paused a moment while she composed herself and then continued.

"By the time she contacted me, the family had already held the memorial service and had him cremated."

I could see it coming, but I couldn't do anything about it. It was like those long-dormant volcanoes that suddenly wake up. You feel the rumble of the earth. Steam begins to rise out of the top. Then, all hell breaks loose and the lava begins to flow.

That's how it was with her. First her body began to shake. Then came the sobbing and the tears. Between gasps of breath, her chest heaving, she managed, "I. Couldn't. Even. Visit. His. Grave."

I let it run its course. Finally, she took a deep breath and let it out very slowly. "I'm sorry. I guess I'm still not over it. I was devastated, of course, and I fell into a funk that lasted almost a month. It was even worse than before we met."

"What was the cause of death?"

"An aneurism. Kate told me he didn't even make it to the hospital. He died in the ambulance."

"Tough luck."

The minute those words tumbled out of my mouth I realized how callous they must have sounded. But I couldn't help it. Let's face it, I don't do grief well. I didn't do it when my own wife died a dozen years ago. I didn't do it well when I released my son from my care. I didn't even do it well when my mother died ten years ago and certainly not when my father died a few years back. But with him there was a good reason. I hated the sonuvabitch. He was a wretched human being. An ex-cop who was a drunk most of the time and when he was he was a classic abuser. I don't hate him anymore. Way too much bad stuff has gone down in my life since then. Enough bad stuff goes down and somehow some of the early crap loses its power. Memory is like that. Pain is like that. Emily Dickinson said it has "an element of blank." She was right. When you're in the midst of it, you can't think of anything else. The intensity is so powerful it's as if you were never without it. But once it's gone you can't conjure up that intensity anymore. You know you felt it, you just can't recreate it. That's probably a good thing. Now, for me, it's morphed into something worse: indifference. No anger. No hatred. No fear. Certainly, no love. I suppose I must feel something but I guess there's some kind of disconnect between the information and the feeling, whatever it might be. It's just a blank.

I could see teardrops still nesting at the inside corners of Rachel's eyes. I would have given her something to wipe them with only I didn't have anything, so they remained there, in suspended animation, just waiting for another eruption I hoped would never come. I can stand up to a behemoth looking to beat my brains out, and that's happened more times than I'd like to remember. But for some reason I cringe at the sight of a woman's tears. I am paralyzed. I don't know what to say. I don't know what to do. I don't know what to feel.

I didn't want to give Rachel a chance to feel sorrier for herself so I did what I do best: I changed the subject.

"Tell me how this fortune teller came into the picture?"

She took a tissue from her purse and dabbed her eyes. "I tried to hold it together, but I wasn't doing too well. I couldn't sleep. I couldn't eat. I lost seven pounds in a week."

"The grief diet. I hear it's very effective."

She smiled. I was getting her back.

"I certainly wouldn't recommend it. I was talking to Kate on the phone one day. She'd call me every so often, to see how I was doing. It was so sweet. By this time, I suppose you could say we'd become friends. Maybe not friends in the normal sense, since we never actually met. It was more of a connection. Through grief. I'd always feel better after talking to her. I guess it was because it made me feel closer to Michael. One day, when I was going through a particularly bad patch, she mentioned this woman who'd helped her through some rough spots in the past and she thought she might be able to help me, too.

"Madame Sofia."

She gave me that patented girlie eye roll, a gesture I took to mean that I shouldn't judge her. I didn't. The only one I judge is me, and that never turns out well.

"I know what you're thinking."

"Many women have tried, few have been successful, Rachel. They usually give me a lot more credit than I deserve for actually thinking anything."

She laughed. "At first I was resistant to the idea. I mean, a fortune teller? Please!" The girlie eye roll again. "But Kate kept insisting so I figured, what could it hurt? It was surreal. I mean, me going to a fortune teller. I admit I've tried some pretty whacky things most people would find just plain weird, you know like kinda way 'out there.' Certainly, my ex-husband would think that. But I was in such pain I figured I didn't have anything to lose. Right?"

"So, you made an appointment to see her."

"I couldn't bring myself to call her, so Kate did it for me. And you know what, after seeing her the first time I actually did feel a little better. "

"How's that?"

"I hope you're not going to judge me, Henry."

"I try not to judge anyone, Rachel," I lied. Truth is, I judge everyone, all the time. Especially myself. I just don't make a habit of broadcasting what that judgment is.

"That's good. Because after that first visit I felt as if somehow through her I'd connected with Michael. She knew so much about me, about him, about us. Things she couldn't possibly have known about me, about us. It was uncanny. I know this sounds foolish but..."

"I try to be open-minded, Rachel. Pascal's wager."

"What's that?"

"Pascal was a French mathematician and philosopher who once said, 'Belief is a wager. Granted that faith cannot be proved, what harm will come to you if you gamble on its truth and it proves false? If you gain, you gain all; if you lose, you lose nothing. Wager, then, without hesitation, that He exists.' I don't see the harm in applying that to just about everything in life."

"You memorized all that?"

"I did."

"I'm impressed."

"Don't be. The result of too much free time and the need to impress women."

"It works."

"Not when it counted."

"I'll have to remember that. Pascal, right?"

I nodded.

"I'm a little bit more positive in my faith, but still, most people would think I was a..."

She didn't finish her sentence. She didn't have to. Judgment or not she was still embarrassed and humiliated by what she'd done. I wanted to tell her she had nothing to be ashamed of. People have been taking advantage of other people since Adam and Eve. But I knew she wouldn't believe me.

"Weirdo?"

She had a nice smile. Her deep, chocolate brown eyes sparkled when the sunlight hit them just right. You know, like in those Disney cartoons. I didn't hear the twinkling sound but I half-expected a bunch of robins to land on her shoulder and start chirping "Zip-a-Dee-Doo-Dah."

"How much did she wind up taking from you?"

"You mean the first time?"

It was worse than I thought.

"Yeah. The first time."

"It was fifty thousand dollars."

"They start slow. And the total?"

"By the end, it was pretty much everything I had."

"How much?"

"I'm embarrassed to say."

"It's something I need to know."

"Close to seventy-five thousand dollars. But," she quickly added, "like I said, it wasn't all at once."

"It never is, Rachel. You're not the first person to be taken and you won't be the last. People who do this for a living are damn good at it. They aren't called confidence men without reason. That's how they work. They steal your confidence and once they've got it, they steal your money. They have an uncanny knack of knowing who to target and, once they find the right person, they're very skillful at working them for pretty much everything they have."

Her head dropped. "Yes, I suppose I was 'worked.'"

"You didn't do anything wrong. She did." I put my hand on her shoulder. "But I'm going to see if I can make it right."

"Can you? Can you really make it right?"

"I can't promise anything, but I'm going to try. But you have to be totally honest with me, no matter how uncomfortable it might get. It's part of my job to be blunt and ask questions about private matters, questions you might not want to answer, questions you think the answers to might be none of my business."

"I know. I'm prepared."

I squeezed her shoulder. "Just remember, I'm on your side. Okay. First question. How'd you come up with that kind of money?"

"It was from an inheritance from my father. I wasn't able to get my hands on it until about a year ago, when I turned thirty-five."

"Why not?"

"He wasn't a big fan of my lifestyle. He thought I was gullible and he probably knew exactly what would happen to it. He used to say I didn't have the healthy respect for money I was supposed to. I'm sure he was hoping by the time I reached thirty-five I'd be a little more grounded. I guess he was wrong. Why is that important?"

"Because people like Madame Sofia don't waste their time on people who are broke. Somehow, she knew you had money."

"What does that mean?"

"It means one of two things. Either she really does have super-powers and divined you had dough, or she researched you. Or it was a coincidence."

"Which do you think it was?"

"You tell me."

"If it was research, how would she do it?"

"There are lots of ways and finding out. How she did it might help lead me to her. I hope she didn't take everything."

She shook her head. "I have a little left. I know I was foolish and irresponsible, but I was in pain and when you're in pain, you'll do just about anything you can to alleviate it. And to be honest, she did help me. At least in the beginning. Talking to her about Michael was very therapeutic. And then, when she was actually able to 'reach' him, or I thought she reached him...I don't know, it just helped."

"Placebo effect."

"You mean it was all in my head?"

"Sometimes that's enough to make us feel better. Sugar pills sometimes do the trick. I read an article not long ago that said even when doctors tell patients they're giving them a placebo, it still has a healing effect. It doesn't make any sense, but it's true."

She smiled. "So, there is such a thing as magic."

"Magic means it's a trick, Rachel. It's manipulation. And so yes, you were manipulated, so yes, it was magic."

"You're a very cynical man, Henry Swann."

"I can't argue with that."

"So little about the world makes sense, Henry. That's why I believe you have to be open to everything."

Yeah, and on your guard, too. But I didn't say that. I've come across plenty of people like Rachel. No matter how hard you try, no matter how much proof you provide, you can't talk them out of a belief. People are always looking for answers and when there are none, they make them up. Somehow, having an answer, even if it's the wrong one, seems to help. Me, I'm different. Things have to make sense and when they don't, I'm compelled to make them make sense. Maybe that's why I do what I do. I'm someone who needs the answer, but it has to be the right answer, the provable answer. It's always there. You just have to scrape away the shit that sometimes obscures it.

"Tell me about this Madame Sofia character. What did she look like? Any quirks that make her stand apart?"

"She certainly didn't fit the stereotype of gypsy fortune teller. You know, dark hair, long, gypsy dress, silver bracelets. She looked more like a Park Avenue trophy wife, or Wall Street business woman. Like she shopped at Ann Taylor. Attractive woman. She was tall, about five-eight. A classic look, like Jacqueline Bissett or Charlotte Rampling. I'd say she was in her late forties. She certainly didn't look like she should be working out of a storefront..."

"Not anymore."

"What do you mean?"

"It's a Subway sandwich shop now. These scammers don't stick around in one place too long. Was there anything about her personally that stood out?"

She closed her eyes. "Yes, there was one thing. She had a tattoo on the inside of each wrist. One of them looked like that sign for infinity. The other one was some kind of Chinese symbol, I think."

"Anything else?"

"When it came up where I met Michael, she mentioned she was originally from Northern California."

We spent nearly half an hour more sitting on the bench as I probed further, trying to get as much information as I could about Madame Sofia and her magical ability to connect with the "other" world. I've got to admit it was strange talking to Rachel about it because even though I think she believed she'd been hustled, she didn't totally disbelieve the possibility that we can, in fact, connect with the dead. If Goldblatt hadn't convinced her she'd been ripped off, I'm not so sure she would have hired someone like me to go after the dough. If you pinned her down, I think she believed that some of us can actually converse with this "other level of consciousness," as she referred to it, and she probably bought into that "other room" crap, too.

Suddenly, in the middle of a sentence, her eyes glazed over, her head sank, and she became very still. It was as if she'd fallen into some altered state. I don't know where she was, but it wasn't with me. She was done, like one of those little wind-up toys that just comes to a dead stop. I knew that to question her any further would only have resulted in diminishing returns.

But before I left her alone, I decided to take a shot at one very important subject.

"So, tell me about you and Goldblatt."

Her back stiffened, her face hardened.

"There's nothing to tell."

"Sure, there is."

The expression on her face might have been described by passersby as a smile, only up close it was anything but. It was as if an impenetrable wall shot up. "He warned me about this."

"About what?"

"About you trying to pump me for information about him."

"I'm not pumping, Rachel. I'm just asking. He's my partner. I'd just like to get to know him a little better. You know, until this came up I didn't even know he was married."

"Why don't you just ask him yourself?"

"You ever try to get answers out of Goldblatt when he doesn't want to give them?"

"Maybe there's a reason."

"Like what?"

"I don't know. You should ask him."

"I've tried. So, tell me, was he ever in the CIA?"

"If he was, he wouldn't be able to tell me...or you, would he?"

"He knows some interesting characters."

"He's an interesting character himself. Here's what I can say about him. He's very loyal and he cares. And you know, Henry, when the chips are down, he's the kind of guy you can count on."

"You're not going to tell me anything else about him, are you?'

"There's nothing to tell. You know as much about him as he wants you to know."

I knew when I was whipped.

"All right. I think I've got enough to get started. But you'll be hearing from me if I have any more questions."

"Do you think you can find her and get my money back, or at least part of it?"

"I don't know about the money part, but if she's still around, I'll find her."

"How can you be so sure?"

"Like the boxer Joe Louis once said about one of his opponents, 'He can run but he can't hide.' No one can hide forever, Rachel."

Even Goldblatt.

3
WITNESS FOR THE DEFENSE

"So, how'd it go, my man?" Goldblatt asked cheerily, as he stuck his head in through the crack in the doorway to the office I keep in Klavan's apartment. It's the small fourth bedroom off the kitchen that had once served as maid's quarters back in the thirties when this beaux art, prewar co-op was constructed. It suits me well. It's far enough away from Klavan's living area so as not to disturb him and his wife, Mary, nor close enough to get in the way of the huge library housing his impressive collection of rare books. The room is not much larger than a prison cell but it provides me just enough room for a small desk, a double-drawer file cabinet and a couple chairs. Other than a few bucks I pay to cover my share of the utilities and to chip in for the cleaning woman who came once a week, my only other responsibility is to make sure Goldblatt makes only infrequent appearances on the property, as the two of them got along about as well as the Israelis and Arabs fighting over the West Bank.

I'd shown up uncharacteristically early, a few minutes before nine a.m., and had been working at the computer for nearly an hour, feeding in the names of Rachel's dead boyfriend and Madame Sofia, while searching for some of the popular types of scams people like her run on marks. It turned out Madame Sofia, who had a seemingly infinite number of aliases, including Diane Flynn, Kerrie King, Wendy Klein, and Debra Flaherty, was not unknown to the authorities. It appeared she'd never spent any time in the Graybar Hotel, despite the numerous charges filed against her. Somehow, she'd always managed to elude prosecution. Charges were dropped. Complainants changed their minds. Witnesses didn't show up in court. Like that. I was impressed. It meant I was not dealing with a lightweight. This was a woman who was quite adept at working the legal system instead of it working her. It appeared as if I was not in for an easy time.

What she worked on Rachel was a variation on a number of other tried and true bunko schemes. It never ceases to amaze me how gullible people can be. Not just folks like Rachel. Let's face it, at one time or another we've all been conned, whether it be for money or love. If someone gets us at the right moment, when we're most vulnerable, when we're at our neediest, whether it be financially or emotionally, and they're halfway decent at what they do, they can get us to buy just any story, no matter how outlandish it might seem. We believe what we want to believe when we want to believe it, and a good con artist can figure out what it is we want to believe and then sell it to us. That's why I tried not to judge Rachel, for who among us hasn't had the wool pulled over our eyes at one time or another? Who among us hasn't bought some version of the Brooklyn Bridge?

By the time Goldblatt stuck his head into the room, I was just about finished with my online research and had pieced together a pretty good picture of what I was up against.

"How the hell did you get in here? You don't have a key and I didn't hear the doorbell."

By this time, the rest of his bulky frame had invaded the room and, with a big, shit-eating grin on his face, he said, "What makes you think I don't have a key?"

"Because I didn't give you one and I'm damn sure Ross didn't either."

I was pretty sure he hadn't, but if he had I was going to read him the riot act. The last thing I wanted was Goldblatt coming around when I wasn't there and pawing through my papers. It wasn't that I had anything to hide. It was that I wanted to have the option to.

"You think that's the only way I could've gotten a key?"

"What's that supposed to mean?"

He smiled. "Relax, Swannee, I'm just pulling your chain. The missus let me in. Not that I couldn't put my hands on a key if I wanted to. You don't think I could?"

"To be honest. I haven't wasted a moment's thought on it. Get in here and close the door behind you, will ya? And quietly, please."

"What's a matter? Afraid Klavan's gonna find me here and kick me out? I can handle myself, you know. Besides, I have every right to be here. We're partners, remember?"

He grabbed the only other chair in the room and sat down. He reached for some papers on my desk and I slapped his hand away.

"Hey, what's your problem?"

"No problem. Next time ask before you touch anything."

"We're partners. This is work product, right? I have every right to see what's going on."

"Take me to court, Goldblatt. In the meantime, just keep your hands to yourself. Now what are you doing here?"

"How'd it go with Rachel?"

"You already know how it went."

I was annoyed that Goldblatt was interrupting the work rhythm I'd established, and I was afraid Klavan might walk in on us and that any goodwill I'd built up between my good friend and I would evaporate, resulting in him kicking me to the curb. Office space was expensive in Manhattan and I didn't feel like being deported to one of the outer gulags. Besides, not only did I like having an office in a classy neighborhood, Gramercy Park, but I also liked being in close proximity to Klavan's immense collection of rare books. It reminded me I had a brain and that at some point in the future I might even get an opportunity to use it again in ways not connected to finding people who didn't want to be found and righting wrongs that didn't want to be righted. Working here gave some credence to the lie I told myself: that this job was temporary and that soon I would be on the life track I was really meant to be on. Not that I had any idea what that track might be.

"What do you mean?" he asked so innocently I might have believed him if I didn't know him as well as I did.

"I'll bet the first thing Rachel did after I left her was call you."

He puffed up his chest. "You think you're so smart. Actually, I was the one who called her. So, you're going to help us, right?"

"You mean her."

"I'm the client, remember?"

"That mean you're going to be the one who's paying me?"

"In a manner of speaking."

"What manner is that?"

He waved his hand in a sweeping gesture. "Let's not ruin a perfectly good morning by talking remuneration now."

"Yes. By all means, let's ruin it. Because if you think I'm working pro bono, you are sadly mistaken. So, it's either you or Rachel that's going to be ponying up some dough. Make no mistake, my friend, this is no freebie."

"We're partners, remember? Ever hear of professional courtesy? When I was an attorney I swapped services with my brother attorneys all the time."

"That was then, this is now."

"It's known as the barter system, Swann. You scratch my back, I'll scratch yours. This is a family affair. Besides, I'll be part of the investigation."

"Really? Just how do you intend to help?"

"Let me count the ways. For one thing, I'll be your leg man. You need something checked out, you need to reach someone who's unreachable, you need 'muscle,' I'm your boy."

I laughed. How could I not?

"You're gonna provide muscle?"

"I didn't say it would be me specifically, although I am a master in Krav Maga, among other things."

"In what?"

"Finally. Something the great Henry Swann doesn't know," he crowed, with about the biggest smile I'd ever seen plastered across his face. His chest puffed up like an automobile airbag.

"There's plenty I don't know, Goldblatt, and you know what, I'm man enough to admit it."

"It's Israeli martial arts. It's a tactical mixed martial arts and combative self-defense system, combining boxing, judo, jujitsu, and aikido."

"Really? I'd like to see a demonstration someday."

"That would only be possible if you witnessed me actually having to make use of it. It's not for show or amusement, Swann. It's for self-defense. We take a sacred oath, you know."

"That so? Suddenly, I feel so much safer around you."

"Yeah, well, you should. But don't go spreading this around, okay? It works a lot better when people aren't expecting it."

"My lips are sealed."

"So, what's our plan of action?"

"Rachel hired me, not you. If I share strategy with anyone it'll be with her. You should know by now that's how I work."

"Yeah, you seem to forget when it comes to business there is no you. There's only us."

At that point, before I regurgitated the breakfast I'd had a couple hours earlier, the door opened a crack and Klavan stuck his glistening, newly shaved head into the office.

"Brain trust meeting, I presume," he said. "I mean I could practically feel the room pulsating with intellectual energy from all the way across the apartment."

"This is a private meeting, Klavan," snapped Goldblatt.

"As in privately conducted in my apartment. You might have a point if you guys were actually paying rent but since you're not..."

"So, you're going to throw that in our..." Goldblatt sputtered, his facing turning bright red.

"What's up, Ross?" I asked, looking to defuse the situation before the boys escalated the confrontation beyond insults. After all, I didn't want to be responsible for Goldblatt having to perform his Krav Maga on Klavan. The room seemed much too small for that sideshow and I certainly didn't want to be responsible for someone getting hurt.

"Message for you. And by the way, maybe you guys should invest in an answering machine because I didn't sign on to be part of your agency or whatever the hell it is you're calling yourselves."

"As soon as we hit the lottery, we'll be out of your hair and moving to that Park Avenue suite," I said, thankful Klavan hadn't pressed me to define exactly what our relationship was. "What's the message?"

"Guy named Paul Rudder."

"Who's that?" asked Goldblatt.

"Did he say what he wanted?" I asked, ignoring Goldblatt's question.

"He has a job for you. Said to call him at his office or stop by when you get a chance. Said he'd be there most of the afternoon."

"Who is he?" Goldblatt repeated, practically vibrating with excitement. And if you can picture a blob of jelly on a plate you'd have a pretty good idea of what that looked like.

"A lawyer I used to do some work for back in the day."

"What day was that?" asked Klavan.

"Pre..." I jerked a thumb toward Goldblatt who didn't seem to notice. I assumed he was too busy trying to figure out how he could benefit from Rudder's call by setting up an imaginary fee schedule.

"Call him back," barked Goldblatt.

"Excuse me," I said sharply. I don't like being ordered around. Especially not by Goldblatt.

"I mean, he probably has some work for us. You should call him back ASAP, before he takes it someplace else," he said, softening his tone considerably.

"Us? I'm sure he hasn't the foggiest idea who you are."

"Maybe not, but whether you like it or not, Swann, we're an us now. Swann. What's good for the Swann is good for the gander," he said through a wide grin. He was very proud of himself. He'd made a joke. And it wasn't a bad one. I tried not to smile—it would only encourage him—but I wasn't very successful.

"I'm pretty busy right now, remember? I'm working for you."

"You're working for this doofus?" said Klavan.

"Who you calling a doofus," said Goldblatt, puffing out his chest and glaring at Klavan, as if ready to go to the mat. Even with his professed skill in Krav Maga, I'd still lay my money on Klavan, who works out daily and whose solid physique shows the results. He's no more than five-nine, weighs in around one hundred seventy-five pounds and not an ounce of it is fat.

"Hey, you two can slap your dicks on the table and measure them later. Right now, I'm going down to Rudder's office to see what's on his mind."

"I'll go with you," said Goldblatt.

"No, you won't. Just go wherever you go and I'll meet you at your favorite coffee shop around one. This is nonnegotiable. And Goldblatt..."

"Yeah?"

"I need you to do a job for me," I added, realizing I had to throw him a bone every once in a while, if only to keep him off my back.

A suspicious smile crept slowly across his face. "Yeah? Like what?"

"I want you to find out who owns the building where Rachel's fortune teller had her storefront. Then, I want you to make an appointment for me to meet with the owner as soon as possible. Just make up some phony story as to why I want to meet with him."

"You think I'm an idiot, Swann?" he said, his face turning a shade of crimson I hadn't seen before. "You think this is the first time I've done," he threw up air quotes, "undercover work? And don't you mean *we* meet with him?"

"I have no idea what kind of experience you've had."

"I tell you all the time."

"You tell me lots of stuff, but I have no idea if any of it's real."

"You think I'm a liar? You think I make shit up?"

I looked over at Klavan who, by the look on his face, was really enjoying this. With no good end in sight, I put up both hands in a gesture of defeat. "Okay, okay. Everything you tell me is true. And as for you tagging along, I figured you'd probably have better things to do."

He was silent a moment and I could practically see the wheels spinning. "You're right. I do have some irons in the fire. We'll see how it goes when the time comes."

I wondered what those irons might be, but I wasn't going to ask. I did promise myself one thing. I was going to spend some time trying to figure out just who—and what—Goldblatt really was and try to separate truth from fiction. Not an easy task, under any circumstances. It wasn't because I really cared. It was because I hate not knowing the truth.

Paul Rudder is a highly regarded criminal attorney and one of the more honorable practitioners of his profession I've crossed paths with. He's got something most of the others sorely lack: principles. I've never seen him give anything less than his best for a client no matter who that client might be or what that client might have done. Unlike me, it's not solely about the dough. "I owe it to them and the judicial system, Swann," he once explained. "Everyone's entitled to competent counsel. It's the only thing that makes the system work. I don't buy into this bullshit where only the rich can game the system even though it's true. I know it's corny but it's got to be equal justice for everyone or there's no justice at all."

It was corny, but it was also true and I respected and admired him for it. I'm glad there are still Paul Rudders around principled enough to believe that crap so guys like me don't have to.

We met twenty years ago. Paul was fresh out of law school and working for Legal Aid and I was just getting started in the skip trade. A big man, several inches over six-feet and weighing in around a deuce, he still has the solid build of a point guard which is exactly what he was at Yale, where he played college ball. His pleasant, gentle demeanor belies his size which can be a little intimidating. Soft-spoken, with just a hint of a south Jersey accent, where he was born and raised, he still manages to command a room, especially when that room holds a judge and jury. If I were ever in serious criminal trouble, and believe me, I've come close, Paul is the guy I'd like in my corner. He's smart, hard-working, diligent, honest, creative yet not afraid to find and work find the angles. I like to think of him as the yin to Goldblatt's yang.

But despite his principles he's got a practical streak and so after his second kid was born he segued from the public sector to private practice. Now he's able to command big bucks for his services. He's worth it. Over the years, he's taken on some high-profile mob cases—not his favorites, he admits. "The money's too good to ignore and you know, someone's got to make sure the government follows the rules." He shies away from white-collar crime "because it's usually the little guy who gets screwed and that doesn't sit too well with me," and domestic cases, "I don't like the idea of making money on the backs of human misery." Instead, he specializes in the less subtle crimes like high-end robbery and murder. "They still get the old juices flowing," he explains, "and frankly the higher the stakes the better I concentrate and the more money I can make." Music to my greedy, little ears.

Paul's office is in downtown Manhattan, just a few blocks from the courthouses at 60 Centre Street. A no-frills guy, he has one junior partner (a recent law school grad, who he grooms for a couple years then rotates out) and Norma, the long-time secretary slash receptionist he's had ever since he went out on his own. Norma knows the criminal court system better than most attorneys and I wouldn't be surprised if she also knows the law better than most of them. I kidded her once that she could probably pass the bar and start her own practice and she answered, "And what, take a pay cut?"

The office itself is nothing special. "I don't have to impress anyone but myself," Rudder once explained when I kidded him about spending a little of that newfound money on a classier office. "They're paying for this," he said, tapping his temple, "not the furniture, man."

"Okay to go in?" I asked Norma, who was squeezing the phone between her chin and her shoulder as she filed her nails. She's a beautiful woman, a petite redhead, who takes particular pride in her appearance. She's gotta be in her fifties, but she sure doesn't look it.

She flashed a smile and nodded toward Paul's office while still managing to keep the phone in place and the file moving steadily.

Paul, dressed casually in jeans and a white, button-down shirt with the sleeves rolled up, was stretched out on the couch across from his desk, reading legal documents. He got up and shook my hand.

"Hey, Henry, good to see you, man. Been a while, hasn't it?"

"Couple years, probably."

"Thanks for coming."

"Yeah, well, I can always use the work. I assume that's why you got me here."

"I thought maybe you retired."

"Fat chance."

"When I heard you finally gave up that rathole up in Spanish Harlem, I thought maybe you'd finally decided to get a real job."

I shrugged. "It suited me at the time."

"Where you working out of now?"

"I've got a place on Grammercy."

"Moving up in the world, ay?"

"More like sideways."

"I hear you've taken on a partner since the last time I saw you."

Oh, man. My heart sank. Word was out on the street. I don't know why I thought my association with Goldblatt would remain a secret. Wishful thinking, I guess.

"I wouldn't exactly call him a partner."

"What would you call him?"

"I'll get back to you on that one."

He smiled. It wasn't one of those funny, ha-ha smiles. It was one of those mischievous smiles that let you know they know you're screwed. Yeah, he knew all about Goldblatt. I don't know how, but he did.

"What can I do for you, Paul?"

"Have a seat," he said, gesturing toward a chair in front of his desk. "Can Norma get something for you?"

"I'm good."

He slid into his chair behind his desk and leaned back, his hands cradling the back of his head, as he swung his legs up on his desk. "Even though you've evidently moved downtown, I take it you're still the best in the business of finding people."

"I took one of those aptitude tests and found I was qualified to do nothing else except collect garbage, which is pretty much what I wind up doing anyway. So yeah, I'm afraid the answer is yes."

"Good. Because I need someone found and I think you're the man to do it."

"I take it we're not talking about some run-of-the-mill bail jumper."

"It's a little more important than that. It's for a case I'm working on. I need you to find a witness who's disappeared."

"Someone make him..."

"It's a her, actually."

"Her disappear?"

He shrugged. "Not sure, but I believe it's more likely she took it upon herself to skip town."

"I sense a story here."

"Haven't lost that uncanny sixth sense, have you? Sure you don't want coffee? I might even be able to scrounge up some of that designer water crap."

"I'm good."

He swung his legs off his desk, leaned forward, and pulled his chair closer to his desk. "This is confidential, of course."

"You're in luck. Hardly anyone listens to me and I don't have any friends."

"This associate of yours. Goldblatt, right? What about him?"

"You know him?"

"Let's say I know of him."

"Really? He's actually got a reputation?"

"We've all got reputations, Henry. But if you're asking how much I know about him in terms of fact, the answer is not much. He was a fixture around the courthouse five, six years ago. I got to know about him because of a fed case a few years back a friend of mine was trying. Stock fraud. Not my thing, but it was an interesting case so I paid attention. My pal represented one of the minor defendants, but his guy never made it to trial. He pled out. Word is Goldblatt was the middleman responsible for getting him a pretty sweet deal. I don't know the details, but my pal was very impressed."

Maybe Goldblatt was more effective and better connected than I gave him credit for. Perhaps there was some untapped potential there. I would've asked Rudder for more details, but that's not what I was there for. But he wasn't finished, and I wasn't about to stop him.

"If I'm not mistaken, he's not practicing anymore and it wasn't by choice," Rudder continued, as he got up and moved toward a half-refrigerator in the corner of the office. He opened it and took out a can of Coke. "You sure you don't want anything?"

"I'm sure."

He popped it open.

"He got into some kind of trouble, right?"

"So I understand."

"Disbarred?"

"Could be," I said, knowing full well that he'd had his ticket pulled. But the less I let on I knew about my 'partner,' the less I'd be held responsible for him. At least that's what I hoped.

Rudder settled back into his chair and took a swig of his Coke. "In the long run, they probably did him a favor. This profession sucks. I just wish I'd known that before I got in too deep." He put down the soda can and crossed his wrists in front of him as if handcuffed.

"Listen, Paul, if you don't want him involved in this whatever it is, I won't let him get anywhere near it."

Rudder shrugged and took another swig of Coke.

"I don't really care if he's involved or not. If he can help, why not? I'll leave that to you. I just need the job done and I need it done as quick as possible. I got into this late in the game and the DA has fast-tracked it. It's a really big get for them."

"Who'm I looking for and why?"

"My client's up on a murder rap."

"I thought you'd laid off those a while back. Who's he supposed to have killed?"

"It's complicated."

"Why's everything I touch turn out to be 'complicated'?"

"It has to do with what he does for a living."

"Which is?"

Rudder paused. "He's a hit man."

"You're kidding me."

"No. It's true."

"You mean like he lists hit man as his occupation on his resume?"

"He might as well since it's probably the worst kept secret in town, at least among the law enforcement community."

"Now I see why it's complicated."

"Yeah. He doesn't exactly have clean hands. But I think it's possible he's not guilty of this particular murder."

"I hope you're not hiring me to dig up evidence proving he didn't do it, Paul, because that's not the kind of thing I do."

"I know. But you have a special knack for finding people. I need you to find a witness my client says can prove he couldn't have been where the cops say he was when the murder was committed. Only problem is, she's disappeared."

"Maybe you should start from the beginning."

"Right. My client's name is Nicky Diamond. Not the name he was born with, by the way, but it's legal now so we might as well refer to him that way. He grew up in Brooklyn and started out as a small-time hood, shoplifting, fraud, extortion, that kind of thing. Eventually, he worked his way up to freelancing bigger jobs mostly for the Russian mob working out of Brighton Beach. I don't know this for sure, but I hear he might have branched out and has been doing some work for the Armenians, too."

"And by bigger jobs I take it you mean murder."

"I do."

"I thought you stayed away from organized crime cases, Paul."

"This one's different. First off, I owe someone a favor and second, I really do think there's a good chance he didn't do it. I don't want the government to get away with nailing this guy for something he didn't do. Let them nail him for something he did do. Besides, the DA they've assigned to this case is a real arrogant son of a bitch and I'd like to stick it to him."

"Who's the favor for?"

"Not important."

"Which means you don't want to tell me."

"That's right. But don't let your imagination run away from you, pal. It's not some 'Mr. Big,' if that's what you're worried about."

"Out of curiosity, how many murders is this guy supposedly good for?"

"He hasn't handed me a scorecard, but it probably runs into the dozens. He doesn't deny what he does for a living. In fact, he's kind of proud of it. And he's good enough at it that they've never been able to nail him. Until now. Of course, he claims he's never killed anyone who didn't deserve it."

"He thinks he's performing a public service?"

"Yeah. Pest control."

"But this one he claims he didn't do?"

"Right."

"How do you know he's not lying?"

"Look, Henry, guys like Nicky wouldn't know the truth if it jumped up and smacked them in the face, so I can't be sure. But I'm defending him so the default position is he's telling the truth until I find otherwise. But that's not something I need to know. Whether I believe him or not is irrelevant."

"But between you and me..."

"Yeah, I do believe him. But even if I didn't, it's my duty to defend him, which means doing everything I can to find this witness he says was with him at the time of the murder."

"Who is she?"

"His girlfriend."

"How convenient. Have you met her?"

He shook his head.

"Then how do you know she even exists?"

"I won't know for sure until you find her. And if you can't find her, then I'll know she doesn't exist."

"What happened to his former lawyer?"

He smiled. "Creative differences."

"Which means?"

"Let's call it a mutual parting of the ways. The judge allowed it but only after I agreed to take over on short notice. After one meeting with him I could see why his previous lawyer threw in the towel. He won't win any congeniality awards."

"Let's say I find her, how will you know she's telling the truth? I mean, she's his girlfriend, which means she'd lie for him."

"A guy like Diamond wouldn't have to make this up. He's perfectly capable of finding someone to vouch for him, so why come up with someone who isn't around? It doesn't make a whole lot of sense unless he's telling the truth."

"The guy's a killer, Paul. He brags about it. Lying is easy once you've jumped to the Thou Shalt Not Kill commandment. But let's say he didn't kill this particular victim. Let's say the cops got this one wrong. What's the difference? He goes down for this one instead of another one. Are we supposed to shed a tear? In the end, it all equals out, right?"

"It's not about guilt or innocence, Henry. The state has to prove beyond a shadow of a doubt Diamond did it. If we find his witness, and I think she's credible, and I put her on the stand, and a jury believes her, then there's plenty of doubt and he's off the hook. Let the government nail him for one they can prove not for one they can't."

"Okay. I'm in. So long as I get paid, what do I care?"

"Obviously moving downtown hasn't changed you."

"I've put in for a personality transplant but evidently I'm way down on the list. What's the chick's name? What do you know about her? And why do you think she ran?"

"Name's Jana Monroe. Twenty-seven years old. She's a cocktail waitress slash actress works at the Hilton on Sixth Avenue. At least she did until she disappeared. Lives in Park Slope with a couple roommates. Takes night classes at NYU. Here's all the information." He handed me a page of handwritten notes.

"As to why she took off, your guess is as good as mine. The easy answer is she didn't want to get involved. Any other answer is more complicated and something you're going to have to find out for yourself. I asked Nicky, but I can't get a decent answer out of him. Maybe you can, though I doubt it."

"Of course, there's another possibility."

"You mean that she didn't disappear voluntarily?"

"Right."

"Considering the circles Diamond runs in that has to be on the table. But if it was someone else's doing, that's something I'd like to know because it's someone I can plan B. One way or another, you're going to earn your fee."

"What have they got on him? Witnesses? Physical evidence?"

"Yeah, well, I guess I should have mentioned that. They've got someone who rolled over on him. A guy who says he was there when Nicky was hired to do the job. And they claim they've got the murder weapon with his prints on it."

"You think one witness who's his girlfriend is gonna counteract all that?"

"It's my job to make it work. But she's got to be willing to testify and she's got to be believable. I'm working on a narrative where, if all the pieces fall in place, I can sell to a jury and it might get him off. And, if you find her and she's credible, I might even be able to convince the DA to drop the charges."

"That's one hell of a narrative, Paul."

"In case you don't know, I'm very good at what I do. But it all hinges on you finding Jana Monroe."

"What if I don't? Or what if I find out she's dead?"

"We'll cross that bridge when or if we come to it."

"If I know what that theory is I might be able to look for things along the way that support it."

"I'd rather not get into details now, but bottom line, I think he's being set up. I don't know why and I don't know by who. If Nicky does, he's certainly not sharing that information with me. He's a stubborn sonuvabitch. Sometimes, I think he doesn't give a shit whether he lives or dies." Paul took another slug of Coke. "Maybe that's what makes him so damn good at what he does."

"If he doesn't give a shit, why should you? Why should I?"

"Because it's our job. And the less he cares the more I do. Don't ask me to explain it, because I'm not sure I could."

"Okay. I'm in. Since it's a murder rap and he's got the resume he has, I assume bail was out of the question."

"That's right."

"So, he's at Rikers?"

"Yeah."

"I need to see him."

"I don't think you'll get much more than I'm giving you here, but I'll make sure you're put on the Riker's 'guest list' as my investigator. That'll get you inside."

I checked my watch. It was only one-thirty, still enough time to get my ass out there and get the ball rolling.

"Now for my favorite part."

"Your fee, right?"

I nodded.

"What's your day rate now?"

"Seven-fifty."

"Liar," with a big, fat grin on his face.

"Oh, hell, it's not my money. Nicky's got plenty of dough. Norma will cut you a check for a week in advance on your way out. I wish I had more for you to go on, but this is all I've got. You'll find all you need to know about Jana on that paper I gave you. I'm afraid this is the only photo I was able to come up with. I pulled it off the web, her Facebook profile picture. I'm not sure how up-to-date it is."

He was right. It appeared to be some kind of college gradua-tion photo. She was wearing a cap and gown and one of those silly hats and she was clowning around with a few of her fellow grads. She was a pretty girl, a brunette, with a cute smile. She looked like every attractive young woman who comes to New York filled with dreams of making it as an actor. Nice cheek-bones. Mary Tyler Moore nose. Straight, white teeth. She was the whole package.

"Better than nothing."

"You might be able to get a better photo from her room-mates. Or maybe you can pull something off the web."

"Nothing with Nicky, I presume?"

He shook his head.

"Okay, I'll get started."

"And Henry, one more thing."

"Yeah?"

"We're kind of on the clock on this one. The judge allowed the switch of attorneys but refused to give us much of a continuance. Two weeks. That means we go to trial a week from this coming Monday. I can stall for a few days while we pick a jury, but after that..."

"Okay. It's not the first time I've had to work with the clock ticking. Remember, Paul, I'm no miracle worker."

I got up and headed toward the door. Before I left, I turned and ask, "By the way, just out of curiosity, what were those 'creative differences' Diamond had with his first lawyer?"

"He didn't like the way he looked."

4

THE HEART OF DARKNESS

It wasn't my first trip out to Rikers, but I never stop hoping it will be my last.

Today, I was not alone in that hope.

As soon as I got off the bus I had to pick my way through a noisy demonstration of a couple dozen protestors, mostly women of color, a few holding the hands of small children, all of whom looked like they would rather have been almost anywhere else. Those not cradling babies in their arms held homemade signs demanding the closing down of the facility, with clever slogans like, *Educate, Don't Incarcerate.*

Rikers is a New York City prison located on a strip of land on the East River that sits between Queens and the Bronx. Depending on the day, the notorious jail houses between ten and twelve thousand prisoners, making it a cesspool likely to breed more crime rather than less. Yet I couldn't help wondering what alternative these folks had in mind for the city's criminal population awaiting what rarely wound up being the promised speedy trial.

After almost an hour of waiting, I finally made it through security and was directed to a small, airless room with a table and two chairs, usually reserved for attorney-client meetings.

Nicky Diamond, his hands cuffed in front of him and led in by two guards wasn't what I'd expected. He might have been a tough guy on the street but now, dressed in his tan jumpsuit that was several sizes too big for him, he sure didn't look it. Instead of some hulking, mouth-breathing behemoth, he was scrawny, weighing maybe a hundred and forty pounds, tops. He stood five-six on a good day, which meant a day when he was wearing shoes with proper heels instead of a pair of designer track shoes. He reminded me of the skinny Sinatra who played Maggio in *From Here to Eternity*. Before his incarceration, he probably boasted a healthy head of hair, but today he sported a state-sponsored buzz cut (there had been a recent plague of head lice according to the *New York Post,* my favorite New York City tabloid, and prison officials were obviously taking no chances of it spreading), accompanied by that annoyingly pseudo-hip three-day unshaved look favored by models for men's fashion magazines like *GQ* and *Details.* Why anyone would think I'd buy a particular shirt or pair of pants because some dude neglected to shave for a few days is beyond me. But maybe that's what most women, especially those with a hankering for bad boys, consider a good-looking guy. Nicky completed the uninspiring package with prominent cheekbones, a sharp nose, full lips and a perfect set of choppers. Hollywood casting directors would probably have pegged him as the James Franco type.

I checked his arms and neck for tattoos because it's a quick and easy way to map out shortcuts to a guy's life history. Surprisingly, there were none. This was unusual for the average mobbed-up guy who didn't mind advertising that it would be healthy to steer clear. But on second thought, Nicky Diamond struck me as the kind of guy who didn't need or want to telegraph danger signals. He was the kind of guy you didn't fuck with just on principle.

From the looks of him, Diamond didn't fit the stereotype of a stone-cold killer, but therein lay a good example of a valuable lesson learned early on. Epictetus had it right. "Things either are what they appear to be; or they are not, nor do they appear to be; or they are, yet do not appear to be; or they are not, and yet appear to be." In the end, it didn't matter much what Diamond looked like. It was who he was and what he could do to you that mattered.

At first glance, there was nothing particularly frightening about this little man. But that changed as soon as he sat down opposite me and I could look him in the eye. Only then did I get a glimpse into the soul of Nicky Diamond.

Ariel's song from Shakespeare's *The Tempest* immediately came to mind.

"Those are pearls that were his eyes."

Only Nicky Diamond's eyes were definitely not pearls, but rather steely black pellets that sucked you into a dark abyss. Only then could you possibly know for certain the black hole that was Nicky Diamond. It was not somewhere I wanted to be. It was not somewhere anyone should want to be. I hadn't ex-changed a single word with Diamond, yet I had to admit this wiry, little punk scared the bejesus out of me.

Even if you were able to avoid those perilous eyes it wouldn't take long to pick up on his tough-guy vibe. You only had to sit across from him and try to engage him in conversation to feel a paralyzing chill.

I could see Diamond was used to being in charge. Before I could even introduce myself properly he hissed, in a raspy voice not much above a Kiefer Sutherland whisper, "You're Swann."

It wasn't a question. It was a statement. No, strike that. It was more like a warning. The kind warning that at that moment made me wish I wasn't Swann.

"That's right."

"I'm Nicky Diamond."

"Yeah. I know. Any particular reason you're whispering?"

He looked around. "The fucking walls have ears," he hissed, as if I were an idiot for not recognizing the obvious.

"If you mean the room is bugged, I don't think so. It's for lawyers and clients. It would be against the law to bug them. You know, that confidentiality thing."

He snorted, like a bull. "You think that fucking stops them?"

He looked up and seemed to continue the conversation with some unseen entity. "Rudder send me some kind of moron? Besides, you're a private dick, not a lawyer."

"That's only half right. I'm not a lawyer but I'm not a private dick either."

"Then who the hell are you and why the hell are you wasting my time?"

Intimidation was obviously a technique Diamond had mastered. It was time to rock his world and show him who the real alpha dog was in this pack.

"I'm the guy who's going to help get you out of here and if you think I'm wasting your time and, more important, my time, I can get back on the damn bus and leave this shithole island."

He shrugged, his shoulders rising so high it looked as if his head would sink back into his body.

"I got nowhere else to be, so I'll listen to what you got to say. But we gotta watch it. Like I said, I don't trust these motherfuckers." He looked around the room again. "Rudder says, whatever the hell you call yourself, you're good at finding people."

"I have a knack."

"We'll see. You don't got long to get the job done, you know."

"That's why I'm here. I need your help so I can find Jana before you go to trial."

"I think you oughtta know something. I'm not a helpful guy."

"Maybe we can change that. Tell me about Jana."

"What's to tell?"

"I know where she works. I know where she lives. I know where she goes to school. I need the stuff your lawyer didn't write down. I want to know where she's from. Where her family lives. Who her friends are. What her habits are. What her favorite food is. What she likes to do for fun." I tactfully left out, *what the hell she sees in you.*

Diamond stared at me, or rather through me. If he blinked, I missed it. It was scary how focused this guy could be. I felt a chill not for me but for his victims, past and future. They didn't stand a chance.

"What the fuck is this, the *Dating Game?*"

"Okay, let's take this one step at a time. Where do you think she might be?"

"If I knew that I wouldn't fucking need you, would I?"

"But you do need me, Nicky, and since we're stuck with each other, you might as well make my job as easy as possible. Especially since it's your ass on the line, not mine. I can go through the motions and still cash my check. It's your dough. If you want me to earn it, you'd be smart to cooperate."

Diamond glared at me. Suddenly, I knew where that expression *looked daggers at me* came from. It made me uncomfortable. But I wasn't going to let him get the upper hand, so I just stared right back at him. For what seemed like several minutes but was probably less than one, neither of us said a word. I was thinking about all the meals I'd had in the last couple days. I have no idea what he was thinking about. I won. He blinked first.

"You know something, Swann, I don't fucking like you."

I shrugged. "Suit yourself, Nicky. Usually takes people a little longer than a few minutes to get there, but I guess you're more perceptive than the average guy. And when I get home, I'll spend the rest of the night crying into my pillow because you don't fucking like me. Fortunately for both of us, as soon as I leave here there's a pretty good chance we'll never have to lay eyes on each other again."

"What a fucking shame that would be."

"Anyone ever tell you you've got a hostility problem, Nicky?"

"All the fucking time." He snorted again. "But I make it work for me so's it ain't my problem."

He leaned back, a giant smirk on his face. He thought he was back in control and he was enjoying himself. This was a monumental waste of my time and it pissed me off. But there was very little I could do about it other than ignore him and try to move things along.

"You're paying me by the hour, Nicky," I lied. "So, what say we move this train down the tracks?"

"You think I give a fuck about your time? I'm the one doing the time, pal. You think money's ever been a problem for me? Look, let's get this straight. I'll tell you what I can, but no questions about me, understand? I don't need no two-bit psychoanalyzing. You know, like where did this boy go wrong crap. Or what makes this poor boy tick. Or what did his mommy and daddy do to him to make him such a bad boy. Or anything about what I do for a living. Because if you do ask those questions, you'd be wasting my time, because you're not going to get any fucking answers."

"I hope this doesn't come as a shock, Nicky, but I don't give a damn about you. I'm not your social worker and I'm not your mother. And while we're at it, we might as well get something else straight. I'm not here for you. I'm here to help an old friend who happens to be your lawyer. I don't care if you did it or didn't do it. I don't care if you fry or spend the rest of your life seeing the world through iron bars. Frankly, I think we'd all be better off if either of those things happened. None of that concerns me. I'm being paid to find Jana. It's what I do and I do it well. So, despite what I think about you and how you've spent your sad, pathetic life, you're going to get your money's worth. And if it happens that as the result of my doing my job you get out of this hellhole and back on the street to do whatever it is you do, well, I can live with that. And you know why?"

He looked like he was about to say something but I didn't give him a chance. I had to show him who was really in control. At least while he was the one in chains.

"I have more than enough of my own shit to carry. I don't have any more room to carry around someone else's."

He grinned. But it wasn't one of those happy grins. Or share a joke grins. I was learning pretty quick that the only thing worse than him being hostile when you were around Nicky Diamond was when he appeared to be amused. I'm no shrink but I've been around enough head cases in my time to recognize a host of psychological syndromes, among them borderline and narcissistic personalities spiked with an unhealthy touch of sociopathic tendencies. Translated, this meant not only was Nicky Diamond fucking nuts, but he didn't care about anyone other than himself.

"I think maybe we're going to get along after all, Swann," he whispered.

"I wouldn't start shopping for friendship rings. How about we get down to answering some questions?"

He leaned back in his seat and lifted his handcuffed hands over his head and placed them behind his head.

"Yeah. Sure. Why not?"

"How long have you and Jana been together?"

"Three, maybe four months. Maybe six."

"You're not sure?"

"Time flies when you're having fun, pal. Besides, I lead a very full life. I don't have time to keep track of dates."

"How'd you meet?"

"At the Hilton, the joint where she works. I liked the way she served drinks."

"What brought you there?"

"What difference does that make?"

"Just answer the questions, Nicky. If you try to deconstruct every one of them we'll be here all night and only one of us is checked in."

"I got a few places I like to hang out. That's one of them."

"You had business there?"

He hesitated a moment. "You might say that."

"What kind of business?"

He didn't bother to answer, which was answer enough for me.

"You get along pretty good with her?"

"Good enough."

"You two ever fight?"

"Everyone fights, pal. They say they don't, they're lying. But we never had a drag out or nothing like that." He hesitated a moment. "I never hit her or nothing, if that's what you're asking.

That's not the way I roll. Guys do that are fucking cowards, man."

"So, there's no reason she should be afraid of you?"

"No. I treat her good, man. She never had no reason to be afraid of me. We been together this long without breaking up, so what do you think?"

"Does she know what you do for a living?"

There was that glare again.

"Like I said, I don't talk business outside of business."

"I'll take that as a no, When was the last time you saw her?"

"She visited a couple months ago."

"How long have you been in here?"

"You kinda lose track of time in the joint. It's not like you gotta keep a calendar of appointments, if you know what I mean."

"Guess."

"Three, four months. They don't give bail on murder raps."

"Did she visit you often?"

"She came that one time and that was it. I told her to stay away."

"You knew she was your alibi so why didn't you have her tell the cops, or your lawyer? Why did you keep it a secret?"

"I didn't want to get her involved. I didn't do it, man, so I figured why the fuck bother."

"What changed your mind?"

"My lawyer told me what they had on me."

"Rudder?"

"No. The other one."

"And that's when you realized you needed Jana?"

"Yeah."

"Did you talk to her about testifying?"

"I don't remember."

"What's that supposed to mean?"

"It means I don't remember if I told her I needed her. I told my lawyer. I figured that was enough. Besides, I couldn't get hold of Jana by then."

"Did Jana stay in touch after she visited? Phone? Letters?"

"Not really."

"So, once you realized what the state had, that's when you told your lawyer about Jana as your alibi?"

"Yeah."

"And he tried to contact her?"

"I guess."

"But he couldn't reach her?"

"Yeah. Something like that."

"And that was how long ago?"

"Couple weeks, maybe."

"That's just before Paul took over."

"Yeah. I was the one told him about her. He tried to reach her but he couldn't find her. That's why we hired you."

"Why'd you fire your first lawyer?"

"Creative differences."

"What's that supposed to mean?"

"It means I didn't like him. I thought he was an asshole."

"How'd you come to Rudder?"

"Word of mouth. What's this got to do with Jana?"

I didn't want to tell him nothing, so I ignored his question.

"Ever meet any of Jana's friends or her roommates?"

"We didn't double-date, if that's what you mean."

"So, what did you do for fun?"

He cracked a wicked-looking smile. "What do you do with your girlfriend for fun, Swann? Assuming you've ever had one."

"Yeah, well, the difference between you and me is I hold onto mine, Nicky. You're not going to make this easy for me, are you?"

"Where's it say I got to make it easy for you? I can only tell you what I can tell you. You already know where she works. You already know where she lives. Talk to the people who work with her. Talk to the people who live with her. Maybe they can point you in the right direction. Me, I'm in here. There's not much I can tell you about what happens out there." He jerked a thumb in the general direction of somewhere else.

"Is she your only girlfriend, Nicky?"

"What's that supposed to mean?"

"It means are you sleeping with other women the same time you're sleeping with Jana?"

"We're not married, if that's what you're asking. Not that that would make a difference. In case you haven't figured it out yet, I ain't no saint. What's that got to do with anything?"

"Maybe she found out you're seeing other women, got pissed and decided she doesn't want to help you out."

"She'd have to be pretty pissed to do something like that, wouldn't she?"

"You look like you could piss someone off pretty bad, Nicky."

"Yeah. I probably could. But that's not the way it went down."

"How did it go down? Why do you think she disappeared? Did she disappear on her own or do you think someone else was involved, someone who might have something against you? Or her?"

"How the fuck should I know?"

"Because she's your girlfriend. Because she's the one who could get you out of this mess. Now either she took off on her own or somebody made sure she wasn't around to help you."

"Why don't you ask her when you find her?"

"That's the best you can do?"

"Yeah," he said, nailing me with those damn eyes. "That's the best I can do."

I had a very strong sense Diamond was holding something back, but I knew no matter how long I questioned him I wasn't about to get it out of him. I asked a few more general questions just to see if he'd loosen up, but he pretty much shut down. The law of diminishing returns kicked in. He'd told me everything he was going to tell me. Maybe he knew more, maybe he didn't. But there was no reason for me to stick around any longer. So, I left hoping I'd seen the last of Nicky Diamond the same way I always hoped I'd never see Riker's Island again.

5
LIBERTY AND JUSTICE FOR ALL

Nicky Diamond was scum, a coldblooded killer for hire who belonged off the streets. Not just for a while, but forever. And yet, I was very much aware that if I were successful in finding Jana Monroe and she could, in fact, provide him with the alibi he needed, I'd be responsible for putting him back out there, a real menace to society. If that happened it wouldn't be much of a stretch to hold me responsible for a string of murders he'd commit in the future. He wasn't, in the strict sense of the word, a serial killer. He was worse. He was a killer for hire. A mass murderer. And if I did enable him by providing the alibi he needed to go free, how much different from him would I be?

Did it bother me? Yeah. Maybe. A little, I guess. But enough to make a difference? Obviously not.

Let's face it, I've done plenty of things I wasn't proud of in my life, solely for the money. And there's little doubt I'd do them again and will continue to do them in the future. It's the life I've chosen for myself. Or was it the life that, after the untimely death (is any death really timely?) of my wife, chose me?

All I had to do to get through it and continue to sleep at night, no matter how fitfully, was to keep reminding myself that finding Jana Monroe was a job, just like so many other jobs I'd had over the years. How different was it from repo-ing cars? It wasn't personal. It was business. It wasn't necessary for me to like my client, or condone how he lived his life. Besides, I was working for Paul Rudder, not Nicky Diamond. And if I tried hard enough, maybe I'd even be able to convince myself that by helping exonerate Diamond, I was doing my part to make the American judicial system work like it was supposed to. I've known plenty of good cops and some bad, which would include my own father, and if the cops were wrong on this one then it was up to me to help prove it. Yeah, that's what I was, all right. Just another superhero doing his job to help keep America safe, by providing liberty and justice for all.

What made this job trickier than most was that I didn't know if Jana Monroe disappeared on her own or whether someone else was behind it. If it was the latter then I had to consider the possibility that she was no longer alive. If that was the case, I was wasting my time and Nicky Diamond was sunk. Unless, of course, Rudder, who was a very clever defense attorney, could use her death to provide that shred of doubt needed to convince a jury Nicky Diamond shouldn't be put away for life.

Once I got off Rikers the plan was to visit the hotel lounge where Jana Monroe worked and then, later in the evening, head out to Brooklyn and talk to her roommates. After that, well, there was no after that. I could only hope one of those stops would steer me in the right direction because if it didn't I had no idea what I'd do next. But that didn't bother me. It has always been the way I work. Over the years, I've found if I do too much planning it stifles creativity. I get locked into a plan and often that stops me from seeing the big picture. As Thelonious Monk once said, "Man, sometimes I play things even I've never heard before." That pretty much sums up the way I work. It's instinctual, straight from the gut. I plan no further ahead than tomorrow and even that's not guaranteed. Most folks can't work this way. They need to know where they're going and how they're getting there. They need the security of a well-worked out plan. Not me. If I do it that way and wind up headed in the wrong direction, it paralyzes me. Doubt creeps up and from doubt there is the debilitating specter of failure, which inevitably leads to inaction. If that happens, all is lost. I am lost.

Once back in Manhattan, I headed over to the Hilton on Fifty-fourth Street and the Avenue of the Americas where Jana Monroe worked as a cocktail waitress. As I was crossing Fifth Avenue headed west, my pocket vibrated. It was a text from Goldblatt. Simple and to the point: "Call me."

My first instinct was to ignore him, but I knew if I did there'd be a series of angry texts and finally an annoying phone call.

"What's up?" I texted back, hoping I wouldn't have to talk to him. No such luck. My phone rang.

"I tracked down the owner of the building where Madame Sofia ran her operation," he said. He could hardly contain his glee.

"Text me the information."

"No need. I made an appointment for us to meet with the guy tomorrow morning. I cleared my schedule."

"Unclear it. I prefer to work alone."

"You're afraid I'm going to get in the way?"

"The thought occurred to me."

"Don't worry. I'm just along for the ride. Promise I won't interfere. I'm your partner, Swann. I need to know how you work. I bet I could learn a lot from you."

"Cut the bullshit, Goldblatt."

"No, man, I'm serious. You know, like if you're busy we could get twice as much done. Besides, what if you're incapacitated and I have to take over."

"You know something I don't?"

"Of course not."

"Then maybe you're thinking of going into business for yourself?"

"I got no interest in your part of the business. Besides, I'm much too valuable as your inside man."

"I'm guessing this is nonnegotiable."

"That's a good bet. I'll text you the four-one-one and we'll meet there ten o'clock tomorrow morning."

"What did you tell him?"

"That we're looking for office space. I know you think other-wise, Swannee, but I ain't no chimpanzee, pal. So, I'll see you tomorrow morning in the lobby of his building. Unless you want to meet a little earlier and grab breakfast."

My stomach involuntarily began to churn.

"Despite how much I love watching you eat, I think I'll pass on that. I'm not really a breakfast person."

"You on that thing for Rudder now?"

"Yeah."

"You can fill me in on that tomorrow."

I didn't bother arguing with him. Goldblatt was like a cat with a ball of string. When the time came, I could always keep him occupied by waving something in front of him.

It was in the middle of the cocktail hour and the Hilton lounge was buzzing. The bar area was two and three deep and nearly every table was occupied. Not the best time to find someone to talk to me, but I didn't have much choice. The obvious place to start was with the manager, since the waitresses were in con-stant motion and look much too harassed to talk.

The bartender pointed me in the direction of the manager's office, which turned out to be a room not much larger than a utility closet. The door was ajar, but I still knocked. A guy seated behind a desk, whom I presumed was the manager, was on the phone. When he heard the knock, he looked up and motioned for me to come in.

He was a good-looking Latino who appeared to be in his mid to late thirties. He wore his jet-black hair slicked back and tied in a short ponytail and he was neatly dressed in dark slacks, a white button-down shirt and black tie.

He put his hand over the mouthpiece. "Have a seat. I'll be with you in a minute."

True to his word, a minute later he hung up and smiled at me.

"Name's Luis," he said, pointing to the nameplate on his breast pocket. "How may I help you?"

"Name's Henry Swann and I want to talk to you about one of your employees."

"Well, Mr. Swann, as you can see it's a madhouse out there, and I'm short staffed." He pointed to the phone. "I was just trying to find someone to come in last minute."

"This won't take long."

"You wouldn't happen to be a cop, would you, Mr. Swann?"

"I look like a cop?"

He shrugged. "Even cops don't look like cops anymore."

"Would there be a problem if I was the law?"

"Nope. Just curious."

"I'm just a guy looking for one of your employees."

"Who'd that be?"

"Jana Monroe."

"Jana, huh?" He sized me up. He was weighing whether he should help me or get rid of me. It was a look I'd experienced many times before. I'm always surprised when I pass muster but somehow I always seem to manage it. "Mind if I ask why you're looking for her?"

"Is it important you know why?"

"I'm protective of my girls, sir. Jana's a good girl. I like her. I don't want to make trouble for her."

"She's not in trouble."

"Then why are you looking for her."

"She's a possible witness in a criminal case and I've been hired to find her."

His hands went to his throat to fix a tie that didn't need fixing. Then he nervously did this fake hand-washing thing with his hands. I knew the body language well. He was weighing his options. He didn't want to get involved but he wasn't sure he could stay out of it.

"What kind of crime are we talking about here?" he asked.

"I'm afraid I can't say."

"Why not? Is it something serious?"

I could have told him the truth, but I was afraid it might freak him out, which would only make my job tougher.

"Frankly, Luis..." I let the name settle in the air a moment for dramatic effect, "I haven't been authorized to talk about the case with anyone other than my client and, of course, Ms. Monroe. So, I'd really appreciate a helping hand here."

"I don't know. It just don't seem right. I mean I got a responsibility to my employees. I can't just be handing out information about them without knowing why. Or without authorization from my superiors." He stopped, waiting for me to convince. Did he want an incentive? A few dollars? I hesitated to do that unless as a last resort. Not so much because I had scruples preventing me from paying for information, but rather because you can never be sure the information you're paying for is true. Sure, I'd stick my hand in my pocket, but only if I had to.

"You got some identification?" he asked, breaking the silence. "Maybe that'll help."

"Sure." I pulled out my wallet and handed him the only business card I had, one I'd made up years ago, when I was still working out of that ratty office up in Spanish Harlem. It had that old address, my cell number, and my email address. The chick who designed it—it was her way of paying for services rendered, since she was flat broke—made it look official. Like I was a man of importance. Goldblatt had been threatening for a while to make us business cards, but it hadn't happened yet, and I wasn't pushing the matter. Why? Because somehow in my mind having business cards with his and my name on it would make our alliance more serious and more permanent than I wanted it to be. It was the difference between living together and getting married. This card, frayed at the edges from being pulled in and out of my wallet for God knows how long, was hardly worth the paper it was printed on, but it usually did the trick. You show people something that looks even mildly official they buy it. Mostly, because they want to.

"Looks okay. But I still don't know why you can't tell me why you want to speak to her. It don't make a lot of sense."

I shrugged. "What can I say, Luis? Sometimes, no matter how hard we try, life just doesn't make sense. Look, like you say, it's a madhouse out there and I'm sure you've got better things to do, so why don't we wrap this up?"

"It's the Italian shoe convention. They keep my girls hopping and because they're European, they think tips are included. I have to watch that the girls don't add tips to the check…"

"Tell me what I need to know and I'll get out of your hair. I promise, Jana's not in trouble. I just need to find her so an innocent" (the word almost stuck in my throat) "man doesn't get convicted."

"Of what?"

"Like I said, I'm under a strict gag rule. How long has Jana worked here?"

"'Bout a year, I guess."

"She cause any trouble?"

"What kind of trouble?"

"You know, coming in late? Missing shifts? Getting into it with customers?"

He shook his head. "Nah, not Jana. She's a doll. Very reliable. Never missed a shift and she was always ready to take on someone else's if they needed to switch."

"You're talking in the past tense, Luis. In like she doesn't work here anymore."

He didn't answer which was an answer.

"How long since she's been in?"

"Few weeks, maybe. But that don't mean she don't work here anymore."

"Did she give notice?"

He laughed. "These girls come and go, man. They don't give notice. They just don't show up. And you think I keep track of 'em?" He shook his head. "Don't want to. Couldn't even if I did."

"Does not showing up and not calling in to tell you seem out of character for her?"

"Haven't given it much thought."

"Have you tried to get in touch with her?"

He shook his head.

"Why's that?"

"I didn't take this job to be no one's babysitter. Someone don't come in that usually means they're quitting and ain't coming back. Listen, she's a good-looking girl. They meet some guy wants to take care of them, or they get a part in a show or a commercial or a movie—most of 'em are wannabe actresses—they up and quit. They don't feel like they got to give notice or anything like that. They just servers, man. They didn't sign no contract."

"You think that's what happened with her?"

"What's that?"

"She got another gig somewhere."

He shrugged. "Sure. Why not?"

"Aren't you worried something bad might have happened to her?"

I could tell by the look on his face I was pissing him off. Wasting his time. That's what I was aiming for. When people are pissed they sometimes say things they wouldn't ordinarily say. He might give me important information just to get me out of his hair.

"You think this job's easy, man? Working with the public in the hospitality industry sucks. You wouldn't believe what goes on here, what I gotta deal with as manager, every, single, frigging day. I can't hold everyone's hand. I gotta move on. Jana doesn't come in, I figure that's her way of quitting. So, I just find someone to take her place. Believe me, it ain't hard. Servers are a dime a dozen in this town. You know how many actors, writers, musicians, artists we got here?"

It was a rhetorical question that didn't require an answer.

"Anyone ever come in to see her during working hours?"

He shook his head. "We got rules about that. Management calls it fraternization."

"I didn't ask about rules, Luis. I asked if she ever had visitors. Like a boyfriend, maybe?"

"Yeah. Maybe once or twice a guy came in. Maybe he was her boyfriend. Maybe he was just someone she knew. I had to tell her to cut that out. I didn't want no trouble. The other girls see that and they think this is some kind of social club. Besides, I didn't want her to get in trouble and that dude had trouble written all over his face. I know the type. I grew up with them."

That had to be Nicky Diamond, but I needed to make sure.

"Remember what he looked like?"

"Little guy. Tough looking. The kinda guy you don't want to mess with, because guys like that are unpredictable. You know the kind. They blow your head off for looking at 'em the wrong way. You say something, they knock your head off. You bump into them on the subway, they hit you with a club."

Yeah, that was Nicky Diamond, all right.

"She ever talk to you about him?"

"It ain't good to get personal with staff. You don't want it to look like you're playing favorites. You know, with scheduling and whatnot. There are good shifts and there are bad shifts. Naturally, all the girls want the good ones. There's a lot of jealousy you got to deal with. Especially with these girls. This ain't a career for them, man. Besides, you got to be extra careful 'cause of this sexual harassment stuff. You know, the me-too shit. We get special training. It's a sensitive thing. Getting friendly with the staff is a big, fat no-no. Gets in the way, and it spells trouble."

"Did she have any particular friends among the staff?"

"I think maybe she and Susie were kind of close."

"Susie here tonight?"

"She's the tall blonde. But look, it's a busy night. Like I said, we got that shoe thing in town...So, I can't be having you take Susie off the floor just to rap with her."

"I get it. I'll get her contact information and I'll catch her after work."

"I can't give you that, man."

"I know, Luis. Rules. I'll get her contact information from her."

"Okay, but just see you make it quick."

I found Susie just as she was dropping off a tray of drinks to a table of guys in Italian suits who could have been shoe sales-men or in the mob. Or both. I told her I was looking for Jana because I was worried about her. I got her number and told her I'd be in touch the next day. She warned me she was on the late shift and not to call till after noon.

By now it was almost six-thirty. I was hungry, so I grabbed a hot dog and a Coke from the Sabrett cart on the corner, then hopped the train out to Park Slope. I was hoping at least one of Jana's roommates might be home by the time I got there. I didn't want to go all the way out to Brooklyn for nothing.

6

Girls in the 'hood

"We've been pretty worried about her, but we didn't know what to do about it," said Cassie, one of Jana Monroe's roommates.

We were sitting in the living room of their second-floor walk-up apartment in Park Slope. The room was eclectically furnished, thanks to a cacophony of furniture that looked like it had been rescued from the sidewalk, before being picked up by New York's Strongest.

I was sitting on a fold-up chair facing Cassie and Trish who were seated next to each other on the threadbare couch. At first, they were reticent to talk, but after I explained I was there because I was worried about Jana, they opened up.

"Basically, we didn't know who to call," added Trish. Or was it Cassie? To be honest, I couldn't tell them apart so it might have been Trish who spoke first and Cassie second, though I'm pretty sure it was the other way around. They were both about the same age, mid-twenties, cute, petite and bubbly. One Betty, the other Veronica. They were dressed alike, in sweat pants and loose-fitting sweatshirts. Not only did they share the same body type but shared the same personality: chipper and upbeat. It didn't matter which was which and it wasn't worth the effort it would have taken to tell them apart. One of them, Cassie, I think, was in grad school at NYU, getting her MA in business. The other, which would have been Trish, was in a MA program for social work at Hunter. Both were quick to inform me they shared Jana's enthusiasm for theater. Both had come to the city right after college, hoping to make it as Broadway performers—Cassie was a singer, Trish an actor. Now, after a couple frustrating years pounding the pavement, they were more realistic about their chances at stardom and had chosen backup professions. The city is chockful of talented kids like these, pursuing their dreams, and I admired these two for getting real about their chances.

"Do you think we should have called the police?" asked the one I'll call Cassie.

"It wouldn't have done much good. Since neither of you is related and they had no reason to suspect anything criminal, they would have just blown you off."

"So how come you're looking for her? I mean, how'd you even know she was missing?" asked Trish, who I pegged as the alpha chick in the apartment.

"Come to think of it, how'd you find us?" added Cassie.

"Her parents hadn't heard from her and were worried. I'm a family friend, so they asked me to check up on her, to make sure everything was okay." Sometimes I scare myself at how easily lies pass through my lips. "Either of you ever met her boyfriend?"

"Boyfriend?" said Cassie, crinkling her nose.

"Didn't you know she had one?"

Both shook their heads in unison, like a well-practiced synchronized swim routine. I once read somewhere that when women live together they can get on the same menstrual cycle.

"She never talked about the guy she was dating? I mean, you girls talk about stuff like that, right?"

"Yeah...but we really don't spend that much time together," said Cassie. "Our schedules don't match up. She works nights. Both of us have part-time day jobs, and the rest of the time we have classes or we're in the library."

"We're teaching assistants..." Trish added.

"Otherwise there's be no way we could afford—"

"So, the name Nicky Diamond doesn't mean anything to you?" I interrupted. We were rapidly reaching the point of TMI, as the kids say, and I didn't have all day.

"No," said Trish, shaking her head.

"Me, neither…oh, wait, now that I think of it she might have mentioned the name Nicky once or twice," said Cassie. "Right, Trish?"

"If you say so," said Trish, who, obviously bored by the conversation, had picked up a fashion magazine and was flipping through it.

"Do you remember the context?"

"Not really," said Cassie.

"Oh, wait. I remember," said Trish. "One night she called and said she wouldn't make it home. Remember, Cassie? She said she'd be working late and had an early audition in the morning so she might as well stay in the city. She said she'd stay with Nicky. I guess I assumed it was one of her girlfriends. You know, like Nicky, could be short for Nicole.

"Jana never really talked about boyfriends or anything like that. She wasn't very big on small talk," said Cassie.

"She was very sweet and very considerate. She wouldn't want us to worry about her," added Trish, who looked up from her magazine. "You know, in case we woke up and she wasn't here."

"Not that we would have worried," said Cassie. "I mean we're all adults here."

"She didn't say anything else about him?"

"I don't think so. Do you think he has anything to do with her disappearance?" said Cassie.

"I don't want you girls to jump to any conclusions. This isn't an episode of *Dateline*."

They giggled. In unison, of course.

"Either of you got any idea where she might be?"

Both girls shook their heads.

"Come on, girls, use your imagination. You must have talked

about places you'd like to go if you could. You know, dream trips? Or places you've been before that you'd you like to go back to. Or people she'd like to visit?"

"I guess maybe like she could be visiting a relative?" said Cassie.

"It obviously can't be her parents," said Trish, "since they're the ones who asked you to look for her."

"How about friends? You know, from before she moved here," I asked, trying to move the conversation along.

"She did talk about a best friend who was from some place down south. I think it was Alabama. Jana went to college down there," said Trish.

"I think so," said Cassie.

"It might have been one of her classmates."

"I think she went to Tulane," said Cassie.

"That's in New Orleans, right?" said Trish.

"But you said Alabama."

"Yes. She went to Tulane, but her friend was from Alabama."

"You wouldn't happen to have the name of that friend, would you?"

Cassie looked at Trish. Trish looked back at Cassie.

"I think maybe her name was Janet something or other."

"That's right," said Trish. "Like, Janet...Kirby? That's it. Kirby. I think she was originally from Mobile, but now she was living in a small beach town across the bay. Fair-something."

"That's right," said Cassie. "I remember she talked about it once and it sounded great. A beach town. She said it reminded her of the Hamptons."

"The Redneck Riviera, right?" said Trish.

"No! Don't you remember. She said it wasn't the Redneck Riviera. That was on the Gulf and the place she was talking about was on the Bay."

"Oh, yeah, that's right. I remember now. We like Google mapped it one night. Remember?"

"Hope, that's what it was," said Trish.

"Hope, Alabama?" I said.

"No, no. It was Fairhope."

"Right, that was it," said Cassie.

These girls seemed kind of ditzy, and I didn't know how reliable their information was. But it was a possible lead.

"You've been a big help, girls. I'll check that out."

"I sure hope she's okay," said Trish. "Won't you tell us the real reason you're looking for her? I mean, you don't expect us to believe that story about her parents asking you to find her, do you?"

"Why not?"

"Because her father's dead and she hasn't spoken to her mother in years, that's why," said Cassie.

I smiled. They were playing me. I kinda liked that.

"You girls are really something else. I guess you got me."

"So, what's the real story?" asked Cassie, leaning forward as if getting closer to me would ensure my telling her the "real story."

"I can't say much, but it has to do with her boyfriend, Nicky."

"But who really asked you to find her?" asked Trish.

"And why can't you tell us what's really going on?" added Cassie.

"To be honest with you, girls, the less you know the better."

"Are you kidding?"

"Trust me, girls, this is not something to kid about. Jana could be in serious trouble, so you've got to promise me if you hear from her you'll let me know right away. And please, don't talk to anyone else about this."

I took out my pad and pen. "I'm going to write down my contact information and I want you to get in touch with me if you hear from her or if you think of anything else that might help me find her. Understand?"

They nodded.

"Do you think she's in real danger?" asked Cassie.

"It's possible. That's why I've got to find her as quick as I can."

"I sure hope you find her," said Trish.

"It's nice to know you guys are worried about her."

"Oh, it's not that," said Cassie. "The rent is due in a week and we need to get her share."

7
RENT STRIKE

One thing about Goldblatt I can always count on is his being on time. Sometimes a blessing, sometimes a curse.

We met in front of a nondescript prewar office building on West Thirty-seventh Street, just west of Seventh Avenue, in what's known as the Garment Center. For one particularly hot summer in my teens I worked here for a factoring company, delivering large checks to companies who sold their invoices for a discounted price to the company I worked for. It was one of the best jobs I ever had because no one kept tabs on our time, just so long as we got the checks where they were meant to go. This meant so long as I made the delivery, carrying checks sometimes in the amount of fifty to a hundred grand, I could aimlessly wander the streets on company time.

I even recognized this as one of the buildings where I made deliveries several decades earlier. The building hadn't changed much. It was rundown then, it was rundown now. I wondered if the landlord we were meeting owned the building where he had his office. If so and it was representative of his other properties, he qualified as a commercial slumlord. For one thing, the lobby hadn't been painted since one of the wars, take your pick as to which one, and the elevator, so small it could hardly hold more than four people at a time, smelled of a combination of piss and curry, the latter odor compliments of the takeout Indian joint next door.

The agonizingly slow elevator seemed to take forever to get to the seventh floor, where Frank Becker had his office.

"So, what did you tell him?" I asked Goldblatt, as the elevator lurched skyward.

"That we were looking to open a store and were interested in the location of one of his buildings. Don't worry, I've got the backstory all worked out. So, you might as well let me start the ball rolling. I'll give you the high sign when you can take over."

"Not a chance."

"What's that supposed to mean?"

"First of all, we don't need a backstory. There's no need to waste time playing games. Once we're in the office I'll ask him what we need to know. So, I'm not going to bother asking what the high sign is."

"But that's half the fun," he whined. "You know, playing the game."

"We're not here to play games, Goldblatt. We're here to find Madame Sofia."

I could see from the expression on his face he was disappointed. For a split second I was tempted to let him off the leash just so I could see him in action. The truth is, my curiosity about my partner was beginning to get the best of me. I was fascinated by the discrepancy between who he was and who he says he was. But now was not the time to find out.

"So, you really don't want me to say anything?"

"I'm not serving you with a gag order. If you think you can add something constructive to the conversation, go ahead. But I'm warning you, think before you speak. Understand?"

"You think I'm some kind of out-of-control moron?"

"I didn't say that. But let's face it, sometimes you act like one."

His face morphed into a pout. Me, all I could do was smile, though I tried not to make it too obvious. I know. I know. Sometimes I can be a real, low-down son of a bitch.

"If I do, it's because I think it's a productive strategy. People underestimate me, Swann, and you're one of them. You'd be wise to remember this: I always know what I'm doing and why I'm doing it."

"That's valuable information for me to have," I said, hoping that, in fact, it was true. In the future I might be more likely to give him the benefit of the doubt, but I wasn't totally convinced.

As the elevator door opened onto the seventh floor, Goldblatt turned and said, "This guy's a real scumbag. I ran a background check and I wouldn't be surprised if he knew what was going on when he rented her the place."

"I'm used to dealing with scumbags," I said, as we stepped off the elevator.

I'd also run Frank Becker through a Google search and Goldblatt was right. As a landlord his shady tactics included emptying rent-controlled and stabilized apartment buildings of longstanding tenants while racking up a record-breaking number of code violations in a city where the competition for this position was pretty impressive. He even had the distinction of making the *Village Voice's* list of worst landlords four years running, quite a distinction in a city like ours. Somehow, he'd managed to keep himself well-protected either by greasing the right palms or by operating under an umbrella of shell corporations or holding companies, several of which were printed on his office door.

Enterprise Corporation
American Realty Company
Manhattan Connection
Apartments 4 Everyone
Universal Home Corporation

My hand was on the doorknob when I happened to glance over at Goldblatt, who had a big, fat smile on his face.

"What's so funny?"

"I used to do some work for guys like him," Goldblatt said. "It's like they got no soul."

I took my hand off the doorknob.

"Then why'd you work for them?"

He shrugged. "I guess those were my scumbag days. I'm guessing you haven't always worked for saints."

I couldn't argue with him there. Case in point: Nicky Diamond.

"I know how easy it is to play these guys. You sure you don't want me to handle this?"

"Why don't we see how I do then, if I need help, you can jump in."

"I'm ready, partner," he said, giving me a condescending pat on my shoulder.

The office was one large room and reeked of that musty odor you find in the basements of older buildings. There was a large desk up against the wall opposite the front door. A couple folding chairs were set up against the wall on our right. A bookcase stuffed with folders and loose papers that reached my belt buckle and two smaller desks were up against opposite walls. The two small desks were empty while the larger one was occupied by a middle-aged white guy, wearing a white button-down shirt, sleeves rolled up, no tie, obvious toupee, mustache, horn-rimmed glasses, sporting an over-sized gold pinky ring. This, I assumed, was our man.

"Becker?" I asked.

He glared at me.

"Swann?" he growled.

He was a miserable-looking sonuvabitch but then in this city most slumlords fit this description. My theory is that they're born looking like the rest of us and grow into looking like this. But maybe it's the other way around. Nurture or nature? In the end, does it really matter?

"That's right."

"Who's this? Your bodyguard?" he asked, jerking a thumb in Goldblatt's direction.

I glanced back at Goldblatt, whose face had suddenly turned to stone.

"Does it look like I need protection?" I didn't bother adding, *"and if I did, do you think this would be the guy I'd choose?"*

"In this city, everyone needs protection," he said, probably speaking from experience. His chair squeaked as he leaned back, cupping his hands behind his head. Haughty bastard. If my plate wasn't already full I'd take this asshole down and enjoy every damn second of it. But I had other fish to fry.

"Especially landlords."

"I guess you think that's funny." He leaned forward. "Because I don't. Let's get down to business. I understand you're looking for a spot to open a store. What kind of place we talking about?"

"That's what my associate here told you but it's not the truth."

Becker's body tensed. He dropped one of his hands below the desk and I could see him moving it slowly toward the side desk drawer. Was he going for a weapon? A panic button?

"Relax. We're not here to make trouble, so if you're reaching for a weapon or a silent alarm, you can save yourself the trouble."

His hand stopped moving, hovering over the top of the desk. "You think so?"

Obviously, he'd had his fair share of threats, probably from irate tenants. I pulled open my jacket, so he could see I wasn't carrying. "I do."

"If you're not looking to do business, what the hell are you here for?"

"I need some information about the storefront you rented on First and Sixty-first."

"I don't know what you're talking about."

"Madame Sofia mean anything to you?"

"What's your game, Swann?"

"No game. I need information and, one way or another, I'll get it. So, why not make it easy on both of us, tell me what I want to know, and we'll get out of your hair?"

"I run a big organization. You think I personally handle every goddamn rental we make?" He picked up a stack of papers and moved them around, trying to signal we were done. "I'm afraid you're shit out of luck. Now, if you'll excuse me, I've got a lot of…"

"I'm sure you've got flunkies who do your dirty work for you, Becker. But you look like a guy whose fingerprints are on every piece of paper, every decision. So, no matter how many names you plaster on your door," I jerked my finger toward the front door, "you're the only name that matters."

His body relaxed. A smile began to form on his lips but quickly morphed into a sneer. Suddenly, he seemed more comfortable, most likely because I'd given him the respect he craved.

"Why do you need this information?"

"Because I need to find Madame Sofia."

He laughed. "I got news for you. That ain't no real name. Even if it was, like I told you, I don't know anyone like that. If I did, what makes you think I'd tell you?"

"I don't see any good citizenship awards on your wall so I know it wouldn't be civic duty. But I'm guessing you're not the kind of guy who's looking for more trouble than you already have."

He laughed. It wasn't a ha-ha laugh. It was one of those laughs that's supposed to intimidate whoever's in the room. The kind of laugh that's supposed to send the message that you don't know who you're fucking with. That's the kind of laugh it was. Only, those kinds of laughs don't work on me. At least they don't work the way they're supposed to. To me, they're what I call a cover-up laugh. It's a laugh that signals you've got something to hide. It's the kind of laugh that makes me even more determined to get what I want.

"What kind of trouble you think I've got?" he said, cocking his head to one side.

I've got some looks of my own, so I shot him the one that says, *you gotta be kidding.* He knew what I meant. He was a lowlife blood sucker, but he wasn't stupid.

"So, I've got a reputation. Big fucking deal. You think anything you do or say can make it any worse?"

"Me? Probably not much. But him," I jerked my thumb toward Goldblatt. "He's the one I'd be worried about I were you."

"Who the hell's he?" Becker said, wagging a finger in Goldblatt's direction.

I could see from Goldblatt's body language that was itching to jump in. Up to now, he'd done a fine job of restraining himself, but now the game was afoot and he'd caught on as to what his role was, I could tell from the twitching of his fingers he was anxious to join in. I shot him another one of my looks. The one that says, *play it cool*. I hoped it was a look that would squelch temptation, at least for the moment. I had Becker on the ropes and didn't want to risk Goldblatt might saying the wrong thing and screwing things up.

"His name's not important. What's important is who he knows, what they owe him, and what he can do with that information. He's very familiar with the kind of people can make life difficult for you. The kind of people you don't want to piss off. And I'm not talking about getting your ugly kisser on the front page of the *Village Voice*."

I turned back to Goldblatt. What I saw surprised me. Suddenly, from his usual look as the Pillsbury Doughboy, he'd morphed into Tony Tough Guy. His face had hardened into a menacing growl, a look I'd never seen before, and he seemed to have added a couple of inches while dropping a few pounds. He was, for lack of a better word, intimidating. Maybe I'd underestimated my partner. Maybe he really could be as useful as he repeatedly claimed he could be. Was the real Goldblatt, my new secret weapon?

His eyes fixed firmly on Becker, Goldblatt nodded slowly, almost imperceptibly, in a way so understated yet chilling that even I was starting to believe my threat was not an idle one.

"Okay. Okay. I don't need no trouble," muttered Becker, who seemed to have shrunk in size as Goldblatt swelled.

"That's good, 'cause neither do we. All we want is information on this Madame Sofia. Who is she? Where is she?"

"Her name's Susan Finch."

"How do you know her?"

"Business. She was referred by a mutual friend. She's rented a few apartments and a couple storefronts from me over the years."

"You know what she uses them for?"

He shrugged. "That's none of my business."

"It is if she's breaking the law."

"How the hell would I know if she's breaking the law? I ain't her keeper."

"She was running a bunco operation out of that storefront on Sixty-first Street. That Madame Sofia, fortune teller thing was a scam."

"I already told you, I don't know nothing about no Madame Sofia and I certainly don't know nothing about fortune tellers. Like I said, I rented that place to Susan Finch. That's the name she gave me, that's the name she signed the lease with, that's the name she signed on her checks. That's the name on her driver's license. What she did with the store was her business."

"Is she still renting from you?"

"No."

"You're sure?"

"I don't have to be sure because I'm under no obligation to tell you if she was. People are entitled to privacy. You ain't the law."

"That's why you should be worried. The law doesn't care, but I do. So does my friend over here," I jerked a thumb back in Goldblatt's direction, who was still in character, his arms folded across his chest, his expression grim, his eyes glued to Becker.

"How can I reach her?"

"You guys think you're gonna make trouble for me if I don't tell you?"

"If we have to."

I was bluffing. What could we do to him? But his imagination was my best weapon. Whatever he could imagine was a lot worse than the reality.

He bit his lip. He was weighing his options. He was going to give us something. Anything to get us out of there. The truth? A lie? It didn't matter. We'd walk away with something and that was better than nothing. Because even a lie would ultimately get us closer to Susan Finch. Most people aren't good enough liars to be able to make up everything. They always fall back on a kernel of truth in their story and that kernel was often enough.

"I might be able to come up with an address for her. I think maybe she's subletting a place from someone I know. Not one of mine. This would be something more high-end than I handle. I made the connection with a business acquaintance of mine who was leaving town for six months. He was going to sublet his apartment to her, but I don't know for sure that it went through or, if it did, that she's still there."

"Where?"

"You gonna keep me out of this, right?"

I nodded.

"It's over somewhere on West End."

"The address?"

"You think I got it memorized?"

"Get it for me." I took out my last business card and tossed it on the table. "I don't hear from you within the hour, my friend here will be making a few calls of his own."

"I don't like being threatened."

"These would be consequences not threats."

"You think I don't got some juice in this town?"

I smiled. It wasn't that I didn't believe him, it was that he couldn't possibly do anything to me that would make my life any worse than it already was.

"Once you find this woman it's over, right?"

"As far as you're concerned, it is."

"Yeah, I'll see what I can do."

He put it that way because it would have killed him to let me think I'd gotten the best of him. That's the way guys like him operate. Even when they lose they have to make it seem as if they've won. What did I care? So long as he got me closer to Susan Finch, he could feel any damn way he liked.

8
THAT'S JUST THE WAY, THE WAY I LIKE IT

L.P. Hartley wrote that "the past is a foreign country; they do things differently there."

He was right.

Like it or not, everyone has a past.

Some remember it. Some don't. Some learn from it. Some refuse to. Some believe they can change it. Some know they can't. Some try to rewrite it. Some deny it. Some live in it. Some are obsessed by it. Some prefer to ignore it.

Me? I know it's there. I try to learn from it. But I don't dwell in it. The past is a fiction. It is there only to lead us to the present which is a pathway to the future.

The present is where we all live, though some of us will do anything we can to avoid it. We tell lies to ourselves. We tell lies to others. Some of us are under the impression we can control it. Those of us who are smart enough know we can't. The more we try to control the past the more uncontrollable it becomes. The present is nothing more than a shadow. It's here and then, in a flash, it's gone. Quickly and seamlessly it disappears and becomes part of the past. No matter how hard we try to hold onto the present, we can't.

I've spent time living in the past and it's not a pleasant place to be. So, now I try to be in the present as much as possible, no matter how uncomfortable or unsatisfying it is. Why? Because living in the past can be dangerous. Sometimes, when I allow my mind to wander, I find myself drifting away, back into a past that can send me, if I remain there too long, into a tailspin that's tough to recover from.

The best way to beat the present is to embrace it, knowing that at the very moment you do it becomes intertwined with both the past and the future.

Ah, yes, the future.

Some fear it. Some prefer not think about it. Some fantasize about it, pinning hopes on it. Some depend upon it. Some believe we can predict it. Some believe that if we imagine it hard enough it will become what we want it to become. These are the people who believe in fate. These are the people who believe that what is written is what will happen. Some go so far as to think there is an actual book somewhere, a book where our future is written and once written it cannot be changed.

I am not one of these people.

I believe the future is written in the present which then becomes the past.

I wish I could predict the future. I can't. I don't think anyone can. There's the possibility, of course, that one can predict the likelihood of something happening by studying the past. But at best that would count as little more than an educated guess. If we could reliably predict the future that would mean we live in an orderly, predictable world. And we all know that's not the case.

I can't predict the future and chances are no one else can. At least I haven't seen any proof of it yet. There may be crystal balls out there that claim to do the job, but as far as I'm concerned, they work about as well as that 8-Ball toy I had as a kid. You asked it a question, shook it up, and you got your answer. And somehow, the answer you got always seemed to fit the question. That was no accident. It was designed that way, as are we. We continually look for answers and if they're not readily available, we invent them. We make them fit that 8-Ball prediction. It makes us feel good. It makes us feel safe. It makes us believe there are answers to everything. It maintains the illusion that life has meaning.

Let's face it, that's why I stay in business: the hope that there are answers to every question, solutions to every problem.

But if you ask me, I don't think anyone has a pipeline to the future.

With this in mind, it should come as no surprise that I'm skeptical when it comes to believing anyone can commune with the dead, or that in turn the dead are capable of chatting with us. The only spirit guides I know of come out of a bottle. As far as I'm concerned, once you're gone, you're gone. Ashes to ashes, dust to dust, and all that crap. And yet, I'm someone who likes to think of himself as having an open mind. Let's face it, not everything can be explained logically. I mean, try to explain me to someone and see how that goes for you.

I didn't always think this way. I learned my lesson the hard way, a long time ago, on a case that took me half way around the world and wound up landing me right back where I started from, and in a lot worse shape.

I'm not one of those people who thinks he knows everything. Don't get me wrong. I'd like to be that person, but I'm smart enough to find someone who knows more than I do and try to learn some of what I don't know.

I believed Susan Finch, or Madame Sofia as she called herself, was a fraud, a con artist, a fake, a charlatan. She was a lowlife who preyed on the vulnerabilities of others. She lacked basic morals and ethics. She was a woman despicable enough to victimize another human being at a low point in her life by taking away something she had no business taking. And I'm not only talking about the dough. Even worse, she robbed trust and once that's taken, it's virtually impossible to get it back.

Before I tracked her down, I had to know what made Susan Finch and people like her tick, how they worked, how they thought. Only then could I begin my search. That, my friends, is where preparation comes in. It's the perfect example of making use of the past in the present to deal with the future.

That's where my friend Freddie Patton came in.

I suppose calling Freddie a friend is stretching it a bit. He's really more of an acquaintance, since I've only seen him a handful of times. We met a dozen or so years ago when I heard him speak at a Barnes & Noble on the Upper West Side. He'd just come out with a book entitled, *Phonies, Fakes and Charlatans, My Life in the OtherWorld.* I hadn't planned on attending, but as I strolled past the bookstore headed up to my old office in Spanish Harlem, a large poster caught my eye. It was a picture of a man in formal wear, including a top hat, dressed as if he were going to some kind of fancy affair. He was gazing into a crystal ball, while holding a copy of his book, and under the photo were the words, *The Great Debunker.*

Freddie is a professional skeptic who began his career as a magician. From the time he was a kid he was fascinated, then consumed, by magic. He idolized Harry Houdini and Harry Blackstone. He spent all his money on tricks and books that taught him the art of prestidigitation and he soon became an expert on the history of the black arts. In his late teens, he began booking local gigs, billing himself as The Fantastic Freddie and it didn't take long before he lived up to his name. After traveling from city to city while still in his early twenties working the magic circuit, he finally settled in Vegas, where he became a popular lounge act. Eventually, he got bored with that life ("Vegas is for suckers," he once told me, "and there's no one more pathetic and boring than a sucker") and became what he calls "a professional skeptic." "I got tired of seeing folks taken by so-called psychics and professional seers who claim to speak to the dead and give advice to the living," he told me.

He began to appear on local talk shows illustrating to the public how these charlatans pulled off their outrageous scams. Eventually, he grabbed the attention of the national media when he offered half a million dollars to anyone who could prove they could read minds or commune with the departed. Eventually, he

upped it to a million bucks. His challenge: he'd hand over a certi-
fied check for the dough to anyone could perform some feat of
paranormal mumbo jumbo that he couldn't duplicate by simply
using tried and true magic techniques, with utter transparency,
showing the public how it was accomplished. Of course, this
didn't make him particularly popular with his professional
brethren or those claiming extraordinary powers of the mind,
but as Freddie said, "I couldn't care less. They're all a bunch of
self-important poseurs anyway."

After a short discussion followed by a lively Q and A, I approached him, introduced myself, and asked if we could meet
for coffee some time to talk about a case I was working on. At
the time, I was looking for a runaway husband and wasn't
having much luck. His wife insisted I talk to her psychic who,
she said, might have some helpful information for me. I wanted
to know if Freddie thought I'd be wasting my time. But what I
really wanted to know is if Freddie had any doubts at all as to
whether there was an afterlife or whether there was such a thing
as ESP or paranormal phenomena.

Why? Not because I gave a shit about this woman's husband,
that's for sure. The real reason was because I was still struggling
with the loss of my wife, snatched from me in a freak accident—a
manhole cover blowing up, hitting her as she crossed Madison
Avenue, and practically slicing her in half. Was there a God and
if so, why would He or She do something so arbitrary, so meaningless, so cruel? Was there an afterlife and if there was, was my
wife there and could I reach out to her? Was there hope of our
ever being reunited? In my heart (and mind) I knew these questions would probably never be answered but like Rachel, I had
been in a particularly vulnerable place and needed something to
hold onto, even if that something was nothing more than an
empty promise.

I know this sounds ridiculous. And weak. And embarrassing.
And there was no way I was going to come out and just ask him
those questions. But that was the lowest point in my life, and I

was pretty desperate for answers. That's why I was drawn into that Barnes & Noble that evening to see what Freddie Patton had to say. That's why I screwed up my nerve and approached Freddie. And that's why I went out on a limb and invited him to have coffee with me.

I didn't expect him to say yes, but he surprised me and so out of my pain and confusion grew an odd friendship. Over the years, we've stayed in touch. I don't see him often, but several times a year I reach out to him just to maintain the connection. He's someone I can talk to about the real mysteries of life. Not where someone is hiding or how the lost get found, but whether or not there is such a thing as a soul and if there is one, what happens to it after there is no longer a physical container to hold it. Has he provided answers that have satisfied me? Of course not. But somehow just asking the questions seems to help.

This time, there was a far more practical reason to seek out Freddie's help.

In his heyday as a magician, Freddie was on the road ten months of the year. But his life changed dramatically when he gave up performing. Now, he primarily works from his home in rural New Jersey, about an hour and a half from Manhattan. He rarely ventures out anymore, using his time to write books and articles. Occasionally, he does venture forth, when the money is good enough, to give lectures on the subject of the occult.

And yes, that million-buck offer is still on the table and, as of yet, no one has been able to claim it.

I gave Freddie a call and explained what I was working on. He invited me to visit, a rare occurrence since he does not welcome visitors often. In fact, by choice, he's leading something of a hermetic existence. The rumors as to why run the gamut from his suffering a stroke, to developing a serious case of agoraphobia, or he's in the throes of a deep depression the result of a broken heart. I had no skin in that game, so I didn't ask him about it, especially since he was willing to help me and didn't mind having me in his home. But knowing Freddie as well as I do I suspect it's none of those but rather rumors he has spread around himself, enjoying every wild speculation that arises.

Freddie left Vegas, a town he never liked, and settled into a small, nondescript, two-story home in a working-class neighborhood in Paterson, not far from where he grew up. The former mill town was the birthplace of, among other notables, Lou Costello. It was also the hometown of the poet William Carlos Williams and his red wheelbarrow, as well as the famed boxer and convicted killer, Hurricane Carter. In Jack Kerouac's novel *On the Road,* his protagonist, Sal Paradise, lives with his aunt in Paterson, and the city is the setting for many of Junot Diaz's short stories as well as his novel, *The Brief Wondrous Life of Oscar Wao,* as well as John Updike's novel, *In the Beauty of the Lilies.* Why a city in such obvious decay deserves such a distinguished literary history is beyond me, but I have to admit there's a bit of a thrill for me every time I step off the bus or the train and see the city signage.

Freddie greeted me at the front door wearing a pair of faded, baggy blue jeans held up by a pair of Bugs Bunny/Tweety-Bird suspenders, and a tattered, red-and-blue plaid shirt. He'd let his frizzy, gray hair grow out since I'd last seen him, giving him an Einsteinian look, and the gray stubble on his face indicated he hadn't bothered to shave in several days. He looked like a scary cross between a mad scientist and a Midwestern farmer cum serial killer.

"Jesus, Freddie, you look like you haven't been out of the house in weeks."

He grinned, baring a startlingly white set of choppers. He'd had some work done since the last time I'd seen him. "I like to call it the bunker and that's not far from the truth. I'm working on this new book and I'm already way past the deadline which is why, by the way, if the phone rings I won't be answering it. It'll either be my damn agent or my goddamn editor hounding me for the finished manuscript. That's what happens when you make the best-seller list. They can't get the next one out fast enough. I promised myself I wouldn't leave the goddamn house till I finished it. I figure I got a good week or two left to go."

"Sorry to mess with your rhythm. I promise this won't take long."

"Are you kidding? You're the best damn thing that could happen to me, Swann. First off, it's always good to see you." He patted me hard on the shoulder and pulled me in through the doorway. "Fact is, it's good to see anyone. But mostly your visit gives me a legit excuse to take a break from what I'm supposed to be doing. Have I ever told you I have a problem with authority? I hate being told what to do."

"I believe you have."

Suddenly, a big, black lab, panting loudly, appeared at his side. As Freddie bent down to pet him, he made the introduction. "Swann, meet Mephistopheles. Best damn dog in Passaic County."

The dog wagged his tail wildly and spun around several times, as if trying to cast a demonic spell over me. After a subtle hand signal from Freddie, he sat and raised a paw. I took it as a peace offering and shook it.

"Not much of a guard dog, is he?"

"He sees someone lurking outside he's more likely to invite him in for a drink. Let's go into the kitchen. It's my favorite room in the house."

I followed him as we moved through his living room, cluttered with books, magazines and newspapers, covering practically every surface. Mephistopheles was right behind me, bouncing around, his nails clicking on the wooden floor, literally nipping at my heels.

"When was the last time you cleaned up this dump?" I asked, as I sidestepped a pile of newspapers.

He stopped and looked around. "I've got news for you, pal. This is cleaned up."

"How long is it you've lived alone now?"

"We resent that. Mephistopheles may not pay rent, but he's

a full-time occupant. Besides, I think two marriages is more than enough for anyone, don't you?"

"I do, although my partner doesn't seem to agree."

"Partner?"

"Long story. Best told another time."

We reached the kitchen which held the requisite refrigerator, stove, sink, and kitchen table large enough to seat four. There was a dishwasher, too, but I didn't see much point since the sink was piled high with dirty, food-encrusted dishes. The kitchen table was covered with all kinds of books and papers and a laptop. Obviously, this was where Freddie did his writing.

"You really ought to get someone in to clean this place up. You're lucky the board of health doesn't condemn it."

"They'd have to have stomach enough to check it out first. But I'd get a pass anyway. Don't you know, I'm the neighborhood eccentric? I'm the most famous guy left in Paterson. I'm even on the goddamn tour. Every Saturday and Sunday, twice a day, a goddamn bus passes by and they point out this house as the home of The Fantastic Freddie. I'm thinking of changing it to The Fascinating Freddie. What do you think?" He didn't wait for an answer. "Anyway, I called them up one day and told them that Freddie wasn't very fantastic anymore, that he hasn't been for a while, but it didn't seem to sink in since those tour buses still keep me on the route. I hear they're even trying to designate this shithole as an historic home. Can you believe that?"

"You're a famous guy, Freddie. Whether you like it or not."

He shrugged. "It's got its perks. Here, Fisto," he yelled, and within seconds the dog burst into the kitchen, tail wagging, spinning in circles. Freddie grabbed him by the collar and led him toward the back door.

"If I don't let him out back he'll be all over us." He opened the door, tossed out one of those chewy bone toys, let go of the dog's collar, and Fisto barked gleefully a few times as he bolted outside.

"He loves it out there, so long as I let him in before dark."

"Mephistopheles is afraid of the dark?"

"He's a strange dog. If I believed in those kind of things, I'd think he was the reincarnation of my Aunt Tillie. Woman was afraid to go out of the house, lest some disaster befall her. Hey, how'd you like a piece of birthday cake?"

"What are you doing with birthday cake?"

"It was my birthday last week. Seventy fucking years old. Can you fucking believe it? The ex dropped by the other day and ambushed me with this cake. It was a pure act of sadism. She knew damn well I didn't want to be reminded of it. But could she let it go? Nope. She showed up out of spite. Besides, she knows I'm prediabetic. So, at the same time she's reminding me what an old fart I am, she's trying to kill me. I didn't have the heart to tell her she's not in the will anymore. Not that I have all that much to leave."

"But you ate it anyway, didn't you?"

"Damn right I did. I'm seventy fucking years old. I can eat any damn thing I want. You only go through this world once, you know." He smiled.

"Which brings us to why I'm here."

"I figured it was something like that. What about that piece of cake? And something to wash it down with? That way I won't feel so guilty about having another slice."

"In that case, just to be hospitable, sure. And maybe a glass of water."

"I can do better than that, Swann."

"I'm sure you can, but that'll be fine. There's no room on this table, you know?"

"Oh, yeah. Sorry about that." He picked up a bunch of papers and books and carried them over to the counter where he dropped them. He came back, closed up the laptop, opened up the oven, and put it there.

"Hey, aren't you afraid you'll forget you put it there, turn on the oven..."

"No chance of that. I haven't cooked anything in there since I moved in."

He went to the refrigerator and pulled what was left of one of those irresistible, tacky, store-bought birthday cakes. It had a couple candles on it and was still sitting on its cardboard slab. He cut a slice for me and one for himself, took what I hoped was a clean glass from the cabinet, poured a glass of water for me, plunked some ice into it then popped open a can of Tecate for himself.

"Should I sing 'Happy Birthday'?"

"You do and I'll throw you out on your ass."

I took a bite of the slightly stale, sickeningly sweet cake. "Not bad."

"She didn't make it herself, if that's what you're wondering. Cooking was not one of her strong points. What's that old joke Henny Youngman used to tell? 'My wife asked me to take her someplace she'd never been before, so I took her to the kitchen.'"

I smiled and suddenly an image of Goldblatt eating what was left of the cake sitting on the counter flashed through my mind. Why did it feel like I was cheating on him?

"I won't ask you what her strong points were."

"Yeah, no need to go there. Okay, pal," he leaned back in his chair, "tell papa all your problems."

"There's not enough time for that, but what I am here to talk to you about is this case I'm working on. It involves a woman who went to a fortune teller..."

He smiled and smacked his forehead with his hand.

"As my neighbor, Mrs. Horowitz would say, 'Oy...'"

"Yeah, well, there were circumstances. I guess there always are. That's what these folks count on, right?"

He nodded, took a swig of his beer, then wiped his mouth with his sleeve.

"I think I've got a lead on how to locate this chick, but before I do I want to find out as much as I can on how people like her operate and I figure if there's anyone who can fill me in..."

"It's yours truly."

"Right." I raised my glass. He raised his beer bottle. We clinked.

He finished off his cake with two large forkfuls, pushed the plate away from him, took another swig of beer, then wiped his mouth with his sleeve again. "To begin with, you can't go wrong with Occam's razor. You're familiar with that, right?"

"The simplest explanation is usually the correct explanation."

"Precisely. That means that someone has fed the con man, or in your case con woman, information before the mark showed up. Either they've researched them, which with the web is easier than it's ever been, or they've done it in a personal way without the mark even knowing they were cooperating, or if not them, someone else."

"How's that work?"

"Here's an example. Take those TV talk shows where the person with the so-called extra-sensory powers is a guest. Before the show, people with tickets are lined up outside the theater. A cohort is sent to stand on line with the audience members and they can pick up important information in one of two ways. They can either overhear conversations and pick up little tidbits or they can actually strike up a conversation."

"Don't people figure that out pretty easily?"

"You'd think so, but the answer's no. What you've got to understand is most people want to believe in an afterlife, or the ability to predict the future. Or in the supernatural. I think maybe we're hardwired for it. All we're looking for is proof. Any kind of proof. We want to find it. In order to believe we have to suspend our disbelief. If you do that you'll believe anything and then you're perfect fodder for these con artists. A skilled interviewer knows how to get information without the person even knowing what they're giving out or how important it might be. I'm sure that's something you're good at, Swann. It's probably an essential part of what you do."

I nodded. He was right. Over the years, I've found the problem isn't getting people to talk, it's getting them to shut up.

"They make notes and if they don't see their boss before his or her appearance to go over the information, they're hooked up to them electronically and they can transmit the information that way. They also provide them a detailed physical description, so the 'performer' can pick the mark out of the audience. But there are other methods, as well."

"Like?"

"You know those TV shows where the person who claims to talk to the dead chooses someone out of the audience by divulging some seemingly very personal information about them?"

"Sure."

"That ain't random, my friend. It's all technique. Here's how they work. They'll say something like, 'I see the letter R. and the letter L. Is there anyone out there that means anything to?' Here's what happens. Everyone, and I mean everyone, in the audience searches their memory bank for anyone they might know with those initials. First, they start close to home. Family. Mother. Father. Grandparents. Kids. Uncle. Aunt. Cousin. Then close friends. People they work with. Trust me, in an audience of a hundred fifty, two-fifty, there's bound to be plenty of people who can connect to those initials. And if no one rises to the bait, the next thing out of their mouth will be, 'Wait, it's not an R it's a B.' Smart. 'Cause an R can resemble a B, right? But they rarely have to go that far. When someone raises his or her hand, then our guy goes to work. He throws out several general observations until slowly he's able to home in on a profile of someone. The best are experts at reading faces and body language. They can tell right away when they're onto something. And once they smell blood, they keep going. They circle around and around until they home in on vital information that when you think about it is very easy to deduce, but to the audience and even to the mark it appears as if this incredible thing is happening. That they're being told information that absolutely no one else could possibly know. You'd be shocked at how easy it is and how the real pros make it look both difficult and easy at the same time. The more difficult it appears to be, the more they stumble, the more genuine it appears to be. Hell, with a little training I could teach you to do it like a pro. Any halfway intelligent person can master the technique. I've recreated it dozens of times, but still people fall for it."

"It seems so..."

"Fake? Yeah, it is. But it takes talent. It's also a craft that can be learned. All it takes is a good con man...or woman, who has heightened powers of perception. Not everyone can pull it off. The bigger bullshitter you are the better you're going to be at it. And believe me, the good ones are really, really good. But none of them have been able to fool me."

"Not yet."

He shook his head and smiled. "Not ever. Because I've spent my entire life proving there is no such thing. If you start at that point, all you have to do is figure out how they do it. I haven't been stumped yet. The ones who are particularly adept at this are those who know it's all a mind game."

"What do you mean?"

He thought for a moment. "Okay, maybe I can explain it this way. This victim you're talking about, she goes to see this con woman when she's in a certain state of mind. The mere fact she goes there means that she's in the state of mind of wanting to believe. Otherwise, she wouldn't have been there, right? Once she's in that state of mind it's easy for the 'fortune teller.'" He used air quotes. "It becomes a form of hypnosis. The psychic makes suggestions and those suggestions are accepted by the person in the audience. A narrative is established. In this case, it's the narrative that people don't die, they just go to another place. That narrative is constantly reinforced and the victim finds him or herself in a state very close to being hypnotized. It's all about the power of suggestion. If you can get someone in a certain state, they are very susceptible to these suggestions, which means they start to believe what you want them to believe.

Once that state is reached, you can pretty much get someone to do anything you want them to do, to believe anything you want them to believe."

"This is diabolical."

"If you believe in the devil, I suppose it is."

"But how can you be so sure there isn't something more out there?"

"For one thing, common sense. After all these years, has there ever been any convincing proof? I haven't seen any. It's the same thing with visits from the little green men and alien abductions. Ever wonder how come all these sightings always happen in out of the way rural areas? But don't get me wrong, you don't have to be stupid or gullible to believe. Arthur Conan Doyle was a believer. I think even Houdini, who was a real hero of mine, was a believer of sorts. He thought he'd come back from the dead and deliver a message. Or at least he considered it a possibility. Somewhere along the way that message got lost. Between you and me, he would have been better off dropping it in the mail, and we all know how competent the US Postal Service is."

"And God?"

He shrugged. "You want to believe in God, or a Supreme Being, that's fine with me. But I haven't seen any convincing evidence of that, either."

"Some people say all you have to do is look around and you'll see plenty of evidence everywhere you look."

"I have the one-word answer to that, my friend: science. All of what you see can either be explained scientifically or by magic. And by magic, I mean sleight of hand or trickery. Copperfield can make it appear as if the Statue of Liberty has disappeared but we all know it's still there, where we left it, on Liberty Island. Believe what you want to believe, Swann, but as far as I'm concerned, religion and the paranormal is for suckers."

"I guess maybe I've got more of an open mind than you do, although in this particular case I know it's just a bunch of crap. This woman stole from my client and it's up to me to find her and try and get back at least some of the money."

"I wish you luck, my friend, and if there's anything I can do to help, just give a holler. But in the meantime, how about another piece of cake?"

I accepted his offer, not because I really wanted one but because I figured one more slice for me was one less slice for him and with his health being what it was, I was helping save a life. Although, I wasn't so sure Freddie wasn't itching to die just to prove his point about there being no afterlife.

I stuck around another half hour or so, talking about this and that, Freddie regaling me with all kinds of tales of debunking and tricks of the trade, lest I needed help once I connected with Madam Sofia.

By the time we finished, it was dark. Freddie called for a cab to take me to the train station and an hour and a half later, I was back in my apartment watching *The Exorcist* on TV.

I didn't fall asleep till almost three and I couldn't say whether it was the movie that kept me up or all that talk about God and the possibility (or impossibility) of the afterlife.

Either way, it was surprisingly disturbing.

9
A FRIEND INDEED IS A FRIEND IN NEED

The next morning the vibration of my cell phone as it jiggled closer to the edge of my night table was enough to wake me from a fitful sleep. I caught the damn thing just as it was about to shimmy over the edge and crash onto the floor. It would not have been the first time that happened. For the past six months I'd been having sleep problems, waking up at four in the morning and not being able to get back to sleep for a couple hours and then never able to sleep past eight a.m. But when I grabbed the phone I saw it was already nine-twelve a.m.

And whose name should be staring at me when I brought it to eye level? Goldblatt, of course.

"What do you want?" I asked, annoyed that he'd interrupted what might have been another hour or two of much needed sleep.

"I didn't wake you, did I?"

"It's after nine."

"Yeah. That's what I mean. I can tell from your voice you just got up. What the hell are you doing sleeping in at nine o'clock? Rough night?"

I didn't see the need to go into my sleeping habits with Goldblatt, so I took the easy way out.

"Yeah, that's right. What's up?" I asked, swinging my feet over the side of my sleeper couch, which hadn't seen use as an actual couch for at least a couple weeks. What was the point of closing it up each morning when I'd just have to open it again that night? As far as appearances were concerned, well, the only person who'd been in the apartment other than me in months, maybe longer, would have been the super when he came to fix a dripping faucet in the bathroom that promptly returned to its unfixed state within a matter of hours. I'm not complaining. You get what you pay for.

"Any word from Becker yet? You know, like with an address for that Susan Finch chick."

My mind was still enveloped in the fog of sleep, so I had to think for a moment who he was talking about. Oh, yeah, the landlord. And Madame Sofia. Before I answered I held the phone away from my head and took a quick look at my text messages. Nothing.

"Not yet."

"You think we ought to apply a little pressure? I could go over there and…"

"I know you're itching to use that Israeli martial arts thing, but let's give him till this afternoon. If I haven't heard from him by then, I'll send you over there and let you practice some of that shit on him."

I thought I heard a grunt, then it got quiet.

"Goldblatt, you still there?"

"What do you mean, send me? Like I'm some kind of employee, or something."

Oh-oh. I'd ruffled his feathers, fragile flower that he was.

"Wrong word, okay. Remember, I just got up. My mouth isn't quite aligned with my brain. And I've got that other thing on my mind."

"What other thing?"

"The thing for Rudder."

"Oh, yeah, the missing witness."

I'd flashed a shiny thing in front of his eyes and taken his mind off my slight.

"Yeah."

"What about it?"

"There's a tight deadline on that one. I've got to get moving on it."

"You don't think Rachel's case is important?"

Oh, man. Now I was in for at least five more minutes of conversation I didn't want or need. All I could do was try to wriggle out of it.

"Of course, it is. But it's not time sensitive. This one is."

There was a moment of silence. Had I escaped?

"Okay. Yeah. Maybe you're right. So, what's going on with that one?"

I didn't see a drawback in filling him in, even though the idea of making him any more a part of my life than he had to be made me a little nervous. It was that give him an inch thing. But he had earned a little more respect from me. It wasn't the Israeli martial arts. It was more his surprisingly impressive performance in Becker's office the other day. It was a side of Goldblatt I hadn't seen before and it had me asking myself if perhaps I wasn't giving him enough credit.

"I think I've got a lead on finding this runaway witness."

"What kind of lead?"

"A childhood friend of hers. I've tracked her down to some beach town across the bay from Mobile, Alabama."

"So, you're going down there?"

"I think I have to."

"Have you cleared it with Rudder?"

Goldblatt wasn't being protective of me. He was worried about his cut of the deal. He didn't want me to go over budget, whatever that might be. Fair enough. We were partners. At least for now.

"I was going to do it this morning."

"You want me to go down there with you?"

"I appreciate the offer, but I don't think that's necessary. Besides, we need someone up here to watch the store. And if we don't hear from Becker by this afternoon it wouldn't hurt for you to remind our friend that we need that information."

Another moment of silence.

"Yeah. I guess you're right. Someone's gotta stay on top of the sonuvabitch. How long you think you're gonna be gone?"

"Probably no more than a couple days."

"I know some folks down in Pensacola, in case you run into trouble. It's only an hour, forty-five minutes or so outside Mobile."

"How do you know that?"

"I know a lot of stuff, Swann. There's a Naval base down there."

"How do you connect with a Naval base?"

He chuckled.

"That's a story for another time. Anyway, let me know if you come up with anything down there. Meanwhile, I'll keep you posted on what's going on up here. Before you go, maybe you ought to let Klavan know I might need to stop by and use the office every now and then."

Alarm bells went off.

"That's not gonna go over too well."

"Why not?"

"You know why not."

"Yeah, well, I'm your partner and that's where our office is. I'll stay out of his hair, if that's what you're worried about. And I'll give a heads-up when I want to stop by."

That might make things worse. I knew Goldblatt's "stopping by" might result in my getting kicked out of Klavan's place. But Goldblatt was right. He was my partner. And what kind of man would I be if I didn't stand up to Klavan by standing up for Goldblatt, no matter what kind of doofus he is? It would be a character test for me. Did I have enough character to do the right thing for a change? Did I risk pissing off a friend? And losing the best office I've ever had? Friends come and go and the only person I really had to live with was myself, and I couldn't let Klavan's disapproval stop me from doing something I thought was right. Let's face it, most of these kinds of tests I fail miserably. Maybe it was about time I started a winning streak. One small step for man, one giant leap for Swann.

"Okay. But remember, he not only lives there but he does business there. You've got to stay out of his way."

"You mean make like I'm not even there?"

"Exactly."

"But I will be there."

"I know. And that's what worries me."

"Relax. I'll be very professional. Fact is, I might not even show up. You know me. I've always got plenty to do, plenty to keep me busy. I just like to keep my options open."

Was the doofus just testing me? If so, I probably passed. If not, I'd have to trust Goldblatt really could contain himself and behave in at least a semi-professional manner.

"Okay. I'll give Klavan a shout-out…" I meant warning, of course. "But you gotta promise to check with him first because I'm not giving you my key. He'll either have to make sure someone's home or the concierge lets you in."

"No problemo. You're a prince among men, Swann."

Yeah. Right.

I checked with Rudder to make sure there was enough money in the till for a quick trip down South and when he gave me the green light, I booked an early morning flight through Atlanta to Mobile for the next day. I didn't figure I'd need to be down there more than overnight, but just in case I reserved a couple nights at the Grand Hotel in Fairhope and arranged for a car rental at the airport.

I figured I'd been working hard enough, so I spent the rest of the day going to the movies. I saw three of them back to back to back. They all depicted a much better life than I had, which only made me promise myself that when both these cases were over, I'd take a serious look at how I wanted to spend the rest of my time on this planet, especially since, according to Freddie, it was the only chance I'd get.

* * *

Before leaving the next morning to get to the airport for an eight a.m. flight, I checked to see if there was any word from Becker. Nothing. I didn't want to have to pay him another visit, nor did I want Goldblatt over there on his own, so I decided to give him at least till I landed in Mobile. But to let him know I wasn't letting him off the hook, I sent him a two-word text. "I'm waiting."

I arrived in Mobile around noon. As I was completing the paperwork for my car rental, I looked out into the distance and spotted storm clouds rolling in from the south, the direction in which I was heading. I asked the perky female clerk at the rent-a-car booth about the possibility of rain.

"Sugar, it's that time of year down here. Rains a little pretty much every afternoon. But it ain't nothing to be worried about. Half hour, hour, tops. Twenty minutes later you won't even know it rained at all. If you're driving, y'all jest pull over to the side of the road if it gets so bad you can't see. You won't be sittin' there long."

I was handed the keys and directed to an area in the parking lot where I'd find my car. It was only early June but man, was it hot. And humid. As soon as I got outside I was sucker punched by a gust of baked air that almost took my breath away. By the time I reached the car, my shirt was soaking wet and sweat was rolling down my face. As soon as I got in the car, I turned on the AC and just sat there a few minutes, waiting to cool off.

It was a few minutes past one by the time I finally got on my way. Using the car's GPS to guide me to my destination, I was directed into a tunnel that must have stretched half a mile. Once I cleared it, I found myself on a causeway that crossed Mobile Bay. By this time, the sky had darkened considerably, and an occasional maverick raindrop splattered against the windshield.

It wasn't until I approached a small town called Daphne, only a few miles from Fairhope, that the skies opened up. Suddenly, as if a heavy wool blanket had been thrown over the sun, it turned dark as night. The raindrops were huge, splattering on the windshield, and within minutes it was raining so hard the windshield wipers didn't have a prayer of keeping up. I was afraid I was going to hit something, so I pulled over to the side of the road and sat there listening to country music on the radio until the worst of the weather passed.

The girl at the rent-a-car was right. Within fifteen minutes the sun was out, there was not a cloud in the sky, and I was back on the road.

I'd programmed the GPS for an address I'd copied off the internet for Janet Kirby. I had no idea how up-to-date it was, or if she still resided there, but it was a starting off point.

As I reached the edge of the quaint, little village, my mood, which had been kind of somber, began to lift. I'm not sure why. Maybe because there's something about small town America that to this city-bred kid clicks the nostalgia button. Why it should do that, since it's far from the kind of childhood I led, is beyond me. Besides, I'm not the nostalgic type. For me, the past has always been consistent with the present and the future. It all pretty much sucks.

These beach towns looked familiar, even though I'd never been here before. I realized it was because they could have been any little sleepy beach town on Long Island or up the coast of New England. The only difference seemed to be that there were plenty of pickup trucks with Southern-style bumper stickers. And the fact that we were just a few weeks away from July fourth, Independence Day, meant almost every lawn and store-front had some version of the American flag flapping in the breeze, only highlighted that All-American effect.

I glanced at the dashboard GPS screen and noted I wasn't far from the address I'd punched in. I debated with myself as to whether I should keep going, toward the Grand Hotel, and check in, or head straight to Kirby's address. Since I was anxious to get started and had no idea how long it would take me to locate her, I decided I'd check into the hotel later in the day.

Kirby's address was not far from the Fairhope Municipal Pier where, according to the information I found online and printed out, most of the after sunset festivities took place.

The address turned out to be a small, two-level apartment building within sight of the bay. I parked out front. I found her name on the directory and buzzed her apartment. No answer. It was just past three in the afternoon, so the chances of her being home were slim. I'd come back in a few hours, when she'd be more likely to be home. I had time to kill, so I headed to the Grand Hotel. The sprawling grounds hugged the bay line, and my room, which was in the main building, had a beautiful view of the water.

Once I'd checked in and dropped my bag in the room, I decided to drive into town before heading back to Kirby's place, maybe walk the main strip, grab an ice cream cone, immerse myself in small town America.

I found a spot off the main drag, parked, and started walking. Within a block or two, I found myself in front of a large bookstore called Page and Palette. What better way to waste a little time than in a bookstore? It was what got me through much of my childhood, when I used to hop the train into Manhattan and haunt bookstores like the long since disappeared Brentano's, Scribner's, and Doubleday's.

After browsing through the store for a while, I figured I'd see if I could pick up some information. After all, this was a small town and I figured everyone pretty much knew everyone else's business. I approached the young woman with short brown hair and a pug nose at the cash register and asked if she happened to know Janet Kirby.

"As a matter of fact, I do," she said, in a soft, Southern drawl.

"Would you happen to know where I can find her?"

"Why y'all looking for Janet?"

"We have a friend in common. I figured since I was down here, I'd say hello."

"Have you ever met Janet?"

"Nope."

"Who's this friend y'all supposed to have in common with her? Maybe I know her, too."

I was about to answer when I finally noticed the name on the tag she was wearing pinned to her blouse.

I smiled. "How much longer were you going to lead me on?"

She returned the smile. "I don't know. I was jest having an awful lot of fun."

"I feel like a jerk."

"Well, I'm real sorry, but you know, there's jest not that much to do in this town so when an opportunity like this presents itself..."

"Yeah. I get it."

"So, who is this friend we're supposed to have in common?"

"You wouldn't happen to be on a break soon, would you? If you are, how about I buy you a cup of coffee?" I motioned toward an area to the right of the bookstore where there was a coffee bar and half a dozen tables.

"I'll see if someone can watch the register for a few minutes. Why don't you go over there, order yourself something, me a latte?"

Five minutes later, she arrived at the table I'd chosen near the back. She started to open up her wallet, but I shook her off. "My treat."

"Why do I have the feeling this is going to cost me a lot more than a latte?"

"Not a lot more. I promise."

She sat down across from me.

"So, what's this really about? I mean, I know you don't live around here, and I know this ain't no accident, you showing up looking for me, I mean. Or this friend of mine."

"Finding you here was very much an accident."

"But you were looking for me on purpose, and I'd like to know why."

"Fair enough. I'm actually looking for your friend, Jana Monroe."

She got up. "I need some sweetener. Y'all need something?"

"Thanks. I'm good."

A moment later, she returned, sat, shook a packet of artificial sweetener a couple times, tore it open, and emptied it into her drink.

"You give yourself enough time to figure out what you're going to say?" I said.

"Is that what I was doing?"

"I'm pretty sure it was."

"You're pretty smart for a New Yorker."

"How'd you know I'm from New York?"

"You gotta be kidding? It's written all over you. For one thing, it's your attitude."

"I've got an attitude?"

"You sure do."

"Yeah, I guess maybe I do."

"So, how'd you find me and what makes you think I know Jana?"

"I spoke with her roommates. They told me about you. Thought you might be able to help me."

"Help you with what?"

"Find Jana."

"Why do you want to find her? It must be pretty important if you'd come all the way down here from New York City looking for her."

"It is."

"So, what is it?"

"She's a possible witness for a case and if she is, I need to bring her back to the city."

"You some kind of cop?"

"Nope. Far from it."

She broke into a wide grin. "You're a private dick! Even better. I've never met a private dick before."

"I think they prefer being called private investigators or private eyes, of which I'm neither."

"So, what are y'all?"

"That's the sixty-four-thousand-dollar question, and it's one I've been asking myself for years. But the easy answer is, I'm a skip tracer."

"A skip tracer? What the heck is that?"

"I find people. Things."

"Like when I lose my car keys, I'd give you a call?"

"I'm not sure I'd be cost effective for something like that."

"So, what's this Jana's supposed to have witnessed?"

I didn't know how much Kirby knew and I didn't know how much I should tell her. If she knew nothing, I didn't want to scare her off. Or, she knew and she was shining me on, protecting her friend, trying to throw me off the track. Either way, I had to be careful about what I disclosed. First, I had to figure out where she stood, and that wasn't going to be easy because Janet Kirby, regardless of that "oh, shucks" thing she had going, was sharp.

"Do you know where she is, Janet?"

"Why should I know?"

"Because she's a friend."

"Mister, I got me lots of friends and I don't know where most of them are."

"When was the last time you saw her?"

"Oh, lemme see. Well, I guess it's been a while."

"How much of a while?"

"You know, I just realized something. I don't really have to answer any of your questions. And even if I did, I'm not under oath, so how would you know whether or not I'm lyin'?"

"I've got a pretty good bullshit detector."

"Really? So, am I bullshitting you now?"

"Yeah. I'm pretty sure you are."

"Then why waste your time asking me questions if you know you're not going to get honest answers?"

"I think you care about your friend. That's why you let her come down here and why you're hiding her. And that you're not being honest tells me I'm on the right track."

"You're pretty darn sure of yourself, aren't you?"

I shrugged. "I'm not good at much, but one thing I am good at is judging people. I hate to tell you this, Janet, but I can see right through you."

"That so?"

"That's so."

"And just what do you see?"

"I see a friend trying to protect a friend. Which I admire. But if you really want to help her you'd help me. So, where is she, Janet?"

"We still haven't established that she's down here."

Silence is often a powerful tool. So, I kept my mouth shut and my eyes glued to her eyes.

"Well, maybe she was, but maybe she's not now."

"You think you're helping her out, don't you?"

"Like you said, I am her friend."

"That's obvious. But what if your friend was in trouble. Wouldn't you want to help her? And you wouldn't want someone to be blamed for something they didn't do, would you?"

She didn't answer right away. I could see I had her on the ropes.

"Maybe that someone deserves what that someone gets. Maybe the reason she's hiding out is that she doesn't want to get involved. Maybe she's afraid that if she does something will happen to her."

"That's a lot of maybes, Janet. Like what does she think could happen to her?"

"I don't know. I'm just asking."

"Why don't you let her tell me herself? Look, I'm not out to get anyone in trouble. I have a job to do, but I'm also someone who knows how the world works. Even if I do talk to her, there's no way I can make her come back to New York with me. But I need to know what she has to say. I need her to tell me to my face that she doesn't want to get involved. Then, I can go back knowing I did my job."

"I can't make decisions for her."

"I didn't expect you would. How about this? Just tell her I'm down here and I want to talk to her. Just talk. I'm not about to force her to do anything she doesn't want to do. I'm being paid to find her. Nothing else."

"I guess…"

"Look, I'll give you my cell number." I took a small pad out of my pocket, tore off a sheet, and wrote down my number and my name. "I'm staying over at the Grand Hotel. Either way, she can reach me and let me know what she wants to do. No matter what, I'm heading out tomorrow afternoon. Just have her call me. What can it hurt?"

She took the piece of paper, looked at it, folded it up, and put it into her trouser pocket. I couldn't be sure, but I had a pretty good idea that I'd hear from Jana Monroe before I headed back to New York.

10
I ONCE WAS LOST, BUT NOW I'M FOUND

I left Kirby waiting on a customer who was purchasing a book by Roy Hoffman, one of the many local authors, and headed back to the Grand Hotel. I thought I'd get in a quick swim. It had been a long day and I was so tired I could hardly think straight, not the best time to try figuring things out. I hoped that swimming a few laps might reinvigorate me and maybe even help me focus.

There was something nagging at me. I don't get these feelings often, but when I do I've learned to pay attention. I had this feeling in my gut that I was being manipulated, but I didn't know by who. Was it Nicky Diamond? Jana Monroe? Janet Kirby? In the spirit of fair play, I even added Paul Rudder to the list, which I realized only bolstered the sense that I was too tired to think clearly.

Over the years, I've learned to take very little at face value, which translates into questioning everything and everybody. This case was especially vexing. It was a little like putting on someone else's glasses and finding that everything is slightly out of focus. It's not you, it's the glasses. But until you put on the right glasses, everything is still blurry.

The basic question was, could Jana Monroe actually provide an alibi for her boyfriend? And if she could, why did she run off? And if she couldn't, why didn't she just tell Paul and save everyone all this trouble? And what was Nicky Diamond's role in all this? Was he telling the truth when he marked Monroe as a witness who could exonerate him? And if he wasn't, why name her at all?

Doubts like these get in the way of my being able to do my job. The best way to deal with them is to simply focus on the job I was hired to do: find Jana Monroe and try to bring her back. It wasn't part of my job to figure out if she was telling the truth. And it wasn't my job to prove Diamond's guilt or innocence.

When I arrived back at the hotel close to five p.m., there was a message waiting for me at the front desk. It sounded like a ransom note.

"Meet me, eight o'clock on the pier. Come alone." It was signed *J.M.*

I skipped the swim and showered instead, then grabbed something to eat in the hotel dining room.

When I arrived at the pier, it was seven-forty-five and the sun was beginning to set. I decided to stroll to the end the pier, then back, to make sure she hadn't arrived early. I wasn't sure I'd recognize her, having only the photo Paul provided me with, but I trusted that I'd be able to recognize her.

The pier was empty except for several fishermen who were casting large nets out into the bay, then slowly hoisting them up. I stopped to talk to one of them. He was an elderly gentleman, in his sixties maybe, his face weathered from the sun his white hair clipped short. He had a bit of a belly but his arms were well-muscled indicating that he had done more than his share of heavy lifting. He was wearing overalls and a dirty white T-shirt. At his feet were two large, empty pails.

"What's that you're casting for?" I asked.

He looked up. "Shrimp."

"How ya doing?"

He looked down at his pails. "It's early. Just got here a few minutes ago. Hard to tell how it's gonna be."

"You out here often?"

"Yes, sir, I am. I'm retired, going on two years now, and it's a pretty good way to earn a little extra," he rubbed his thumb and forefinger together, "if you know what I mean. Ain't easy livin' on social security, these days. Those damn thievin' politicians up there in Washington, don't leave much for us regular folk."

He lifted his net and as the water poured out, I saw he'd pulled up a nice haul. He dumped them into one of the pails and with a long, looping arc, tossed the net back in.

"Nice technique," I said.

"Been at this long as I have, you know what you're doing, sonny."

It'd been a long time since I'd been called sonny. The last time was by my old man who followed it up with a smack across the face.

"Wanna give it a try?"

I was tempted. There was something alluring about making a living this way, not chasing halfway around the country looking for people who didn't want to be found.

"Thanks. Another time, maybe. I'm meeting someone here in a few minutes."

He shrugged. "Suit yourself."

I resumed walking toward the end of the pier. It was a nice night. Hot and humid. Fortunately, there was a slight breeze blowing in. Across the bay, I could make out the lights of Mobile, and I was reminded of those famous last lines from *Gatsby*, spoken by the impressionable Nick Carraway: "Gatsby believed in the green light, the orgastic future that year by year recedes before us. It eluded us then, but that's no matter— tomorrow we will run faster, stretch our arms further...So we beat on, boats against the current, borne back ceaselessly into the past."

I don't care much about the future. Don't give it much thought, actually. Maybe that's because I don't think I have much stake in one. But for some reason being away, out of my element, that's exactly what I started thinking about. Was this, I wondered, how I'd be spending the rest of my life? Searching for that little green light, searching for the orgastic future, that kept receding faster and faster with each passing year? I felt like I was that boat battling the current, trying to find a calm place to moor. But, to be honest, I didn't have much faith in my ever being able to find that place, though that probably wouldn't stop me from looking. In the meantime, I had other, more concrete things to search for, things that helped get me out of my own head.

When I got back to the beginning of the pier, I leaned against the railing. I checked my watch. A couple minutes before eight. The light was beginning to fade, but off in the distance, maybe fifty, sixty feet away, I noticed a figure standing in the shadow of a large tree. It was a woman. It had to be Janet Kirby. I didn't want to scare her off, so I stood my ground, hoping she'd come to me.

She saw me staring at her and began to walk toward me. Every few steps she'd stop and look behind her. She was wearing a baseball cap. Her hair was in a blonde ponytail. Kirby was a brunette, but it made sense that she'd change her hair color. She was wearing faded blue jeans and an untucked plaid shirt.

I didn't want to spook her, so I just stood there and waited for her to come to me. About six feet from me she stopped.

"You must be Mr. Swann?"

"That's right. You're Jana. You changed your hair color."

"I wanted to see if blondes really do have more fun."

"Do they?"

"So far, I'd have to say the answer's no."

"You're in hiding."

"I guess I'm not very good at it. You found me."

"It's what I do."

"I know why you're here."

"I figured you did."

"Why don't we go to the end of the pier. It's more private." she said.

"Suits me."

We passed the fisherman who had been joined by a middle-aged woman who was also casting a net. I nodded at him and he nodded back.

"Friend of yours?" she asked.

"We just met."

"I come here a lot, but I don't recognize him."

"Are you afraid someone's watching you, Jana?" I asked, as we came to the end of the pier.

"There's always someone watching."

"That so?"

"Don't you know there are cameras everywhere. There's no such thing as privacy anymore."

"You think someone's watching you for a particular reason?"

"What do you think?"

She pulled a pack of cigarettes out of her back pocket, took one out and offered the pack to me.

I shook my head.

"I didn't think anyone smoked anymore. They say it's bad for the skin."

"You think I should be worried about my skin?"

"Not yet."

"You think I'm vain?" She held the unlit cigarette between her forefinger and index finger.

"No. Not that there's anything wrong with vanity."

She popped the cigarette into her mouth, pulled a pack of matches out of the cigarette package and struck one. She held it inches from the cigarette but before lighting it she waved out the match. She stuffed the pack of matches and the cigarette back into the package.

"I only just started," she said.

"Nerves?"

"Probably. It's something to do."

"It's easier to stop now. You know, before you get hooked."

She stared at me a moment, then turned and tossed the cigarette pack into the bay. She had a pretty good arm. I watched as it floated away from us.

"I guess…" She looked wistfully out across the bay, toward the floating pack of cigarettes. Toward Mobile. Toward the lights, which twinkled like stars in the dusk.

"There was a jubilee yesterday," she said, matter-of-factly, her arms resting on the railing while she stared out over the water.

"Yeah?"

"You know what that is?"

"It's a party."

She smiled. "Not that kind of jubilee. There was one here last night. It's really bizarre. One of those inexplicable things that happens and no one's been able to figure out why."

"So, what is it?"

"It's a natural phenomenon that happens in the bay. An enormous number of crabs, shrimps, flounders, eels, and other fish leave the deeper waters, there are hundreds and hundreds of them, and swarm toward the shallower part of the bay. It's like the mob scene after an Alabama football game. As far as they know, it only happens here, and no one knows why."

She pointed to the shoreline to our left. "Last night it was over there. The fishermen love it because it's like the hand of God delivering all these fish. They don't even have to cast a line, or a net. It's that easy to catch them. They just flop around in the water, until they make it to shore. It doesn't happen that often, and no one can predict it. They don't know why it happens, but when it does it causes quite a stir around here."

"I can imagine."

"It's a real windfall for the local fishermen. Ask your friend back there. I'm sure he was down here. One of them told me he could fill a washtub with shrimp and that he could gig hundreds of flounders and fill up the back of his pickup with a foot deep of crabs. Evidently, they're oxygen deprived and so any fight they might have had is wrung out of them. The fishermen can just knock the fish over the head and put them in their baskets

or coolers. Then they bring them to sell to dealers. One fisherman told me, 'It's like money in the bank.' It seems like cheating
to me."

"Very interesting, Jana. But why bring this up now?"

She shrugged. "It happened last night. I was out here and
saw it. It had an effect on me. I don't know why. It's just one of
those inexplicable things."

I could tell from the look on her face there was a reason she
was telling me this. Was it to prepare me for something that
was going to happen in the future? Whatever it was, she wasn't
going to explain it now and so I let it pass.

"Lucky you were here to see it."

"It wasn't luck. I'm here almost every night."

"Why's that?"

She hesitated a moment. "I don't have much else to do..."

Suddenly, I got it. She was a fish out of water. She didn't
want to be here. She wanted to go back where she belonged,
only there was something keeping her away.

"Jana, you know why I'm here, right?"

She nodded.

"What say we talk about it?"

"I guess, now that you're here, I can't avoid it."

"No. You can't. I'm very tenacious. I once spent fifteen
minutes trying to thread a needle."

She looked at me and smiled. For the first time I noticed her
eyes. I'd never seen eyes that color. Deep blue. The color made
me think of a chemistry set I had as a kid. My favorite element
was the little jar of cobalt crystals. It was so special I took the
jar out of the metal cabinet and kept it on my dresser. It stuck
around a lot longer than that chemistry set did.

"I guess that doesn't surprise me."

"You seem like a good kid, Jana. How does someone like
you get involved with someone like Nicky Diamond?"

"There's a value judgment in there, isn't there?"

"Two of them."

"Have you never hooked up with the wrong woman? A woman who wasn't good for you? A woman who broke your heart?"

"Yeah. Plenty."

"There's your answer. He was tenacious...like you. There was something exciting about him...until there wasn't. Something that made me feel more alive. Until it didn't..."

"He says you can bail him out of a jam."

She didn't answer.

"Can you?"

"I guess. Maybe."

"Why'd you skip?"

She shrugged. "I don't know. Maybe I didn't want to get involved."

"There's a man's life at stake."

She shook her head.

"Does that mean you can't provide an alibi for him? That he's lying about being with you?"

She took a deep breath, then let it out slow. "Nicky's a bad man."

"I know. But that doesn't have anything to do with this. Unless, of course, he's guilty."

She looked down and shuffled her foot back and forth, as if moving dirt around. Only there wasn't any dirt. Just the wood of the pier.

"Is he guilty, Jana?"

"I'm sure he's guilty of a lot of things."

"You know what I mean. How about this particular thing?"

She looked up, pinning me with those incredible blue eyes. "You want me to go back with you, don't you?"

"I'm being paid to find you. The coming back part is totally up to you. But if you're asking me if I think you should..."

"I don't need your permission." Her tone had an edge to it. "And I don't know you well enough to care what you think of me."

"True. Let's back up a little. Why did you take off in the first place?"

She bent over, picked up a small pebble, then tossed it into the water.

"Anything you say will stay with me, Jana. I promise."

She wet her lips with her tongue, as if she was trying to make the words come out easier. "It was like a suggestion."

"You mean someone asked you to take a powder."

She nodded.

"Who?"

"I don't know."

"How did the suggestion come?"

"A telephone call. A man said if I knew what was good for me I'd leave town."

"Sounds like a bad movie to me."

"You think I'm making it up?"

"Are you?"

Silence.

"Did he threaten you?"

"Doesn't that sound like a threat to you?"

"I guess."

"You're not going to feed me any crap about doing my civic duty, are you? I mean, we both know Nicky has done some pretty bad things in his life. Maybe this isn't one of them, but what's the difference? One way or another we all pay for what we do."

"I can't argue with that, Jana, because I've had the same thoughts over the years. But in the end, I've decided it was usually more important to do the right thing."

"You mean, take the money he's paying you and drag me back?"

"First of all, technically, he's not paying me, his lawyer is. Second of all, no one's dragging anyone anywhere. I'm just telling you what the situation is and it's up to you what you do about it. If you do come back with me, I promise you I'll make sure you're safe."

"You can do that?"

"I believe I can," I said, lying through my teeth. I could hardly guarantee my own safety much less someone else's. Although, I have to admit the thought of Goldblatt and all his so-called training did cross my mind. Maybe this was something I could lay in his lap. You know, make him useful for a change.

"What if I don't want to get involved in this?"

"You're already involved, Jana. I can't make you go back. And frankly, I'd understand if you didn't. But I wonder how you'd feel having Nicky going to jail for the rest of his life on your conscience? No matter who he is and what he's done in the past."

"You don't think the world would be better off with Nicky Diamond off the streets for good?"

"I can't argue with you there. But this isn't about Nicky. This is about you. It's your choice, Jana. I'm just here to help if you decide to go back. Tell you what, I'm here for tonight. I've got a ticket to fly back tomorrow at two. So, you've got till eleven to make up your mind."

"What if they're watching me?"

"Who?"

"Whoever threatened me."

"Are you afraid they'll see you at the airport?"

She nodded.

I don't know why I said this, but I did. "Okay. If you decide to go back to the city, we'll rent a car and drive back. That way, no one will know anything. What do you say?"

"You'd do that?"

"Yeah. I'd do it. But I'd also be just as happy getting on that plane tomorrow by myself. It's up to you."

11
ROAD TRIP

I'm not sure why I offered to drive Jana Monroe all the way back to New York. It's not like I looked forward to a long road trip with a virtual stranger. With anyone, in fact. The last time I did something stupid like that was right after I got out of college and thought it might be a good idea to drive cross country. I figured I'd meet interesting people and have something to write about—those were the days when I thought I was going to end up as a writer and, of course, bestow upon the world the Great American Novel. That pipe dream didn't last long. Both the road trip and the Great American Novel thing, I mean. I ran out of gas, literally, around Topeka, Kansas, and had to take a job in a fast food joint. I quit after a couple weeks, when I made enough dough to fill enough tanks of gas to get me back to New York. Once home, I kissed the ground and swore I'd never leave again, which turned out not to be the first broken promise to myself. I did learn two things. One, that seeing the USA in a Chevrolet was way overrated, and two, just because you're driving cross country didn't necessarily mean you're going to meet anyone worth writing about. In fact, most of the people I met along the way were eminently forgettable.

And God knows, it wasn't like I owed anything to Nicky Diamond. I guess, when it came down to it, it was more a matter of finishing something I'd started. I hate loose ends. I'm the kinda guy who once he starts reading a book has to finish it, no matter how bad it might be. Besides, even if Jana's testimony wound up nailing Diamond rather than exonerating him, well, at least that was what's commonly known as, and I hate the word because it reeks of psycho-babble, closure.

It would have been so much easier to hop on a plane with her. But if her fear was well founded, if someone really was out to stop her from testifying, booking a flight would pretty much announce to the world she was coming back. I wasn't so sure that whoever delivered that message didn't already know where she'd fled to. It was even possible they were keeping an eye on me and if they were, I'd led them straight to their target. And if it were me, the airport would be the first place I'd stake out, keeping a special eye on flights back to New York.

Considering her state of mind, I figured there was more chance of her coming with me if we drove. The woman was petrified. I could see it in her eyes. And maybe she had a right to be. After all, Nicky Diamond was a dangerous man who played with other dangerous men. If someone had threatened her, it was someone who could deliver on the threat. But was she actually threatened? Could she be making it all up? If so, why? What was her angle? One unintended result of spending hours and hours alone with her in a car might be getting the real story out of her.

If I had to give odds, I would've said there was a one in four chance she would come back to New York with me. But I didn't want to press her. That would have been counterproductive. Besides, technically I'd completed my job by finding her. Bringing her back wasn't part of the deal. There was part of me that wished she wouldn't come back because if she didn't, chances were pretty good Nicky Diamond would get what he deserved, and I wasn't about to shed any tears as a result of that outcome.

It was close to ten when I got back to my room. I was beat. I wanted nothing more than to fall into bed but I decided to call Rudder and let him know I'd found Jana.

"Will she or won't she alibi him?" he asked.

"I don't know. All I know is she's pretty freaked out."

"Why?"

"Because someone threatened her."

"Who?"

"She says she doesn't know."

"Do you believe her?"

"I haven't spent enough time with her to form an opinion."

"Come on, Swann. You're good at reading people. You telling me you don't know whether or not she's lying?"

"I can tell you this much. She's genuinely spooked."

"Does she know why she was threatened?"

"Nope."

"Is she or isn't she coming back to testify for him?"

"Can't say. I left her with a proposition."

"Which is?"

"I offered to drive her back. I told her she had till tomorrow morning to make up her mind."

"Why the hell did you do that?"

"Like I said, she's scared. She believes she's being watched."

"Come on. What are the chances of that?"

"Practically nil. But they're a hundred percent to her. And you know, it's not impossible. Whoever threatened her might have kept an eye on her when she left the city. They might know where she is. And I didn't think she was going to get on a plane headed back to the city."

"Why not?"

"Because if someone is keeping an eye on her, or me, for that matter, they'd certainly have the airport staked out, either here or back in the city."

"Seems implausible to me."

"It doesn't matter if it's plausible to us, Paul. It's what she thinks that matters."

"So, you'd really drive all the way back here with her?"

"If I have to. I think I can make it in a day and a half, maybe two. But I've got another idea. We can drive to Atlanta and catch a flight there."

"But if she's being watched…"

"They can't cover every airport. If they know she's here, they'd be checking flights from here, and possibly flights arriving from here. I'll know if anyone's following us on the road. And if they do see us take off by car, they're going to assume we'll drive all the way back to the city."

"Listen, Henry, before you go to all that trouble, try to find out what she's going to say. I don't want to get her up here and find that she's useless or, even worse, hurts our case."

"I assume if she's willing to come back, she's willing to testify."

"If you find out who's been threatening her it could help me with his defense. So, keep me posted."

The next morning, after sleeping more than eight hours for the first time in years, I woke around seven-thirty. I checked my phone to see if there was a message from Jana. Nothing. I checked the hotel message center, also nothing. My guess was that fear won out, and that she'd either skipped town or went deeper into hiding. I felt bad for her. Once you start running, it's awfully hard to stop.

I showered, shaved, threw my belongings into my duffle bag, then went downstairs to check out. When I got to the front desk, I spotted Jana sitting in one of the high-backed, upholstered chairs. She was wearing blue jeans, a weathered brown leather motorcycle jacket, and her hair was tucked up into a New York Yankees baseball cap. At her feet was a backpack. She'd made her decision.

"Ten minutes later and I'd be gone," I said, as I grabbed the chair next to hers.

"I've been here since seven this morning. I didn't want to miss you. You meant it about driving?"

"I did."

While Jana waited for me in the lobby, I found a quiet spot and made a few calls. One was to Rudder, to tell him we were headed back. Another was to the rental car company to arrange for the extended time we'd need and the new drop-off point. I called the airline and canceled my ticket. Then I made a quick stop at the business center, got on the internet, and printed out a route back to the city.

By nine, we were on the road, me in the driver's seat, Jana buckled in beside me. I handed her the print-out. "You're my navigator."

"I had an idea."

"What's that?"

"I think we should just drive to Atlanta and take a flight from there."

"Aren't you afraid we'll be spotted?"

"If someone's following us, you'll be able to tell, won't you?"

"I will."

"And you'll be able to get rid of them, won't you?"

I smiled. "I'm not Jim Rockford, Jana."

"Who?"

I realized I'd just dated myself.

"He was a TV private eye who was an ace driver. I barely passed driver's ed."

"But you'll be able to elude whoever might be following us, won't you?"

"Sure," I lied, because maybe I could and maybe I couldn't. "Are you having second thoughts about spending close to twenty hours in a car with me?"

"Maybe. Or maybe the idea of being cooped up in a car that long doesn't appeal to me."

"So your plan is to drive to Atlanta, ditch the car, and hop a flight to New York?"

"Yes. Is there anything wrong with that?"

"Not a thing," I said, although in truth I was kinda getting into the idea of a long road trip sitting next to an attractive young woman, even though I was pretty sure nothing was going to happen.

It was a beautiful day for a road trip. The sun was shining, there wasn't a cloud in the sky, and it was a less than five-hour trip till we made Atlanta.

"How long have you been doing this thing?" she asked.

"What thing?"

"You know, the private eye thing."

"First of all, I'm not a private eye, so try to rid your mind of those movie and TV stereotypes. I'm not Sam Spade. I'm not Philip Marlowe."

"But you could tell if someone was following us? I mean, you have that skill, don't you?"

"Yes, I could. And I've been keeping an eye out. Why are you so frightened, Jana?"

"Someone threatened me. I'm not about to take any chances. If you found me, someone else could, too."

"That doesn't mean anyone else is looking for you."

"When it comes to your life, you can take chances."

"Okay. I get your point."

"By the time we get to Atlanta, we'll know, right?"

"Yes, we'll know," I said.

Once we got out of Mobile and onto I-65 N, Jana relaxed a bit. She obsessively checked the rearview mirror, to make sure no one was following us. But better her than me. Besides, it kept her busy enough to where I didn't have to make idle conversation.

About an hour into our trip, she seemed to be assured no one was following us and so was I. "I think we're going to have to stop soon," she said. "I need a pit stop, plus I'm starved."

"Didn't you have breakfast?"

"I didn't have time. And you know, I'd love to drive for a while, if you don't mind. It relaxes me."

"You're not signed on as an extra driver."

"So?"

"If there's an accident, I'm responsible."

"I'm a great driver. Probably better than you. There won't be any accident."

"It's against the rules."

"Funny, I didn't peg you as the kind of guy who followed the rules."

"Well, sometimes I am," I lied.

She sat back, folded her arms across her chest, and pouted. She probably thought that would work. It wouldn't. I'm well beyond being controlled by what other people think of me. I was hoping she'd forget about her request. I wasn't worried about her getting us into an accident. I was more worried about losing control.

Finally, after fifteen minutes of silence, I asked, "How'd you get involved with Diamond?"

"He came into where I worked and hit on me. But not before hitting on two of the other waitresses."

"So, you were third choice?"

"I guess."

"That must have pissed you off."

"Not really."

"So, his magic worked on you, not them?"

"You think he's some kind of Svengali or something?"

"You're the one hiding out in some small town in Alabama. What should I think?"

"He looked like he'd be fun, okay?" She paused for a moment, staring out the side window. "If he'd seen me first, I would have been the only one."

"I've met him, Jana. The last thing I'd associate with Nicky Diamond is fun. It's like he's got this big flashing neon sign nailed to his chest that says TROUBLE. But maybe you like trouble."

"Well, maybe I do."

She was silent for several minutes, back to staring out the side window at the very uninspiring view.

"I was bored," she said, finally turning her head to me. "Okay? Women do strange things when they're bored. Nicky Diamond was one of those strange things. I'll bet you've done some stupid, strange things in your life."

"Pretty much every day." And this might be one of them.

"Tell me about yourself."

"What?"

"Tell me about you."

"There's not much to tell."

"Where were you born? What did your parents do? What were you like as a kid? Like that."

"I was born in Long Beach, Long Island. My mom was a teacher, my dad was a cop.

"A cop?"

"Yeah. He was also a sonuvabitch. He drank and he gambled and he was always playing the angles."

"What does that mean?"

"It means he was dirty. He took things he shouldn't have, and he took money for things he shouldn't have done...or not done."

"You sound bitter."

"I'm long past bitter."

"And what about you?"

"Simple. I took a wrong turn in life and wound up doing this."

"What's this?"

"Chasing after people and things. Trying to put the world back in order. Cleaning up other people's messes."

"So, you're a do-gooder? Is that what you want me to believe?"

"You can believe whatever you want, but do-gooder is the last thing I am. The sad truth is I'll do pretty much anything for money." I turned and looked at her. "Short of doing what your boyfriend does."

"That's very hurtful. You think I knew what he did and stayed with him? You think I was some kind of Bonnie Parker?"

I shrugged.

"Well, I'm sure as hell not. The minute I found out what he did, I got the hell out of there."

"But that's not why you ran out."

"No. I ran because, like I said, I was told in no uncertain terms that it wouldn't be a good idea for me to stick around. I didn't even know I was supposed to be an alibi for Nicky until people started looking for me."

"How'd the threat come? Phone? In person?"

"Phone call. Anonymous, of course."

"He? She?"

"He."

"What did he say?"

"'If you want to stay healthy, make yourself scarce.'"

"Those were his exact words?"

"You think I taped it?"

I shot her a look.

"Yes. The exact words. And in a tone that didn't leave much doubt what he meant."

"Did you ask what he was talking about?"

"He didn't seem like he wanted to get into a prolonged conversation. Believe me, if you heard what this guy sounded like, and you wanted to stay healthy, you'd have left town, too. Unless you're some kind of hero."

"I'm no hero. Just the opposite. Why do you think I wear these Chucks?"

She looked down at my feet and stared at my red Converse sneakers.

"Are you a fast runner?"

"When I have to be."

We drove in silence for a few minutes, until I saw a sign for the next rest stop ten miles away.

"We'll stop there," I said.

We split up to go to our respective bathrooms. We met back at a McDonald's, where I grabbed coffees and egg McMuffins for both of us. Once she started eating, she seemed to loosen up a bit, so I figured I'd see if I could get her to open up a little.

"Let me ask you a question, Jana."

"Yes, I've always had this appetite."

"Interesting, but not exactly the question I was thinking of."

"What's that?" she said, taking a bite of her sandwich.

"Were you with Nicky the time he was supposed to be ending someone else's life?"

"It depends."

"What's that mean?"

"I was with him the day of the murder, but I don't know what time he was supposed to be killing someone."

"From what I understand, it was the evening."

"Depends on the time."

"What part of the evening were you with him?"

She took a sip of her coffee.

"I don't really want to talk about that now."

"Why not?"

"Do I need a reason?"

"Not as far as I'm concerned, but there's going to come the time when you're going to have to answer one way or another."

She shrugged. "So, maybe that's when I'll do it."

"You're not going to budge, are you?"

She shook her head and smiled.

"You're enjoying this, aren't you?"

"I know this is probably crap, but yes, it tastes so good. Why do you think it tastes so good?"

"It's the love and care they put into all their food, Jana."

She grinned. I'd gotten the point.

When we got back to the car I started to go around to the driver's seat, but she put a hand on my shoulder.

"My turn."

"I told you, I'm not insured for a second driver."

"Time to live dangerously."

"Dangerous is fine. Foolish is not."

"I won't squeal if you won't."

I could see I wasn't going to win this argument, so I handed her the keys and got in on the passenger's side. As she settled herself in the driver's seat, I did what I always do: I took a look around, just to make sure nothing seemed amiss. I took a snapshot with my mind and, as we pulled out onto the highway, I looked back to make sure no one was pulling out the same time we were. It's not that I'd bought into Jana's suspicions; it's just that sometimes paranoia is contagious.

Everything seemed to check out, and we were on our way again, with only a few hours left to go.

It turned out, Jana had a much heavier foot than I did, which was fine with me. The quicker we reached Atlanta, the better.

Once she'd settled in, I figured I'd see if I could somehow get her talking. "Why do you think someone would want you out of the picture?"

"Boy, you really are a dog with a bone, as my mom would say."

"Yes, I am."

"Let me ask you a question."

"Shoot."

"Do you think you're going to wear me down or do you think you're going to charm me into answering your questions?"

"Whatever works."

"What if nothing works?"

"I refuse to entertain that possibility. So, who do you think was behind the call?"

"I guess, if Nicky is innocent, it could be the actual killer. Or someone trying to protect him."

"That's possible."

"Or maybe, it's someone who has it in for Nicky and wants to stick him with the murder."

"Another strong possibility. Or, how about this? It could have been Nicky."

I looked up and saw a startled look on her face in the rear-view mirror.

"Why, if I could swear he was with me, would he want me out of the way?"

"Thing is, Jana, and this is all to your credit, you don't think like a criminal."

"Thank goodness. But I still don't get it."

"Trying someone for a crime is all about reasonable doubt. If Nicky's lawyer can spin a tale that the jury buys as reasonable doubt, that's money in the bank, and Nicky walks."

"I still don't get it."

"Let's say the story is there's this witness who can exonerate him but the witness has taken off. And let's say your attorney plants the seed in the jury's mind that the reason this witness is missing or even dead is because he or she could get you off the hook by providing you with an alibi. But let's say for some reason that witness has disappeared and that maybe that disappearance was engineered by a third party who is either guilty of the crime or wants it to appear as if you're guilty. If your attorney can sell that story to a jury, well that, my dear, innocent Jana, is what's called reasonable doubt."

"You know something, you really do have a devious mind."

"So, they say. But I've earned it. You deal with lowlifes like Nicky Diamond, people who lie, steal, cheat, abandon, resort to violence to get what they want, and have absolutely no remorse for what they've done, no consideration for their victims, you'd be cynical, too."

"You know something, Swann?"

"No, Jana, what?"

"I actually feel sorry for you."

"Why's that?"

"Because you go through life with an attitude like that."

"I yam who I yam and that's all that I yam, Jana. I make no apologies about it, either."

She shook her head. "It must suck to be you."

"Well, it ain't a day at the beach, that's for sure."

"I just hope this isn't contagious." She reached for the radio. "How about some music?"

Just what I need, I thought, *fighting with a millennial over what music to listen to.*

12
SECRET AGENT MAN

It seemed like we were in that car forever, and if it weren't for the classic rock station we finally agreed upon, it might have been worse. Nevertheless, after two more quick pit stops, "I'm sorry, I have this low blood sugar thing where I have to eat something every couple hours, and that means something to drink and I've got this thing where I have to..." we finally made it to the Hartsfield-Jackson Atlanta airport. What with all the stops we had to make, it was pushing six p.m. What should have been a five-hour drive took us closer to eight hours.

Jana claimed she was beat and wanted to check into the airport hotel and leave for New York the next morning, but I was having none of it. The sooner this was over, the better, as far as I was concerned. Besides, a little bit of her paranoia was beginning to settle over me. There was absolutely no reasonable sign that we were being followed and yet, if you look for something hard enough, chances are you're going to find it. And so, after every time we stopped to cater to Jana's basic urges, we both thought we saw familiar vehicles, one an SUV, one a compact, and one a pickup truck, as we pulled away from the rest stops.

I was pretty sure, in a mini-case of folie à deux, we were imagining the whole scenario, but rather than prolong the agony, I wanted to get back to the city as soon as possible.

We grabbed a quick dinner at one of the forgettable airport

restaurants then caught the nine p.m. flight back to LaGuardia. The only seats available were in first class, but I figured Rudder owed me that much, since the job was done so quickly and efficiently. I thought once we were seated we were out of the woods, but as we fastened up she leaned over and whispered, "What if someone's waiting for us when we land?"

"Jana, let's get real. What are the chances of that? They'd have to know our plan and we didn't even know it before we got here. Besides, we were the last ones on the plane and did you see anyone else in the waiting area?"

That seemed to calm her, at least for the moment.

We were both beat, so before the plane reached twenty thousand feet, we'd nodded off. I didn't regain consciousness till the lights in the cabin went on and the pilot announced we were starting our descent.

I looked over at Jana. She was still asleep. She looked so young and pretty and innocent and vulnerable, but maybe because she looked that way a disturbing thought crossed my mind. *What if I'm being played? What if we're all being played?*

I wasn't even sure what this meant. And why would I have this thought at all? Was it because of all that talk about being a cynic, about not trusting anyone or anything? Had my visit with Freddie corrupted me to the extent that I was even worse than usual in terms of believing anyone or anything? Had it now become part of my DNA to mistrust everything and everyone? But I couldn't help myself. Something about the whole situation made me uneasy. I know women, especially young women, often make bad choices, especially when it comes to men, but even from the little time I'd spent with Jana, I just couldn't see her and Nicky Diamond as a couple. It was like one of those jigsaw puzzles where you dump all the pieces on a table. It doesn't look like those pieces could possibly ever make anything coherent and yet as soon as you start putting the pieces in the right places, it begins to take on the appearance of something familiar.

Sartre believed "things are entirely what they appear to be

and behind them…there is nothing." While Epictetus probably nailed it when he wrote, "Things either are what they appear to be; or they neither are, nor appear to be; or they are, and do not appear to be; or they are not, and yet appear to be. Rightly to aim in all these cases is the wise man's task."

The truth is buried in there somewhere.

Rather than make myself crazier than I already was—chalk that up to a lifetime of being me—I decided it didn't matter. I was paid to do a job and I did it. End of story.

It was past midnight by the time we deplaned. There was no way I was sending Jana back to Brooklyn. If someone was keeping an eye out for her, there was a good chance they had her apartment staked out. Or paid someone to alert them if she showed up back at her apartment. I could take her to my place, but that wouldn't be safe either. It was too late to spring her on Klavan, so the only alternative was to check into the airport hotel, then head back into Manhattan early in the morning.

I suggested the idea to Jana and she was fine with it. "Separate rooms, right?"

"Of course," I said. We agreed to meet up in the coffee shop at nine the next morning.

I needed to get some real sleep, not that half-sleep you get on planes, which I wouldn't get sharing a room with her. Not so much because something would happen between us, but because I'd be too wound up worrying it might. Or that it wouldn't.

I booked two rooms on the same floor, across the hall from each other. As soon as she disappeared into her room I began to wonder if I'd find her there in the morning. What if she got cold feet and decided to take off? How would I explain to Rudder how I let her slip through my fingers? Or to Nicky? The idea of him being behind bars didn't guarantee that he wouldn't have friends on the outside eager to stay on his good side.

I was finally able to fall off to sleep, but only by convincing myself that Jana wouldn't come all the way back with me if she had any notion of taking off once we got here.

I awoke at eight. I called Klavan and asked if he minded putting Jana up for a few days. He tossed the decision to Mary. She agreed.

When I got to the coffee shop, Jana was already sitting at a table, sipping a cup of coffee. Her backpack was at her feet. I slid into the seat across from her and gestured to the waitress that I'd have a cup, too.

"How'd you sleep last night?" I asked.

"On and off," she said. I could see her eyes were puffy, either from lack of sleep or crying.

"Tough night, huh?"

"I can't believe I'm back here."

"To be honest, I was hoping you wouldn't run."

"You'd thought I'd take off?"

"I considered it."

She smiled. "I thought about it."

"What changed your mind?"

"I don't really know." She stared at me with those cobalt eyes. "Maybe I didn't want to disappoint you."

Her answer surprised me. She actually cared what other people thought of her. I've long since given a rat's ass about what anyone thinks about me. After all, it can't possibly be any worse than I think of myself.

"I wouldn't have been disappointed. I'd have understood. It might even have been something I'd have done. How about something to eat?"

"I can't eat when I'm anxious. But please, order something for yourself."

"Coffee's enough. Then we'll head back into the city. I didn't think you'd want to go back to your place, so I've arranged for you to stay with friends of mine for at least a couple nights."

I noticed tears starting to form in the corner of her eyes.

"I...I...thank you. Really. That's very...sweet."

She was making me uncomfortable. I wanted to change the subject, but I didn't know how.

"You'll be safe with Ross and Mary. They're good people. They live in a secure building. He's a rare book dealer, so his apartment is well protected. I have an office there. They have an extra bedroom you can stay in."

"I don't want to be a bother..."

"No bother. I'll feel better knowing you're safe. After you settle in, I'll give Paul a call and he can set up a meeting with you."

"Okay. But you know, you don't have to feel responsible for me."

"Sure, I do."

She started to smile but I didn't let her.

"Tell me something, Jana."

"Yes?"

"After I deliver you, I'm done. But I'm curious. Are you going to help Nicky or not?"

She didn't say anything, which worried me. Was she hesitant because she was about to lie? Or because she didn't want to commit herself? Or was it something else?

"You have to think about your answer?"

She ran her tongue along her top lip. "I told you. I don't know exactly when they're talking about."

"You mean you don't know when Nicky's supposed to have offed the guy?"

She nodded.

Against my better judgment and my long-standing promise to myself to remain personally uninvolved in any case I was on, that's exactly what I did.

"There's something screwy going on here, Jana. Something bothering me. How about helping me out?"

"I don't know what you mean."

"Sure, you do. Your boyfriend gets picked up for murder. He claims you're his alibi. You get threatened and leave town. Now, you're back in town even though you're not sure you can help him. Doesn't that smell a little fishy to you?"

"I guess when you put it that way..."

"What other way is there to put it?"

"You've done your job, right?" Her face tightened, as did her tone.

"You're telling me to mind my own business?"

"I guess."

"I want to help you, Jana. But I can't unless I know everything."

"What makes you think I need help?"

"You skip town in the middle of the night. You tell me why I think you need help."

"For your information, it wasn't the middle of the night."

"That's just an expression, honey. You're scared to death someone's following you. You refuse to give me a straight answer. I'd say that qualifies as needing help."

"That's all I have to say right now. If you don't want to help me out, well, that's up to you. Remember, I didn't ask you for help."

"There are no conditions to helping you. I found you and brought you up here, so I'm responsible for you. I'll leave the door open and if you do need help or advice, you can let me know. Otherwise, I'll keep my nose out of your business. What say we head back to the city?"

She nodded, obviously happy to end the conversation.

We grabbed a cab to Klavans'. After I made the introductions, Jana excused herself, claiming she got little sleep the night before and wanted to lie down. I figured I'd head back to my place, clean up, then give Goldblatt a call and see if there were any developments on his ex-wife's case.

Before I left, I took Jana aside.

"Listen, I don't want you leaving this place without checking with me first. I'm gonna call Nicky's lawyer, tell him you're in town. He'll want to talk to you, but I'm gonna to set it up that he either comes here or, if he wants to see you down there, you're waiting for me to go with you. Understand?"

She nodded.

"Jana, this isn't a game. Someone doesn't want you testifying and we don't know how serious they are about stopping you. I'm gonna to try to figure out who it is and why, but until then we're not fooling around, okay?"

"I don't think you should get involved."

"Too late for that. If you need anything, just ask Ross or Mary. They'll take care of you."

"I don't want to be a bother..."

"I don't do guilt well, so let's not test it, okay?"

She nodded.

On my way back to my place, my phone buzzed. It was Goldblatt.

"How'd you know I was back?"

"I didn't. News flash: phones work all over. I wasn't sitting on my hands while you were gone."

"What's that supposed to mean?"

"It means I found Madame Sofia. She lives over on West End and Seventy-second. What say we go over there this evening? You know, ambush her, like one of those *60 Minutes* dudes."

"I'm not sure that's a good idea."

"Why not?"

"I don't want to alienate her from the get-go. We've got to be a lot subtler than that."

"You mean, like going undercover?"

"That makes it sound a lot more dramatic than it is. But yes, that's the general idea."

"I'm up for that."

"I'm sure you are, but that'd be a mistake. You're too close to it. You'd be the bull, she'd be the china shop. She'd see right through you."

"You think I've never worked the room, Swann?"

"What are you talking about?"

"Let's just say I'm no stranger to working undercover."

"Do tell."

"That would be against the rules, wouldn't it? Let's just say I've practiced my fair share of the art of deception."

"Maybe one day you can give me some helpful hints. But since you've hired me, I think it's best you let me deal with this my way. And if that doesn't produce results, then I'll be happy to let you take over."

Silence. One beat. Two beats. Three beats. "Okay. I hear you. But the least you can do is tell me the plan."

"I don't have one yet, but after you text me her address, I'm going to find out as much about her as I can. It's no different from repo-ing cars. You get the lay of the land first, learn everything you can about the owner, then figure out the best time and place to make the pick-up."

The grumbling I heard through the phone indicated he wasn't happy. Finally, he backed off, but only after I promised to keep him in the loop. But let's face it, I've broken too many promises to let that bother me.

I tried to read a book—I was halfway through a pretty good crime novel—to unwind, but my head was filled with thoughts and images that kept bouncing off each other. I wasn't surprised. When I'm on a case, no matter how hard I try, I can't seem to turn my brain off. It was like that back in my Spanish Harlem days, when I spent way too much of my time repo-ing cars. I'd plan everything, right down to the smallest detail, because if something went wrong, I could find myself the victim of the wrath of a deadbeat owner who didn't particularly like the idea of someone yanking back his dream machine, perhaps the only thing in the world that made him feel like a winner. It happened more than once. One guy took after me with a baseball bat. Another threw a trash can at the back of his own car, magically thinking that somehow it would make me stop and he could get his car back. One pissed-off owner even threatened me with a shotgun. I didn't wait around to find out if he'd use it.

Finally, after an hour or so, I gave up trying to read, made myself a strong cup of joe, took a quick shower, and threw my clothes back on. Before leaving the apartment, I grabbed my mini recorder, a notebook, and a couple pens and took off to the Upper West Side, to do some spade work on Madame Sofia.

I like to work from the outside in. That meant canvassing the stores within a six-block area to see if they knew Susan Finch and, if they did, what they knew about her. I copped a couple photos off the internet to help with identification. I didn't waste my time with the big stores, like Duane Reade, Fairway, Trader Joe's, CVS, and Rite Aid. There was too much staff turnover and besides, the folks who work there rarely pay attention to customers. I also left banks off the list because getting information there is a lot tougher. Instead, I opted for dry cleaners, restaurants, small delis, even a couple coffee shops, of which I am very familiar ever since getting involved with my gourmand partner.

According to Becker, Finch had been living in the neighborhood a few months, but after checking the shops and restaurants in the area, I was convinced she was living there at least a year, maybe more.

The profile I was able to compile had Finch being well dressed, stylish, affable, and yet at times demanding. "She isn't the kind of woman you can drop your standards for," said the proprietor of a fancy delicacy shop. "She knows quality and demands it," he added. According to the restaurateurs, she sometimes dined alone, but often she kept company with a distinguished, white-haired gentleman who always picked up the check and tipped generously.

Perhaps the most important piece of information I found was that she had a cute little Havanese named Corky. This meant she was most likely walking the dog at least three times a day.

After a few hours canvassing the neighborhood it was time to home in on her building. This meant talking to the staff of her building, and perhaps neighbors as well. You want to know something about a tenant, you talk to the doorman, the concierge, or the support staff. Problem is, most of them are very discreet. And with good reason. They talk too much about the tenants, they run the risk of either being fired or losing those holiday tips. But in my experience, they all have good people skills, which means they're affable and friendly. They are there to help you. They are there to be your friend.

Still, they are discreet and a tough nut to crack. You have to earn their trust. But I've found if you approach these people the right way, you can finesse some important information.

Most building shifts are from seven a.m. to three p.m. and three p.m. to eleven p.m., and then overnight shift. You can pretty much ignore the late-shift people, because they rarely have much contact with the tenants.

Finch lived in a classic prewar building on the northwest corner of West End Avenue, a long block away from Riverside Park. I settled myself on a stoop across the street, ostensibly reading a newspaper, for about an hour. I watched the entrance to her building, noting people walking in and out, especially focusing on the doorman, as he chatted with tenants, hailed cabs, and greeted visitors. A few minutes past three, when the shift changed, the doorman, a stocky Latino in his mid-to-late forties, wearing baggy jeans and a black leather jacket, and carrying a Trader Joe's shopping bag, came out of the side entrance of the building. He crossed West End, then waited to cross to the south side of Seventy-second street. I sidled up alongside him.

"Excuse me," I said. "But don't you work at two-sixty-three?"

He gave me a suspicious look and hesitated before he said, "Do I know you, man?"

"No. And I really hate to bother you, but I thought I recognized you and I wonder if you have a couple minutes?"

"For what?"

"Well, I've been out of work a while and a friend suggested I might try finding a job in a residential building. I don't know squat about it and don't even know how to get into it. Let's face it, I don't even know if it's something I'd like."

The light changed, but he stood there, listening to me politely, afraid to hurt my feelings. He was probably good at his job.

"Listen, I know this is a lot to ask, but I was wondering if you've got a few minutes to talk about it? Maybe I could buy you a drink? There's the Emerald Inn, over there..." I pointed to the Irish pub across the street. "You'd be doing me a big favor."

He looked at his watch.

"It won't take long. I promise. You know, I'm really kind of desperate. I got two kids. My ex-wife's gonna take me to court for support..."

"I maybe got a half hour. But no more than that. I don't want to get caught in the rush hour. Train's bad enough."

"That's more than enough time. You're a life saver, man. Really."

I extended my hand. "My name's Henry. Yours?"

"Ricky."

"Nice to meet you, Ricky."

The light turned green. We crossed the street, headed toward the Emerald. I dropped in a little Spanish I'd picked up while working uptown, to bond with him.

"Where you learn to speak Spanish, man?"

"I used to work uptown."

"Yeah?. Whereabouts?"

"Up near One-fortieth and Broadway."

"I got me an aunt who lives up there."

"You know the Paradise Bar & Grill?"

"Sure do, man. We used to hang out there, sometimes."

"The owner, Joe Bailey, was a friend of mine."

"Good dude, man. What'd you do up there?"

"I worked for a guy had a PI license. Did some legwork for him. You know, serving papers. Shit like that."

"How come you don't do that no more?"

"He moved to Jersey. Left me high and dry."

We reached the Emerald Inn, an Irish pub a few steps below

street level. I'd been to the joint before. Years ago, it was the All-State Café, and before that, W. M. Tweeds. Its claim to fame was that it was the inspiration for what was called the Goodbar Murder (which was turned into a film, *Looking for Mr. Goodbar*). A young school teacher, named Roseann Quinn used to hang out at the bar and had a habit of taking home men she'd meet there—she actually lived across the street from where Susan Finch now lived. On New Year's Day, 1973, Quinn met a guy named John Wayne Wilson. At the end of the evening, Wilson and Quinn went to her apartment. Evidently, after smoking some weed, Wilson couldn't get hard. He claimed Quinn insulted him and told him to leave. They struggled. Wilson picked up a knife and stabbed Quinn eighteen times in the neck and stomach. Eventually, the cops focused on Wilson, who by then had returned to his mother's house in Indianapolis. While cooling his heels in The Tombs, the holding prison, Wilson got into an argument with a guard and threatened to kill himself. The guard taunted him, even asking if he'd like sheets to do the job with, later tossing the bedsheets into his cell. Wilson used those sheets to hang himself.

I grabbed a couple beers from the bar and carried them to our table in the back.

"How about something to eat, Ricky?"

"No, thanks, man. My wife'd kill me, I don't eat what she makes."

We made small talk about wives and kids and then I got him talking about his job. It wasn't hard. People like to talk and most of them have no one to listen to them. After a couple more beers, it was like we were best buddies.

"What's it like to work where every tenant makes more dough than you do?"

"Whatchoo gonna do, man? That's the way it is in this city. You rich or you poor. There ain't no in between."

"Do you have favorite tenants?"

"Sure. I got the ones I like and the ones I don't like so much.

But most of them are okay."

"The ones you don't like, why's that?"

"They stuck up, man. They expect you to jump when they call and you know what, those are the ones who don't even bother to tip. The richer they are, the tighter they be."

"What do you do if someone doesn't tip you?"

He smiled. "When they need something done, I'll do it, but I'm just real..." he drew out the word "...slow getting it done. If you know what I mean."

"I think a friend of mine used to date someone in your building."

"Yeah? Who dat?"

"Let me see what her name was. Susan something or other. She had this real cute little dog..."

"That'd probly be Miss Finch. Nice lady."

"Really? I don't think my friend thought so. Maybe because she dumped him."

"That'd do it, man. That don't surprise me. She got herself a bunch of boyfriends, coming and going all the time. Women, too. I think maybe she runs some kind of business up there."

"Really?"

"Wait a minute, I don't mean that she's, you know..."

"Promiscuous?"

"Yeah. That's the word. She ain't no whore, or nothing. I think she just got a lot of friends. And maybe she's a therapist, or something like that. We got others in the building who work from their apartments. Them's the ones who tip real good 'cause they're afraid we're gonna rat 'em out."

"Anyone special come to see her?"

"You mean like a boyfriend?"

"Yeah."

"Why you be so interested?"

"It's not me, Ricky. I'm sure my pal would like to know. You know, keeping up on old flames. Between you and me, I think my friend still carries a torch. If she wasn't in something solid, I wouldn't be surprised if he didn't try hitting on her again."

Ricky smiled and shook his head. "Those things don't never work out, man. Once they gone, they gone."

One more beer into our meeting and Ricky had loosened up enough for me to get a pretty good line on Susan Finch. I knew she was in apartment 12C. I knew she had lots of visitors, clients like Rachel, I was sure. She walked her dog, Fifi, at least three times a day. She kept erratic hours and sometimes wasn't home for days at a time.

It was nearly five-thirty as I watched a slightly unsteady Ricky make his way up Seventy-second Street, head toward Broadway and the subway back up to the Bronx, where he lived with his wife and two kids.

Over the years, I've found that people, no matter how un-predictable they think they are, are creatures of habit. It's some-thing I've counted on and it's never failed me. According to Ricky, every evening around six p.m., Finch walked her dog. Fifi was my ticket in and if Ricky was right, in a half hour Madame Sofia and Fifi would be emerging from two hundred sixty-three, headed toward Riverside Park.

I didn't know quite how I was going to approach her, but I figured now was as good a time as any to make my move.

13
MEET AND GREET

At first, I didn't recognize her. Not that I'd ever actually laid eyes on her, but I had managed to dig up what was admittedly an old snapshot. It's amazing what people will post on social media, without realizing once they do, it's there forever.

She was wearing dark sweat pants, a baggy crimson, Harvard sweatshirt, and a New York Mets baseball cap. It was the dog that gave her away.

I let her get about half a block away from the building, walking in the direction of the park, before I swooped in, just as her little dog was sniffing at a fire hydrant.

"Cute dog. Mind if I pet her?"

"Sure."

"I always like to ask because, well, you never know. Even these little ones can give you one hell of a bite, if they don't like strangers touching them."

"Just like people," she said, smiling.

"What's the breed?" I asked, as I bent down and petted the pup.

"Havanese."

"She's a sweetheart. What's her name?"

"Miranda."

"After the daughter of Prospero?"

"You're familiar with Shakespeare?"

"Somewhat. *The Tempest*. Right?"

"Yes. I'm impressed."

"The result of a misspent youth as an English major. As I recall, she was banished to the island, along with her father when she was only three."

"Very good."

"And for what, twelve years, she lived with only her father and the family slave, Caliban, as her only company."

"You really do know your Shakespeare."

"Just enough to impress attractive women. I'm Henry Swann." I offered my hand. She looked at it a moment, as if wondering how long it had been since I washed it, then shook it lightly. I noticed she didn't offer her name. I didn't push.

"I just moved into the neighborhood and I was thinking of getting a dog. But it's awfully windy over there on Riverside and the idea of getting up every morning and braving that, especially in winter, well, it's more than a little daunting."

"If you have to think about it, then it probably isn't for you." The dog started pulling her toward the park. "She has a mind of her own," she said, as she let herself get pulled forward. I kept in step with her.

"I don't mind," she said, continuing the conversation when she could have told me to get lost. "It gets me out of the apartment three times a day. And the exercise isn't bad."

"You don't look like you need the exercise. You a runner?"

"Used to be, but I had to give it up. Bad knees."

"Yeah. I know all about that. I used to play a little hoops, but the knees started to ache pretty bad a couple years ago. I figured I'd quit while I still had them."

The dog stopped and sniffed a tree.

"What is it you do you for a living, Mr. Swann, if you don't mind my asking?"

Either she was hooked or she suspected something wasn't kosher. It didn't matter. I'd engaged her.

"You know, that's a tough one to answer. I do a little of this, a little of that. I guess you'd say I was an entrepreneur."

"Is that some kind of code for being mostly unemployed?"

I laughed. "Sometimes true. But right now, I am involved in a business operation."

"What kind?"

I mimed zipping my lip. "Not supposed to talk about it. Gag order. But, hey, since I'm new in the neighborhood, to the city in fact, and I don't really know anyone, would you like to have coffee some time? Or, better yet, dinner? And then maybe, when you get a few drinks in me, you can get me to spill the beans."

"Do I look that easy, Mr. Swann?"

"Easy?"

"You know, an easy pick up?"

I stepped back. "Just the opposite. You look pretty hard. For instance, you still haven't given me your name."

"I'm not sure yet if I want you to know who I am."

"You don't look like a woman who has something to hide."

"Everyone has something to hide, Mr. Swann."

"Very true. So, how about that dinner—and maybe then you'll actually warm up enough to give me your name."

"I don't usually do this..."

"Neither do I."

"I don't believe that for a second." The dog started to pull again. "All right. Dinner."

"How about tomorrow evening?"

"That should work." She dug into her pocket, removed her wallet, and handed me a card with her name, email, and phone number, but no address and no hint as to how she made her living.

"Well, Susan Finch, why don't we make it around seven o'clock. And since you know the neighborhood, how about you choose the place? I'd give you one of my cards, except I don't have any new ones yet. You know, with my new address."

"Seven is fine. Let's meet at Café Luxembourg. I'll make a reservation."

"You know, that place can get awfully crowded and noisy. Why don't you pick something a little quieter?"

She looked at me and smiled. "This isn't a date, Mr. Swann. Or is it?"

I shook my head. "Absolutely not. I don't like to hear myself talk—or think—but I do like to hear the person on the other end of the table."

"All right. How about Pomodoro Rosso, on Columbus and Seventy-first? I'll get us a table in the back."

"Perfect. See you tomorrow at seven."

Mission accomplished. I had my foot in the door.

I debated whether to tell Goldblatt. Under normal circumstances, I would have kept him out of the loop. But in this case, I was working for him, so I owed him a progress report. I regretted it as soon as I did. He was excited. So excited, that even though I did my best to wriggle out of it, he talked me into meeting him for dinner that night.

Just as I was trudging up the stairs to my apartment, my phone started jiggling in my pocket. It was Jana Monroe. I stopped on the landing, more as an excuse to catch my breath than being anxious to take her call. As soon as she spoke, I caught a sense of anxiety in her voice.

"What's wrong?" I asked.

"Everything."

"I'm very familiar with the feeling, but anything in particular?"

"Mr. Rudder just called."

"Not a surprise, right?"

"No. But...his call kinda made this all seem so real."

"It is real, Jana. Did he set up an appointment to see you?"

"Yes. Tomorrow morning at ten." She hesitated a moment. "You'll go with me, right?"

Technically, I was off the clock and off the hook. But for some odd reason, I felt responsible for her. Well, maybe it wasn't so odd. There was something about her I liked. I don't know what, but something. So, even if I knew I should, I couldn't just drop her. There was this vague sense that she was in danger. I didn't know from who, but that only made it more ominous.

"You know I don't have to," I said, trying to buy time, hoping she'd take me off the hook by making the choice to go it alone.

"I know. But you'll do it, right?"

"Yeah. I'll do it. I'll pick you up around nine and we'll head down there."

"Thank you, Henry. Thank you so much."

The change in the tone of her voice was palpable and even though I wasn't supposed to care, I was relieved. I didn't know if I could trust her or not, but until I found out for sure I felt this obligation to watch out for her. Besides, how much trouble would it be? I'd go down there with her, leave her in Rudder's hands, pick up the rest of what he owed me, and mark the case closed. That's what I told myself, but I couldn't kid myself. I had this strong feeling there was trouble ahead and the only thing that reassured me was the fact that there was at least a fifty percent change I was wrong.

I took a quick shower, changed, and headed out to a local East Village burger joint where I'd promised to meet Goldblatt at seven-thirty. Usually, I'm the first to arrive, but when I walked in, I spotted him already at a table near the back. I expected him to be working his way through the menu, figuring out what he was going to order, but the only thing in front of him was silverware and a glass of water. And, surprise, he was reading a book.

"How long you been here?" I asked, as I pulled up a chair and sat across from him.

"Just a few."

"You turning over a new leaf?"

"What do you mean?"

"You don't already have a plate of food in front of you."

"Very funny."

"We're a little touchy today, aren't we?"

"Sometimes I get the feeling you don't take me seriously, Swann."

"I don't know where you could possibly get that idea. What's that you're reading?"

He closed the book and held it up, so I could see the cover. *Mind Over Matter...And Yes, It Does Matter.*

"What is this?" I asked, as I took it from him.

"It's a book about mind control."

"You're kidding?"

He shook his head. "Serious as a heart attack, my friend."

"You mean like you think you can move this fork just by thinking about it, as opposed to the usual way you deliver food to your mouth?"

"Very funny. It's a lot more than that, and you should be glad I'm reading this book."

"Really? Why's that?"

"Because it's another potentially powerful weapon in our arsenal."

"I didn't realize we had weapons, much less an arsenal."

"You know what I mean."

I kind of did and I kind of didn't, but I wasn't in the mood to let this silly discussion go any further, so I simply nodded.

The waitress arrived and handed us menus.

Goldblatt held up his hand. "Thanks, but I don't need one. I already know what I'm having. The chef salad. What kind of dressing comes with it?"

"Whatever you want."

"What've you got?"

She looked pissed at having to go through the choices, but she did it anyway.

"Russian, ranch, french, thousand islands, honey mustard..."

"What about vinaigrette?"

"Yeah, we got that, too."

"Perfect. But on the side, please. And iced tea. Unsweetened, please. Oh, and would you happen to know if the lettuce is organic?"

She looked at him as if he were speaking another language.

"I honestly don't know. If it's a deal breaker, I can ask the chef."

"No, that's all right. Just make sure it's not Romaine." He turned to me. "There's that botulism scare." He looked back to the waitress. "The salad is gluten-free, right?"

"You mean like are there croutons in it?"

"Yes."

"I'll have the chef take them out."

"Well, I hope it doesn't taint the salad…"

I was, to say the least, in shock. I don't think I'd ever seen anything green in front of Goldblatt, unless it was money. And what about all these new dietary restrictions? Organic. Gluten-free. And since when did diners have chefs? What kind of bizarro world had I stumbled into?

She looked to me. It took me a moment to compose myself before I answered. I was still in shock, so I didn't bother consulting the menu. "Cheeseburger, medium rare, onion on the side."

"Fries or a salad?"

I thought about it a moment then, in defiance to the new and improved Goldblatt, I said, "Fries. Definitely fries."

After she'd walked away Goldblatt said, "Those things are going to kill you."

"What things?"

"Fries. Do you have any idea how much unsaturated fat there is in those things?"

"No. And frankly, I don't know the difference between satu-rated and unsaturated fats. I don't think you do either. What's with all this? Are you on some kind of diet?"

"It's not a diet. It's a lifestyle."

"By any chance, have you been hanging out on that Gwenyth Paltrow Goop site?"

"I have no idea what you're talking about."

"The crazy actress who has that..." What was I thinking? Why was I engaging with him? Goldblatt never made much sense, so why should he now?

"Okay. Okay. Forget it. You want to know what's up with Madame Sofia, right?"

"Absolutely."

"I've made contact with her."

"You mean you've met her? That's great. Tell me everything."

"Not much to tell. I did some legwork in her neighborhood and then, after I nailed her schedule, I made sure I bumped into her when she was walking her pooch."

"Then what?"

"I'm having dinner with her tomorrow night."

"You're kidding?" He reached across the table and patted my shoulder. "You're amazing, Swann. I mean, I always knew you were good but you're even better than that. So, what's the plan?"

"I don't have a plan."

"What do you mean, you don't have a plan? Everyone's gotta have a plan."

"That's not the way I work. I like to wing it. You know, let things happen..." I hesitated and added, with a smile, "organically. Kind of like your new lifestyle."

"Very funny. You think maybe I should tag along? You know, in case you need help."

"No, thanks. I think I can handle it."

During the meal, while Goldblatt devoured his salad, along with three rolls—so much for his new lifestyle—I filled him in on what happened in Alabama. Of course, when I'd finished, he pressed me on the subject of payment.

"I'll pick it up tomorrow, when I take Jana down there."

"That'll include expenses, right?"

I nodded.

"Good. Because you know, Swann, I hate to break it to you,

but you're not a very good businessman."

"Really?"

"Yeah. Really. I mean, I know in the past you say you did anything for money, but look at that office you had. I mean, that wasn't exactly the office of a successful entrepreneur."

"Is that what I was?"

"Sure."

"And that's what we are now?"

"Absolutely. And now that we've got a little working capital, I'm going to make sure I present a more professional face to the public."

"I shudder to think what that means."

"Just leave it to me. You got the nose, I got the brain."

I might have punched him in his professional nose, only I didn't want to make a scene. Besides, if he really did know that Israeli self-defense crap, I might be the one to wind up with a bloody shnozz.

I knew the brand-new Goldblatt was too good to be true. As the waitress was clearing the dishes, she asked if we'd like dessert, and I was surprised to hear Goldblatt say, "We'll take a look at the menu, thanks."

He wound up ordering a slice of chocolate cake with a scoop of vanilla ice cream. If he asked whether it was organic or gluten-free, I didn't hear him.

14
IS SHE OR ISN'T SHE?

The next morning, I picked up Jana a little past nine a.m., giving us plenty of time to get to Rudder's by ten. Wearing a tailored black suit, black stockings, and black heels, she looked both business-like and sexy in that power-fuck-me kind of way. This was in stark contrast to the last time I saw her when she was waif-like, wearing faded jeans and a hoodie. This outfit made her look older, more substantial, and more confident than I knew she actually was.

"Nice," I said, as we rode down in the elevator.

"What?"

"The outfit. It's very…"

"Conservative?"

"I guess that might be one of the words I was looking for."

"Full disclosure. It's not mine. Mary lent it to me. Even the shoes. We're the same size. Not exactly my style, but I suppose it fits the occasion."

"Looks good on you."

"You think?"

"I do."

As soon as we arrived at Rudder's office, Norma announced us then ushered us into Paul's office with a wave of her hand.

He greeted us with a big smile on his face. "You're the best, pal. I knew you could do it," he said, patting me on the shoulder.

He turned to Jana with an extended hand. "And thanks for coming in, Miss Monroe. I'm sure this isn't easy for you."

"No. It isn't."

"Let's sit down and get started. Norma's got your check, Henry. And again, thanks, pal."

I started to turn away but Jana grabbed my arm, just below the elbow. There was a look of panic on her face.

"You're not leaving me, are you?"

"There's no reason to stay, Jana. It's between you and Paul now."

"I'd really rather you stayed, Henry."

I looked at Paul to see if he cared. He shrugged, which I interpreted as, "whatever you want."

"You know, there's this lawyer-client thing," I said.

"I'm not a client. Am I, Mr. Rudder?"

Paul shrugged. "She's right, Henry. She's a witness, not a client. There's nothing to preclude you from staying, if you want to."

I didn't. But one look at Jana's face and I knew I didn't have a choice. I'd bonded with her as her protector, and was stuck with her, whether I liked it or not.

"Okay," I said. "Let's get started."

Paul sat at his desk and Jana in a chair facing him. I grabbed a place on the couch, hoping I'd fade into the furniture while they talked.

"So, Miss Monroe..."

"Jana."

He smiled. "Fair enough. And you can call me Paul. You know why you're here, of course. I understand you were Nicky Diamond's girlfriend and that you might be able to provide some information on where Nicky was at the time of the murder he's accused of committing."

"I don't even know when it happened."

I found this hard to believe, even though that's what she'd been insisting all along. But I kept my mouth shut. I was sure

Rudder had plenty of experience handling reluctant witnesses.

"It happened on Tuesday, February thirteenth, the night before Valentine's Day. Do you happen to recall where you were and if Nicky was with you?"

"I think we had a date that night."

"You have to be sure, Jana. I can't use you as a witness if you're not one hundred percent certain you were with him."

She hesitated a moment. I wished I could see her face, because then I could read it. But I could only see the back of her head and part of her cheek, if she angled her head in my direction. I have developed a knack that tells me when people are lying. They usually take a fraction of a second before answering, as though testing the lie in the mind before delivering it. Their body tenses. Their face flushes. They cross and uncross their legs. They fold their arms in front of them. They never look you straight in the eye. I didn't know what Jana's tell was, but I was sure she had one. Everyone does. But the question was, if she was lying, what would the lie be? That she was with him or that she wasn't?

"It's hard to remember...it was months ago."

"Take your time, Jana. I need you to be sure. I can't put you on the stand if I think you're lying. But how about for the moment we take it in another direction? Why did you leave town without telling anyone where you were going?"

She hesitated a moment. "I was scared."

"Don't worry. That's nothing to be ashamed of. Afraid of what? Or who?"

She shrugged. "Someone called and told me if I didn't leave, something bad could happen to me."

"Do you remember the exact words?"

"Yes. He said, 'accidents happen all the time in this city.' Wouldn't you be frightened if you got a call like that?"

"I would. Do you have any idea who made it?"

"I didn't recognize the voice, if that's what you mean."

"Was it because you could give Nicky an alibi?"

"How should I know?"

There was a hint of irritation in Jana's voice. She didn't want to be here, that's for sure. She didn't want to be answering questions. But I just couldn't figure out why. I mean, she could have bailed out any time between Fairhope and here—no one was holding a gun to her head. So, why didn't she? Why was she making things so difficult?

"Look, Jana, I don't want to get you in trouble. I certainly don't want you to be harmed. But I need to know the truth. Were you or weren't you with Nicky the evening of February thirteenth?"

"No," she said, in almost a whisper.

Rudder was pissed. I could see it on his face. He looked over at me. I shrugged. I didn't know any more than he did. And I certainly didn't know what to say. She was his problem now, not mine.

"And you're telling me the truth?"

"You think I'm lying because I'm telling you something you don't want to hear?"

"I didn't say that. I have no idea why you'd lie, if you are lying. But I don't know why Nicky would lie, either. I believe he thinks you can provide him with an alibi. I don't know why he'd think that unless he was sure you'd back him up or because he knows it's true. But obviously, one of you isn't telling the truth."

She started to say something, but nothing came out of her mouth. Instead, she turned her head toward me. I don't know why. I don't know what she wanted from me. Did she want me to tell her what to say? Did she want me to ride in on a white horse and whisk her away to safety?

Paul wasn't about to give up, which is probably what makes him such a good lawyer.

"I've gone to a big expense to find you, Jana."

"I didn't ask you to."

"I know. I'm doing my job. For the life of me, I just can't figure out why Nicky would say you were with him when you weren't."

"Why don't you ask him?"

"You're right. I should. Listen, why don't you think about it for a while and if you change your mind, please get back to me." He opened his desk drawer, pulled out a business card and handed it to her. She took it from him and, without looking at it, dropped in her purse. "And if all this is because you're frightened, I understand, but we can provide protection for you."

"Is that all?" she asked.

"For now. I really hope you think about this, Jana. A man's life is at stake. You wouldn't want that on your conscience, if you could help him, would you?"

She didn't answer. Instead, she got up, started to walk toward the door, but stopped in front of me.

"Would you mind taking me home, Henry?"

"Sure," I said.

"Henry, before you leave, can I have a few words with you, please?"

"Sure thing. Jana, why don't you just wait out there. I won't be long."

As soon as she left, Rudder pulled a chair up in front of the couch.

"What's going on, Henry?"

"I have no idea."

"Did she talk about this on the way back here?"

"Not a word. And it wasn't my job to question her about it. All I had to do was find her and try to convince her to come back."

"Nothing?"

"I tried, but I didn't get much of an answer. Yours was a lot more emphatic."

Rudder shook his head. "What do you think is going on here?"

"There are two explanations. One, she really wasn't with him. Two, she was but for some reason, maybe because she's scared, she doesn't want to get involved."

"But if it's the first, why would Diamond say she could alibi him?"

"Maybe because he never thought you'd find her."

"How does that make sense?"

"Let's say he comes up with this idea where he names someone he says can vouch for where he was when the killing was going down. But then, he makes sure no one can find that person by having her threatened. If that works, his lawyer, in this case you, can somehow make that known in court using it as reasonable doubt."

"Possible, but far from a sure thing. Especially with Nicky's background, which they're sure to get out there if they can."

"It's your job to make sure they don't, right?"

"It is. But I wouldn't want the case to hinge on that. We've got a tough, law-and-order judge."

"There's another possibility. Let's say she wasn't threatened by him, that she really can vouch for him. What if there's someone else who wants Diamond to take the fall? By getting rid of his only witness, and planting other evidence, that could make sense, couldn't it?"

"Also possible, but again that's an awful lot of supposition."

"And there's one more possibility."

"What's that?"

"What if Jana can alibi him but she doesn't want to? What if she wants him to get nailed for this murder?"

"Why would she want that?"

"You're asking me to see into a woman's mind, Paul, and that's something none of us can do. But revenge is possible."

"Revenge for what?"

"Cheating on her?"

"That's a pretty hefty price. You've spent time with her. You think she's capable of that?"

I thought for a moment. "No. I don't. But that doesn't mean she isn't. Or maybe it's something else. Some connection she has to Nicky that we don't know about."

"Jesus, Henry, that's an awful lot of shit you've just thrown on the table. What does your gut tell you?"

"My gut tells me that whatever the answer is, Jana's just a pawn. She's either working for Nicky or against him. But whatever the truth is, I still have this feeling she really is in danger. You know me. Normally, I'd just cash the check and let it be someone else's problem. But in this case, I feel kinda responsible. So, tell you what, I'll keep an eye on her. And if, while I'm doing that, I find out something helpful, you'll be the first to know."

"How much is this going to cost me?"

"I know I'll regret saying this, but just pay me what you owe me and this one's on the house."

"This is not the 'I'll do anything for money' Henry Swann I know and could possibly under the right circumstances come to admire if not love."

"Yeah, well, I like to be unpredictable. Besides, it's good business practice. You'll feel like you owe me and you'd better believe one day I'll collect. And who knows, maybe when it's all over, you'll get to feeling guilty and slip me a few extra bucks."

15
SYMPATHY FOR THE DEVIL?

"What now?" I asked, as we stood outside Rudder's building.

In the hour we'd been up there, the weather had turned from sunny to gray. The air felt heavy, as if rain wasn't too far in our future.

"I don't know," Jana said, fiddling with a button on Mary's jacket.

"You want to go back to your apartment?"

"Not really."

"Yeah. Probably not such a good idea. Back to Fairhope?"

She moved her head from side to side. "I don't think so. There's nothing for me there. Unless I want to become a shrimper." She smiled. At least she hadn't lost her sense of humor.

"I can probably get you a few more days with the Klavans, if that's what you want."

"I'm confused. I don't know what I want."

"Look, Jana, if you want me to help you, I'm going to have to know the truth."

"What do you mean?"

"I mean, what's the deal with you and Nicky? Are you in this with him or not?"

"In it?"

"You know what I mean. Did you two cook up this whole scheme?"

"What scheme?"

"What is this, an Abbott and Costello routine? Look, either you were with Nicky the time of the murder or you weren't. Either he's asked you to lie for him, or he didn't. I don't even know for sure if you've really been threatened."

"You think I'd make up something like that? Why?"

"I don't know you well enough to know what to think. If I'm going to take things at face value, I'd believe what you just told Paul, that you weren't with Nicky. Which means he's lying about it. If he is, he either thinks you'd back him up or he's going to make sure you're out of the picture. Either way, it doesn't look too good for you."

She wrapped her arms around herself, as if that would protect her. "I'm not the terrible person you make me out to be."

"I didn't say anything about what you are, Jana. I don't know what you are..."

She got very quiet.

"I've got things to do, Jana, so decide where you're going and I'll get you there."

"How about staying with you?"

"I don't think that's a good idea," I said, though in truth for a second or two I actually considered it. Fortunately, my better judgment kicked in almost immediately. "I live like a college student in a small apartment," I lied. Though the first part was undeniably true.

"Do you think I could stay another night or two with Ross and Mary?"

"I don't see why not. You don't look like the type who'll get in the way."

She smiled. "I'll try to be on my best behavior."

"Then I'll make it happen."

When we got back to Klavans', Ross was in his study, going over an auction catalogue. I made a little small talk, just to loosen him up, before I dropped the bomb about Jana.

"What's with you and her?"

"Nothing."

He tapped the side of his nose. "I smell something."

"When you figure out what it is, let me know. How about it? You'd be doing me a favor. I want to keep an eye out for her till I figure this thing out. If I can't stash her here, I'm afraid she'll take off."

"Mary likes the girl. It's the younger sister she never had, home from college. But between you and me, Swann, what's her story?"

"You mean what happened at the lawyer's?"

"Yeah."

"She claims she wasn't with him the time of the murder, but I'm not so sure she's telling the truth. Or at least all of it. That's another reason why I'm for her staying here a couple nights more. With time to think, maybe she'll change her mind and we'll find out what the real story is."

"Unless she's telling the truth now."

"Yeah. Like everyone always tells the truth…"

I left Jana with Ross and Mary, but I promised I'd keep in touch. When she asked when she'd see me again I told her I had another case I was working on and wasn't sure how much time I'd have to devote to that one. She pouted, and then extracted a promise from me that I'd see her the next evening, after my dinner "appointment." Maybe by that time I'd figure out how to get her to come clean.

I'm not sure why I bothered. After all, it was none of my business. Ever since the Harry Janus case almost ten years ago (my God, time passes quick), I've made it a practice to do only what's expected of me. No more, no less.

But this was different. I'm a curious sort and something was nagging at me. Whether Jana was telling the truth or not should have made no difference. Especially since her latest "truth" was likely to result in Nicky Diamond getting what he deserved. But

it did matter. Why? Because I hate loose ends. They scream im-
perfection. I want things to be perfect, to make sense, even
though I know that's pretty much impossible. But when I see
threads, I can't help but pull on them, just to see what's left, if
anything, when it unravels.

This meant an unauthorized trip out to Riker's to do something very distasteful—talk to Nicky Diamond again. I didn't
want Rudder to know what I was doing. He probably would
have hit the ceiling, and he would have had every right. After
all, my job was over and I had no business talking to his client,
meddling in his affair. But what Rudder didn't know wouldn't
hurt me. So, with time on my hands until my dinner that night
with Susan Finch, I headed out to New York City's version of
Devil's Island, hoping no one had bothered to remove my name
from the Riker's "guest list."

I had no trouble getting in, but I still had to cool my heels for
almost an hour amidst a growing group of women and children
visitors, before I was allowed in. Finally, and by now it was
mid-afternoon, I was escorted to the same room where we'd met
last time. A few minutes later, Diamond, his hands cuffed behind his back, was brought in. He sat down across from me, a
heavy wooden table separating us.

"You gonna be all right here?" asked the guard, as he undid
Nicky's cuffs.

"Yeah. I'll be fine."

"You got fifteen minutes. No more. I'll be right outside the
door, if you need me."

I appreciated the offer but it was kind of meaningless, since if
Diamond was going to do something to me, he'd be able to do
plenty of damage before the guard made it back into the room.

Nicky stared at me, those freaky, unnerving black eyes fixed
on me, for what seemed like an eternity, but this was a power
play I needed to win. Finally, he was the one who blinked.
"Never thought I'd see you again," he said, with a wicked little
smile curling across his lips.

"Ditto, Nicky."

Nicky stared back at the guard, who was still standing by the door. He appeared to be intimidated by Nicky, even though he was the one holding all the cards. Why he should be afraid of Diamond puzzled me. But then I realized everyone was probably intimidated by Diamond, or if they weren't, they should be. It was all part of his thing. It's what made him so good at what he did.

It had been less than a week since I'd last seen him, but it appeared as if he'd bulked up a little. Not much else to do in stir than use the weight room, and it was obvious Nicky was taking full advantage of it. He also had several more days' worth of facial hair growth.

"Growing a beard, Nicky?" I said, hoping to mock his attempt at a macho image.

"You writin' a book? Cause that's the only reason I can figure for asking questions about my personal hygiene choices. You find her or not?"

"Did you want me to find her?"

"What're you, some kind of comedian? That's why you were hired, man. To find the bitch."

"I'm not so sure you wanted her found."

"This some kind of fuckin' game to you, Swann? You think I checked into this dump because of the food and four-star accommodations? You fucking better believe I wanted you to find her. And you did, right? That's why you're here."

"I didn't say that."

"Stop jerking my chain, man. I don't have much of a fucking sense of humor and in case you haven't noticed, I'm not a fucking patient guy."

"So, I guess I don't want to get on your bad side."

"Prob'ly not a good idea. I'd tell you to ask someone who did only I don't think you'd find anyone."

"Why do you think she took off in the first place, Nicky? She's your girlfriend, right? You'd think she'd want to help you out. Unless, of course, you were pressuring her to lie and she didn't want to, so she took off."

"Fuck you, man."

I smiled, which was meant to piss him off even more. When people lose control, they're more likely to say something they don't want to say, which is often the truth. I didn't know if Nicky was capable of telling truth and I didn't know if rattling his cage was going to do any good, but what the hell, it was fun. I was guessing it wouldn't take much to get Nicky to lose control.

I tapped on the face of my watch.

"We've got about twelve more minutes, Nicky. What say you get hold of yourself and we make them count?"

"How the fuck would I know why she took off? If you find her, ask her."

"I did find her."

There was a surprised look on his face.

"Yeah? Where?"

I wanted to give Diamond as little information as possible. I didn't trust him—why should I? I wanted to protect Jana. Until I sorted this thing out, I thought it was a bad idea to let Nicky know where he might find her. He was inside, but I was sure there were people on the outside who would do his bidding. Besides, she might wind up going back down to Alabama and the less he knew about her whereabouts, the better.

"Not important."

"How the fuck do you know what's important, man?"

"I make the rules in this game, Nicky, and considering the position you're in, there's not much you can do about it."

"Is she back here now?"

"I'm not going to answer that."

"Why the fuck not?"

"Look in the mirror, asshole, and I'm sure you'll figure it out."

"Funny man."

"So, what do you think she said?"

"What do you mean?"

"I mean, did she say she was with you at the time of the murder, or not?"

"If she was telling the truth, she'd say we were together."

"Why would she lie?"

"She said we weren't?"

"I didn't say that." I tapped my watch again. "Time's a tickin', Nicky. It might be in your best interest to just answer my questions minus the attitude. I don't know why, but I'm trying to help you and to do that I need to figure out a few things."

"Like what?"

"Like who threatened Jana and why."

"What the fuck? You think it was me?"

I shrugged.

"Why the hell would I threaten her, man? She's my get out of jail card."

"Only if she corroborates your story."

"Why the hell would I pay someone to find this chick if I didn't think she would?"

"The world doesn't always make sense, Nicky. Maybe you're trying to pull a fast one. But for argument's sake, let's say you're not. Let's say you really were with her. But now she won't back your story. Why might that be?"

"Is that the way it is?"

"Just play along, Nicky."

"Beats me."

"The way I see it, there's only one reason. She or someone else wants you right where you are. And if it's someone else, who might that someone be?"

"You got all the questions, man, why don't you go out and find the answers?"

"I have no skin in this game, Nicky. But it got me thinking. They've got evidence against you. If you didn't do it, how's that possible?"

His face went blank.

"I'll give you something to chew on. Someone out there has it in for you and you've been set up. Trouble is, the list is probably a mile long."

"What say I hire you to fuckin' find out?"

"I'm not a private investigator, Nicky. I find people, I don't investigate cases."

"Yeah, well, I'm asking you to find someone. I want you to find out either who the fuck is setting me up or who put Jana up to lying her ass off."

"*If* she's lying, you mean."

"She's lying, pal. Believe me, she's lying. I got plenty of dough. I'll pay you whatever you want."

"This presents a bit of a moral conundrum for me, Nicky."

"Conundrum? What the hell's that?"

"A problem that's difficult or confusing."

"So, what the fuck's your conundrum?" he sneered.

"You're murderous scum and you should be locked up for life. I find the answers to those questions and you might go free."

His expression hardened. I knew if his hands weren't cuffed he'd probably try to beat me to death with his chair. And even though I probably outweighed him by close to fifty pounds, he'd probably be able to do it. Especially now that the city was providing him free gym time.

"I'm telling you something you don't already know, Nicky?"

"You gonna help me or not?"

"I'd rather not think of it as helping you. Let's call it getting to the truth. I like the truth, Nicky. It sets us free. There's something here that stinks. And as much as I'll probably hate myself in the morning, I'm going to try to get to the bottom of it."

"How much this going to cost me?"

He had me there. I have never, ever worked for free. Even back when things were so bad I was driven to accepting food stamps in payment, and took so many IOUs I could have papered one wall with them, I never worked for nothing. But to take his money, well, then I'd be morally compromised. I could take the high road and say I'd work for free, that I wouldn't take his dirty money. On the other hand, why should he get a free ride? In the end, it wasn't about if I took his money but rather how much. Look, I told myself, I'll give part of it to charity. Or maybe slip Jana a few bucks—I was sure she could use it. In other words, I'd launder his dough just to ease my conscience.

"Ten grand."

"Are you fucking kidding me, man?"

"Do I look like I'm joking, Nicky? I'm sure that's a lot less than you get for a job. What's your freedom worth to you?"

"Fuck you, man."

I got up.

"Where the fuck you going?"

"No reason to stick around, Nicky. We're done."

"Okay, okay. Ten grand."

"Up front."

"Are you fucking kidding me? How do I know you won't just take the fucking dough and skip, just like the bitch?"

I sat back down. "I guess you don't. Are you feeling lucky?"

He thought for a moment. "Okay. You got a deal."

"I want it all up front and I won't lift a finger until I get the dough. All of it."

He raised his arms in front of him, palms up, in one of those Hallelujah poses. "I'm in here, man, in the fuckin' can. How do you think I'm gonna get you the money? You think I got a checkbook and can just write a check for it? Or maybe you think I've got it in cash hidden behind my toilet?"

"Frankly, I don't give a damn how you get it done, just get it done. You've got friends on the outside. Have them take care of it. And no checks. Cash only."

He made a sour face. "Okay, but half. That's all you're getting up front. You come up with answers, I'll make sure you get the second half before you give them to me."

"Don't say I'm not capable of compromise, Nicky."

"Yeah, well, fuck compromise. You ain't doing me any favors.

It's a take it or leave it deal."

I took a pad out of my pocket, jotted down my phone number, tore it off, and slid it across the table. "Just have someone call me when they've got the dough. We'll set up a meet, and then I'll start the clock."

The door opened and the guard stuck his head in.

"Time's up."

"That's okay, officer, we're just about finished, aren't we, Nicky?"

He stared bullets at me.

"One last thing," I tore out another sheet and shoved it in his direction. "I want you to write down two or three names, along with how to get in touch with them. These are people who know you real well. People who can provide me with information about you and who you work for…"

"You think I'm giving up shit like that?"

"Suit yourself. But the harder you make it for me, the less likely I'm going to figure things out. Remember, Nicky, my time is your time."

16
DID YOU EVER SEE A DREAM WALKING?

I dressed to impress, as if I were going out on a first date. That meant jacket, tie, and newly laundered pair of jeans. I even debated wearing real shoes, but the lure of the comfort of my Chucks was too strong. I did, however, settle on my black, formal-wear pair, the pair I would wear with a tux, if I had one.

Finch had chosen Pomodoro, a Southwestern joint off Columbus and Seventy-first and I was to meet her there at seven-thirty.

It was quarter past seven when I arrived at the restaurant. I chose a table at the very back of the dining room, a separate room past the bustling bar area, which also held a number of tables already filled with customers. The dining room was about half full, which kept the noise level low.

Finch was late, which didn't surprise me. I had an old girlfriend who made it a habit to arrive at least fifteen minutes late for everything. That way, she could not only make an entrance but also, she confided, it put her in what she considered the power position. *I'm important enough to wait for,* was the message and if you complained or, worse yet, bailed, all the better since it meant you weren't comfortable with her having the upper hand, which in turn meant she wasn't interested in the relationship. I didn't argue with her, even though I disagreed with her logic. It wouldn't have made a difference: she won every argument we ever had, which was why we didn't last very long as a couple.

At seven-forty-five, I spotted her, trailing the maître d', as they came through the dining room entrance. If I was dressed for a date, she'd one-upped me. She had on a sexy, elegant, low-cut, black dress, that stopped several inches above her knees. A bunch of silver bracelets dangled from her right wrist, and there were rings on every finger of her left hand, the one I could see. Her dark hair was pulled back and the light in the room reflected off a pair of heavy-looking, silver earrings that dangled down past her chin line. The message I got was, *I am someone to be reckoned with*.

"Sorry I'm late," she said, as the maître d' pulled out her chair. "I had a bit of an emergency."

"Really? What kind?"

She smiled. "The kind that made me fifteen minutes late."

She knew exactly how late she was and she wanted to make sure I knew it, too.

"I'll let it pass...this time," I said, removing my napkin from the table and spreading it out on my lap. The fewer trips I had to make to the laundromat down the block, the better.

"Think there'll be a second time?" I asked, not expecting an answer.

"We'll see, won't we?" she said, smiling.

The waiter arrived, handed us menus and asked if we'd like something to drink. Always the gentleman, I deferred to Finch.

"I'll have a glass of Chardonnay, please."

I opted for a Dos Equis, two slices of lime.

As soon as the waiter left, Finch leaned forward, close enough for me to be engulfed by the sweet, flowery aroma of her perfume, and whispered, "How do you feel about honesty, Mr. Swann."

"Mr.? I thought we'd progressed beyond that point."

"We'll see how far we've progressed. You didn't answer my question."

"I think it's highly overrated."

"Really?"

"I'm a realist. Besides, who knows what the truth is?"

"You're a philosopher."

"Yeah, sure, why not?"

"I think truth is very important because without it there can be no trust. You want me to trust you, don't you...Henry?"

"That's up to you."

Drinks arrived. Hers in a glass, mine in the bottle along with a glass. The waiter hovered, while she sampled hers. "Very nice," she said. He didn't wait for me to give a verdict on my beer.

"I'm not a big fan of games, Henry. So, why don't we cut to the chase. Who hired you to make contact with me and why?"

I wasn't surprised she'd nailed me. In fact, I would have been disappointed if she hadn't. And I didn't think it took supernatural powers. We're living in an age where there are very few secrets.

"What makes you think I'm working for anyone?"

"This is the age of Google, my dear. All I have to do is type in your name and, voila, I can find out so very much about you. That you are, for instance, an expert at finding people and even, along the way, solving a crime or two."

"That's not against the law, is it?"

"Of course not. But it does cast suspicion on your motives for asking me out to dinner, doesn't it?"

"Does it also say I'm a money-grubbing lowlife?"

"I thought I'd find that out myself."

Was it possible I could learn to like this woman?

"You're a good-looking woman. Maybe I bumped into you for that reason."

"As true as that is, I don't think so." She laughed. "But nice try."

She raised her glass and moved it toward me. "Shall we toast?"

"To what?"

"How about, to us?"

"There's an us?"

"For the moment."

I ignored the glass and picked up my bottle, with the two wedges of lime I'd stuffed past the lip. We clinked. She took a sip of her Chardonnay. I took a swig of my beer. She put hers down. I was thirsty, so I didn't.

"What do you want from me, Henry Swann?"

"What makes you think I want something?"

She smiled. "Oh, please, let's not make this any more difficult than it has to be. I'm sure you know what I do for a living, which means you're not going to be very successful keeping things from me, are you?"

"Because you're a fortune teller who can tell the past and see into the future?"

"I hate that term."

"Fortune teller?"

"That's the one."

"How would you describe yourself?"

"Semi-attractive, moderately intelligent, middle-aged woman in her prime with a special gift."

"I can't think of you that way."

"What way would that be?"

"I'd say you're more than semi-attractive and moderately intelligent. And as for the special gift part, let's just say I'm skeptical."

"For the first, I'm flattered. For the second, I'm insulted."

"Why's that?"

"Because I'd hoped you'd be more open-minded than you obviously are."

"Sorry to disappoint you. I'm about as close-minded as it gets."

"I don't think that's true."

"Suit yourself."

"I know a lot about you, Henry Swann."

"Google? Or that 'special gift'?"

"Maybe both. But since you don't have my special gift, you'll never know for sure."

The waiter checked back to take our order. Finch ordered a chipotle shrimp dish. I ordered the chicken fajitas. There's something in me that likes to build stuff...and then destroy it.

"What with that special gift of yours, I'm surprised you don't know why I made contact with you."

"I take it you're not a believer in the paranormal?"

"'There are more things in heaven and earth, Horatio, Than are dreamt of in your philosophy.'"

"You're full of surprises, aren't you?"

"You mean you're surprised I can read?"

"No, surprised that you do, not to mention what you read. I mean, now many men can recite Shakespeare, and put it in the proper context?"

"We're a dying breed."

"So, you're telling me you're open-minded?"

"On the open-minded scale of ten, maybe a soft seven. On the scale of skeptical, a hard ten."

"That's an odd mix. But okay, I can probably make a pretty good guess why you made contact with me."

"I love guessing games."

"Someone's lodged a complaint against me and you've been hired to track me down and make things right."

"Go on."

"Is there more?"

"Aren't you going to tell me who made the complaint? Or are there just too many possibilities?"

She smiled. "Would you mind if we continued this scintillating conversation when I returned from the little girl's room?"

"Be my guest."

While she was gone, I checked my phone for messages. Nothing. I looked back toward the entrance to the dining room, to see if she was on the way back, when tucked away at a corner table, about thirty or forty feet from me, I spotted something that didn't look quite right. Seated back to the wall, was a man wearing a bulky beige sweater and a black beret. He had a beard and as soon as he noticed me looking at him, he picked up his menu and positioned it in front of his face.

Too late. I'd recognize that body anywhere. Goldblatt. What the hell was he doing here? And more important, how did he know I'd be here? I hadn't mentioned it to him. I was sure of that. Had he followed me? Had he planted some kind of GPS device on me? And that ridiculous attempt at disguising himself. What was that all about? I was about to get up and tell him to get the hell out of here, when Finch, coming out of the bathroom, passed his table. I had to do something to stop him before he messed up anything. I considered texting him, but Finch was back before I could do it.

"So, where were we?" she asked, sliding back into her chair.

I was so preoccupied with Goldblatt's presence I had no idea what we were talking about.

"Are you okay?"

"Yeah. I'm fine."

"You don't seem like it. Is something wrong."

"Shouldn't that special gift of yours have the answer?"

"I'm off duty."

"Nothing's wrong." But, of course, there was. I could only hope Goldblatt had sense enough to stay where he was and not come over and muck up everything.

"Oh, yes, I remember. You were going to tell me who you're working for," she said, as I tried desperately to focus.

"You know I can't tell you that."

"Well then, I suspect it's going to be a long evening, because I can't imagine what else we'd talk about."

I was a professional. I couldn't let this throw me.

"You know something, you're right. We're here, so I might as well put my cards on the table."

She smiled and folded her hands in front of her on the table.

"I'm here on behalf of Rachel."

"I know several Rachels. Which one are you referring to?"

"The Rachel who paid you a shitload of dough to reach her dead boyfriend."

"Oh, that Rachel."

"Yeah. That one."

"I haven't heard from her in a while. How is she?"

"She could be better. Especially, if she had her dough back."

"Let me explain this the best way I can, Henry. I provide a service, a very valuable service as far as some people are concerned. Naturally, I get paid for providing that service, the same way, I assume, you get paid for yours. If Rachel was unhappy with my service, she wouldn't have kept coming back."

"You mean your service of getting in touch with her dead boyfriend, who's now safely ensconced in the spirit world? Or, as you like to refer to it, 'another room.'"

"We've moved onto the skeptical scale now, haven't we?"

"We have."

"Let me make this as clear as I possibly can, so even someone like you, someone who doesn't believe in the spirits, or an afterlife, or other dimensions—and believe me, you're not alone. I have a special gift. I didn't ask for it. Sometimes, I'm even sorry I have it—and this might be one of those times. But I do. And I feel obliged to share it whenever possible."

"You mean, sell it, don't you?"

"Are you working for nothing? Now, for instance?"

"I'm not selling air. I have to show results or I wouldn't be able to keep doing what I do."

"You measure results one way, I measure them another. When I give peace of mind to someone, those are results, aren't they? If I make someone feel better about themselves, those are results, aren't they?"

"You make a pretty good argument, Susan, or do you prefer to be called Madame Sofia? Which brings up an interesting point. If you're on the level, why use some silly name like that? Why not just use your own name? Unless, of course, you're trying to hide something."

"Yes. In a way, I suppose I am. If I used my actual name, I wouldn't be able to have a life separate from Madame Sofia. Everyone I met would be colored by what they knew about me. I wouldn't have friends. I wouldn't be able to meet new people without them making assumptions about me. Just like you are. And I've also found that my clients actually like the anonymity the name gives me. They'd prefer to see Madame Sofia rather than Susan."

"You're good, Susan. Very good. But I still think it's a load of crap you're selling. You strung Rachel along for thousands and thousands of dollars, feeding her a line about this guy. In my book, that doesn't put you up there with Mother Teresa. If you were sincere, you wouldn't take money from people. You'd find another way to make a living, and use your so-called 'gift' for good."

"This isn't getting us anywhere, and it's becoming very uncomfortable for me, debating something that's undebatable. So, if you don't mind, I think we should call an end to this."

"Suit yourself. But let me leave you with this, Susan. If I can prove you're a fraud, and I think I can, then unless you give back every cent you took from Rachel, I'm going to go to the DA. And when I do, it's going to be because I have evidence that you're nothing more than a crook."

She got up. "Give it your best shot, Henry. But I don't believe that's going to happen."

She opened her purse and reached for her wallet. But I wasn't going to let her have the last word.

"No, Susan. This one's on me. Next time, though, you'll be the one picking up the check."

17

I'M THINKING OF A NUMBER
BETWEEN ONE AND...OH, FORGET ABOUT IT

"What the hell are you doing here?"

"Having dinner. What does it look like I'm doing?"

I'd stopped at Goldblatt's table on my way out. I was so pissed off, I wasn't going to bother for fear I'd lose my temper. But I couldn't help myself.

"You're spying on me. That's what you're doing."

His face oozed into a big, fat grin. "Relax. Sit down. I was just thinking about dessert. I hear the banana pudding here is terrific."

"Are you fucking kidding me? You're checking up on me and I don't like it. We're supposed to be partners, aren't we? We're supposed to trust each other, right? I mean, that's what you're always preaching to me."

"Take it easy, Swannie. You're gonna have a heart attack. Although, if you do, I happen to be an expert on CPR."

He was right. Not the heart attack part, but the relax part. What was I getting so upset about? After all, he hadn't interfered. And he did have skin in this particular game.

I sat down. Not because I wanted any banana pudding, but because there was no sense damaging our already fragile relationship.

"What's with the ridiculous disguise?"

"You mean this?" he pointed to his fake facial hair.

"Yeah, that. And the thing you're wearing on top of your head."

"I wouldn't exactly call it a disguise. More of a distraction. I believe magicians call it misdirection."

"I don't know how that applies to this situation and I don't care."

"Suit yourself. Every so often I just like to take my alternative identities out for a spin. You know, use it or lose it."

"How many alternative identities do you have?"

"As many as necessary. So, how'd it go? Not swimmingly, I'm guessing, since good old Madame Sofia seemed to leave in a bit of a hurry."

"If you're asking me whether she threw up her hands, said, 'Got me!' and promised to give back the money, the answer's no."

"Well, we didn't expect that, did we?"

"No. We didn't."

"So, what's next? I mean, now that we've found her we're at least within shouting distance of the dough, right?"

I shrugged. The truth is, I wasn't quite sure what to do next. I was still trying to gauge just how pissed off I really was.

"We've got to somehow prove she committed fraud, but I'm not quite sure how we do that."

The waiter appeared. Goldblatt ordered the banana pudding. When he asked if I wanted something, I declined. I'd lost what little appetite I had left.

"Got any ideas?" he asked.

"Look, unless we believe this woman actually is able to talk to the dead, we have to find out how she got all that personal information about Rachel and the guy, whatever his name was."

Goldblatt's face lit up. "I knew I hitched my wagon to the right star. And that's what you are, Swann. A friggin' star."

The waiter delivered Goldblatt's banana pudding, with extra whipped cream.

"What about that lifestyle diet you're supposed to be on?"

"Oh, that. I decided on moderation."

"You call extra whipped cream moderation?"

"No one says I'm going to eat it all. So how are we going to proceed?"

"It's not going to be easy. For one thing, I'm going to have to talk to Rachel again."

"What for?"

"I need to find out exactly what Finch told her about her life and about the boyfriend's. And then maybe see if I can find out if Rachel tipped off anything. I want to take what Rachel told her and then work backwards."

"What's that mean?"

"I want to see if I can use that information to collect more. Once I get that, maybe I can trace it back to how Finch got the rest."

"That's genius, man. Absolute genius. I'll give Rachel a call and find out when she can meet us."

Usually, the word "us" when pertaining to me and Goldblatt would have sent me over the edge, but this time was different. Begrudgingly, I had to admit to myself that he might actually have some value. After all, he knew Rachel a lot better than I did and he could probably tell when she was holding back. If I saw he was getting in the way, I could always send him packing.

"Okay. But make it as soon as possible. I've got this other thing I'm working on."

"I thought you were finished with that."

"I thought so, too. But evidently, not."

"How's tomorrow morning, if she can make it?"

"That'll be fine.

Before turning in for the night, I gave Jana a call. She was unfinished business, but I couldn't do anything till I heard from those people Diamond was supposed to put me in touch with, the ones who might give me a lead on who had it in for him enough to threaten Jana...if she had been, in fact, threatened. I was also worried about getting the dough from Nicky. Frankly, I was skeptical he'd come through, and if he didn't, I was finished. Still, I wanted to know what possible gain Jana could get from having Nicky rot in jail, convicted of murder. Unless, of course, it was payback for something.

Jana was fine. She wanted to know when she could see me again. She claimed she had something important to tell me. She suggested we meet the next evening for dinner. I figured she was probably going a little stir crazy and just wanted to get out of the apartment. I felt bad for the kid. No matter what her story was, her life was in turmoil. She couldn't go back to her apartment. She couldn't go back to her job, assuming she even had one anymore. She couldn't go back to any part of the life she'd had BN, Before Nicky. She was floating aimlessly in space. Believe me, I've been there plenty of times and it was not a pleasant place to be.

The next morning, I awoke to find a couple phone messages. One from Goldblatt. He'd arranged for us to meet with Rachel at noon. "The only time she can get off from work is her lunch hour, so let's take her someplace nice. I'll make a reservation at Dos Caminos, on Fiftieth and Third. If the weather's good, we can dine al fresco."

Yes, he actually used the words "dine" and "al fresco."

The other message was from some guy named Sal, who sounded like his voice had been worked over by sandpaper. "Listen, I'm a friend of Nicky's. He says I should talk to you. And that I should give you somethin'. Tonight. Nine o'clock." He left the name and address of some dive bar in the East Village, not far from where I live. He ordered me to come alone. He didn't ask me to call him back. He didn't seem to care if I confirmed. He had the kind of voice that let you know it wasn't a suggestion.

When I arrived at Dos Caminos, a little before noon, I spotted Goldblatt and Rachel sitting across from each other at one of the outdoor tables that faced Fiftieth Street. It was early, so there was only a smattering of other diners, spread out among the two dozen or so tables. They were in the section furthest from the doors that opened into the restaurant. I assumed Goldblatt had requested as much privacy as possible.

They were deep in conversation, which stopped abruptly when they saw me approach.

"It's good to see you again, Henry," said Rachel, who was wearing tan slacks, and a powder blue sweater. Her hair shorter and a shade somewhere between brunette and blonde. Perhaps she'd been out in the sun. Perhaps she'd done something to it. Sometimes, when women are going through some kind of emotional upheaval, they seem to think changing their hair color or style will help. From my experience, it doesn't.

"Nice to see you, too, Rachel."

"I took the liberty of ordering for everyone, Swann. Everyone likes tacos, right? I got us a selection of chicken, fish, beef, and vegetarian for you, Rachel. And guacamole is on its way. They make the best damn guac in the city."

"Time saved is time earned," I said. I meant it sarcastically, but I don't think Goldblatt took it that way.

A moment later, the waiter arrived with a tray of margaritas and a stone bowl of guacamole. "I see you've taken care of everything," I said.

"Yup. And the drinks are on me."

"I was thinking the whole thing was on you, Goldblatt. This is a business expense, right?"

He ignored me. Why shouldn't he? He knew and I knew that in one way or another, I'd wind up paying for this.

As soon as the waiter disappeared back into the restaurant, Goldblatt took over.

"So, Henry found your Madame Sofia," he said, puffing out his ample chest, with his gut following close behind. Surprisingly, it did seem as if he'd lost a few pounds, but he had more than a few left to go.

"You did? Oh, that's so great, Henry."

"Not so fast, Rachel. Finding her is only the beginning. Getting your money back, well that's something else entirely."

"Oh…"

"But don't worry, honey, we're working on a plan," said Goldblatt, who was busily stirring his drink so the alcohol was distributed evenly.

"Oh, that's so wonderful," said Rachel. "I knew I could depend on you two."

"I want to tamp down expectations. The odds against getting your money back are pretty steep. First of all, it would be your word against hers. Second of all, even if she admitted taking money from you, she'll claim it was for services rendered. The cops would have to prove fraud, if they got involved at all. And frankly, it's not like they're in any rush to help out, especially if they think you were asking for it. A lawyer friend of mine explained to me that if there's no intent to defraud, then there is no fraud."

"You mean if she really believes she can talk to the dead, we're screwed," said Goldblatt who had finally stopped playing with his drink.

I nodded.

"What does that mean? Asking for it?" said Rachel.

"Yeah, what do you mean, Swann? She didn't ask to be swindled."

"Gullibility is not an explanation, unless the cops can prove there's a pattern, that there's a criminal conspiracy to defraud people like you."

"Well, of course she defrauded me."

"She told you she could communicate with the dead. How are you going to prove definitively she didn't?"

"Does that mean I'll never get my money back?"

"Not necessarily," I said.

"Yeah, not necessarily," echoed Goldblatt. "We've got ways…"

"If you mean threats of violence, Goldblatt, we're not going there. Not that it would do any good."

"So, what can we do?"

"If I can prove she doesn't have the power she says she has and she knows it, I can use that to 'suggest' she return the money or..."

"Or what?"

"Or, we take what we have to the authorities. I've met her. I don't see her as a woman who has spending time in the Graybar Hotel on her agenda."

"But how can you possibly prove something like that?"

"I need to find out all the information she told you about you and about your deceased boyfriend. And how much of it might have come from you."

"You think I gave her information and then she just fed it back to me?"

"No. But you could have given her information that she then parlayed into more stuff she told you about your life."

"I see."

"Then, I'll try to trace it back and see how she could possibly have attained it without talking to a dead man."

And so, for the next hour or so I probed into every possible corner of Rachel's and her ex-boyfriend Michael's lives, or at least as much as she was willing, or able, to tell me. I asked her to recall exactly the kinds of things Madam Sofia told her. The list was large, including some very intimate details of their relationship and his life.

Amazingly, Goldblatt, who was busy packing away his three tacos plus two of Rachel's, as well as two pretty powerful margaritas (they seemed to have absolutely no effect on Goldblatt) pretty much stayed out of the conversation.

By one-fifteen, Rachel was spent and anxious to get back to her job, so we let her go. After she left, Goldblatt and I stuck around while he polished off the meal with a Mexican banana split—"Hold the nuts, please"—his idea of moderation. So much for his new lifestyle.

"So, whaddya think?" he asked.

"I think if Finch really 'divined' half that stuff, she'd be pretty amazing."

"What do you mean, 'if'? You really think she's got some kind of special power?"

"No. There's something fishy."

"Like what?"

"I've done a lot of research in my life, but unless I actually interviewed Rachel and this guy Michael, or people very close to them, I don't know how I'd possibly pick up on a lot of the stuff she knew."

"So, you're saying you believe in this mumbo jumbo talking to the dead stuff?"

"Not for a second."

"It's a load of crap, right?"

"Look, I think anything's possible...but there are certain tricks of the trade that make them even more possible."

"Tricks?"

"I've been looking into this thing they call mentalism."

"You mean like that guy, what's his name? Kreskin, right?"

"Him, among others. I've picked up on some tricks they use to make people think they're reading minds."

"Where from?"

"I've got an old pal who specializes in that sort of stuff, and I've been doing some reading."

"So, if she's not on the level, she had to have a source for the information, right?"

"Right."

"And you're gonna find that source, right?"

"I'm gonna try."

"Where do we start?"

"I'm gonna try to track down the dead boyfriend's sister. She's the most likely source for his information."

"You know something, Swann?"

"No. What?"

"I think I made the right decision partnering up with you."

I didn't have to answer him, because I knew he was right.

18
BARKING UP THE RIGHT TREE

After leaving Goldblatt, I went to my office in Klavan's apartment to work the computer. I was looking to find out as much as I could about Rachel's dead boyfriend, Michael Stephenson, and his sister, Kate.

There wasn't much, but using a telephone number Rachel gave me, I tracked down where Kate Stephenson lived. It was an address on the lower edge of East Harlem, a neighborhood recently reclaimed by money-strapped millennials looking to stay in Manhattan. With real estate values skyrocketing all over the city, the plague of rising rents had spread to the far reaches of Brooklyn, a good part of Queens, and even sections of the South Bronx that previously would have been avoided like the plague.

It was a good half hour subway ride from the East Village, but I had plenty of time before my meeting with Sal to see if I could find Stephenson. I assumed she worked during the day, which meant I'd be more likely to find her home in the evening.

I grabbed a burger at the local diner, then hopped the six train at Astor Place and got off at Ninety-sixth Street and Lexington. When I emerged from underground, it was not quite six-thirty. I figured if I was back on the train by eight-thirty, I'd make it back to the East Village in plenty of time to meet Sal.

Kate Stephenson's apartment building was on Ninety-ninth,

a few steps east of Lexington Avenue. I walked the three blocks north. I considered calling first, but decided it was best if she didn't know I was coming. This way, if I did find her home, she wouldn't have time to think about what story she was going to tell me.

It was a recently renovated six-story, red-brick building, with the scaffolding still in place. It had one of those new-fangled virtual doormen where you punch a bunch of numbers of the apartment you're visiting and a camera projects your image to the tenant who can then decide whether to buzz you in or not.

Kate Stephenson wasn't listed. Had she moved since she'd made the calls to Rachel? Unlikely. In this city, once you've got an apartment you rarely move. It was possible she was using another name. There was a K. Stephan listed, which was close enough for me to give it a try.

I punched the code, five-one-three, which I presumed would also be the apartment number, and a female voice answered, "Yes?"

"Are you Kate Stephan?" I asked.

"I'm sorry, you must have the wrong apartment. There's no Kate here."

The tentative, high-pitched tone of her voice gave her away.

"I may have the wrong name, but I think you're right person. You wouldn't happen to have had a brother named Michael, would you?"

Silence.

Finally, after a few seconds the voice returned. "Who are you?"

"Henry Swann."

"That name doesn't mean anything to me."

"How about Rachel Goldblatt?"

Silence.

Finally, "Please, go away."

It dawned on me I might be using the wrong last name. Goldblatt's ex-wife's maiden name was Albert.

"You might know her as Rachel Albert."

Silence.

"I'm still here," I said. "And I'm not leaving till I talk to you, Kate."

"What do you want?"

"I need to ask you a few questions."

"About what?"

"About your brother."

"He's...dead."

"I know."

"Why do you want to know about him?"

"Why don't you let me up and I can explain."

Silence.

I buzzed again.

"You're not going away, are you?"

"Nope."

"I'll call the cops."

"Suit yourself. But it'll be a lot less trouble if you just talk to me."

Silence.

"Show me some identification. Hold it up to the camera."

I held my driver's license up to the camera. A few seconds passed and then there were several clicks in quick succession. I twisted the door handle and was in.

I took the elevator to the fifth floor. Down the hall I saw an apartment door was cracked open. I headed toward it.

"Stop right there. I'm not alone."

I stopped several feet in front of the door. I could see the chain was up and allowing the door to open only a few inches. Whoever was holding the door open had moved out of the sight line.

"I don't mean you any harm, Kate. Can I come in? It'll just be for a few minutes. I promise."

"I don't know."

"I can understand you being nervous, but I promise you're in no danger."

"How can I be sure? You'd say that even if I were."

"True. We could talk this way, with you behind the door and me standing out here in the hall, but I think it would be a lot more comfortable for both of us if you'd let me in. And if you're worried, why don't we just find a Starbucks nearby where we can talk?"

The door closed. I heard the sound of the chain being unlatched. The door opened.

"All right. Come in. But I'm warning you, I can scream very loud if I have to and my neighbors are very protective."

She seemed to have forgotten that she told me she wasn't alone.

"I don't think there's going to be any screaming, unless, it's me. Look..." I raised my arms and turned around. "I'm not armed, so there's really nothing to be afraid of."

She looked me over.

"You don't look dangerous."

"This is not the first time I've heard that, and I promise not to take it as an insult."

"If you're gonna come in, come in."

The front door opened onto a surprisingly large living room. It was sparsely furnished, with a salmon-colored couch, two black leather-and-chrome chairs, and a glass coffee table. There was a bookcase, but there were only a few books in it. Several paintings that looked like they came straight from Ikea, or some other modern furnishings store hung on the walls. To the left, there was a small alcove with a small table and two chairs and next to that a Pullman kitchen. To the right, there was a door which I assumed led to a bathroom and perhaps a bedroom.

Stephenson or Stephan or whatever her name was, was an attractive woman, who appeared to be in her late thirties to early forties. She had short brown hair and had on a pair of black-rimmed glasses that made her plainer looking than she probably was. She was wearing blue jeans and a pink Rolling Stones T-shirt.

"Have a seat."

I chose one of the leather chairs. She sat on the couch, grabbing a pillow and squeezing it in front of her chest, using it as a shield.

"I'd offer you something, but all I have is water."

"I'm fine."

"What is it you want from me?"

"I'm here on behalf of Rachel..."

"You already said that."

"You in a hurry to get somewhere?"

"Just to get on with my life."

"I'm here to find out what you know about Madame Sofia."

"Who?"

"The psychic you recommended to Rachel."

"Oh, her. It's been a while."

"But you know who I'm talking about?"

"Vaguely."

"You've met her, haven't you? I mean, you recommended her to Rachel."

"No. I've never met her."

She was lying. I could see it in her eyes, which she cast downward when she answered.

"If you haven't met her, why did you recommend her to Rachel?"

"I'd heard about her. From a friend."

"Rachel seems to have the impression you used her services."

"Well, Rachel is mistaken. Perhaps she misunderstood me."

"And yet you didn't hesitate to recommend her to Rachel."

"She helped a friend of mine. I thought she might be able to help Rachel. There's nothing wrong with that, is there?"

"You must have known more about her. From what I under-stand, Rachel was in a bad way and you did a nice thing, trying to help her. But you knew how fragile she was, and yet you sent her to a woman like Madame Sofia. The chances were pretty high she was going to get scammed."

"I don't know what you mean, 'a woman like Madame Sofia.' It's not unusual for someone to go to a psychic for help. Or guidance. Or whatever. Lots of people do it."

"I haven't. Have you?"

"I prefer tea leaves."

"It seems to me you were setting her up for disappointment. And maybe something worse."

"She's a grown woman. She can make decisions for herself."

"Were you aware how much money Rachel gave her?"

"No. Why should I? That was between Rachel and Madame Sofia. Let me explain something to you. I've never even met Rachel. We've only spoken on the phone a few times. She was just someone my brother was dating...before he...passed away. It's not like we had any kind of personal relationship."

"I understood different. I thought the relationship between your brother and Rachel was more serious than casual dating."

"To some people that is serious. I've dated lots of men longer than Rachel was seeing my brother, and believe me, I wouldn't call them serious relationships."

"But you've got someone in your life now, right?"

She looked puzzled.

"I don't know what you mean."

"The coat rack, over by the door. That's a man's sport jacket hanging there."

A look of panic crossed her face. And then, just as quick as it arrived, it was gone.

"I don't think that's any of your business but yes, I am seeing someone." She cast a glance toward the closed door, obviously wanting me to believe he or someone else was in there. "Are we done yet?"

"Not quite. Does your boyfriend live with you?"

She pulled the pillow tighter to her chest. "I don't have to answer your questions."

"You're right. I apologize. Just a couple more questions. I notice you don't have any photographs of your brother around. Were you guys close?"

"Yes. Very close. And I have plenty of photos of him. I just haven't put them out because...I don't want to be reminded..."

"Mind if I see a couple? I'm curious what he looked like."

Rachel had already shown me a photo of them together in San Francisco, but I was trying to stall. The longer I stuck around, the more likely I'd pick up something that might be important.

"Yes, actually, I do mind. It's still an open wound."

Most people would jump at the chance to share a photo or memory of someone they've lost. Not her.

"I'm surprised you haven't asked about Rachel. Like how she's doing. Or why I'm helping her."

She started to fidget. She couldn't seem to find a comfortable position. She was losing patience. Her story was starting to unravel. The more I pressed, the more likely I was to find out something she didn't want me to know.

"Look," she said, running her hand through her hair. "The truth is, I hardly knew her. I feel bad she got involved with my brother, you know, like right before the end. But think how I feel. I know him all my life and she just spent a couple of months with him. I'm still in mourning, you know?"

There was something about her answer that seemed off. I couldn't quite put my finger on it. Something about her behavior or demeanor was off.

"You must feel horrible. It was so sudden. Rachel never mentioned how he died."

She hesitated. Only for a split second, but long enough for me to know she wasn't telling the truth.

"It was an aneurysm. There was no warning. The doctor said he might have been dead before he hit the floor. I guess it was a blessing. I don't really like to talk about it. It's very painful."

"I get it. I lost my wife suddenly, too. One minute they're with you," I snapped my fingers, "next minute they're gone. No rhyme. No reason. You get angry..."

That was it. She didn't seem angry. Angry at the injustice and capriciousness of the death of a loved one, something I knew all about. It took me months to get over that feeling. And it's possible I'm still angry about it. Not only did I lose my wife and best friend, but I also lost my son to my in-laws, who were raising him almost fifteen hundred miles away.

"It's really tough, when they go like that," I said.

Her body relaxed. Her face softened. She put the pillow down beside her. She was beginning to see me not as an adversary but as someone who sympathized with her. She probably felt she was over the hump.

"He was so healthy. That's what made it so tragic," she said, leaning back in her chair.

Time to attack.

"Let me ask you one more thing, then I'll get out of your hair. You send a woman you hardly know to a psychic or fortune teller, whatever she is, and as a result, she loses a lot of money and you don't feel the least bit responsible?"

She tensed. The goodwill I'd built up was gone. I was back to being an adversary.

"Look, Mr. Swann. This is a tough city. Everyone's on the make. Everyone's out to get whatever they can. I can only be responsible for myself. Rachel's an adult. She knew what she was getting into. I can't help it if she was gullible enough to give this Madame Sofia person money. She should have known better. I'm sorry, okay? I thought maybe it would help her get through. I guess I was wrong. But I certainly don't feel responsible."

She picked the pillow back up and hugged it to her chest.

I wasn't going to get anything else from her.

I got up to leave. "I'm a man of my word," I said, as I took a few steps toward the door. I stopped and turned back to her.

"I'm sorry, but I've got a long subway ride back downtown, do you think I could use the bathroom?"

"Um, okay. It's through there," she motioned toward the closed door. "It's on your right."

"Thanks."

I opened the door to find there were two others. The one on the right was the bathroom, the other was another bedroom.

The door to the bathroom was open. The door to the bedroom wasn't. I could see a slash of light coming from the space between the door and the floor. Maybe she hadn't lied when she said she wasn't alone. I was tempted to "accidentally" open the bedroom door, claiming I'd made a mistake. But before I could, she appeared behind me and flicked on the hall light. "That's it," she said, trying to hide anger in both her voice and her body, pointing to the john.

"Thanks."

I shut the door behind me. I turned on the faucet, so she couldn't hear anything, in case she was still in the hallway. There were two toothbrushes in a plastic cup. The medicine cabinet was filled with the usual. Vitamins. Aspirin. Prescription drug bottles. Hairbrush. Two razors; one a pink lady razor, the other a man's Gillette. A bra hung from atop the shower curtain. Stephenson, or Stephan, or whoever she was, was obviously not living alone.

19
WITH FRIENDS LIKE THIS

To call Bottoms Up a dive bar would be a generous assessment. It was dark and dingy and reeked from a combination of cheap beer, peanuts, and several other mysterious odors I couldn't quite identify, nor did I want to. I assumed the mutilated peanut shells littered all over were left there so no one had to bother mopping it down every once in a while.

Irish music blared from the jukebox—it sounded to me like the Chieftains. Every seat at the bar that ran the entire length of the room was occupied by older men who seemed hypnotized by a ballgame on the TV hoisted above the bar. There were no more than a dozen round tables scattered throughout the room, and most of them were unoccupied. Those that weren't represented what I like to think of as the pre-yuppy citizens of the East Village, meaning they were all likely candidates for AARP and some kind of government assistance. In short, they made up the kind of clientele I used to service when I worked up in Spanish Harlem. I liked to call them the "forgottens," not because they were forgotten but because they should be.

I had no idea what Sal looked like, but I assumed when he chose the joint he knew I'd stick out like a sore thumb. I took a quick look around, didn't see anyone vaguely resembling a waiter or waitress. The bartender was a tough-looking blonde biker chick in a tight, white T-shirt whose arms were covered with a colorful mish-mash of tats. She sported a nose ring and wore a pair of heavy, dangling earrings, which would have made it virtually impossible to make it through airport security without setting off all kinds of alarms.

I stood at the end of the bar and when she got close enough to make eye contact I ordered "whatever's on tap."

"Feeling lucky, huh?" she cracked, and I took an instant liking to her, even though I was sure she could put me down with one shot, if she wanted to. She drew the beer in what appeared to be a clean glass—hope springs eternal—then handed it to me. I dropped a ten on the bar, told her to "keep the change," and asked if she knew someone named Sal.

"I got a phone book full of guys named Sal," she said.

"Any of them here tonight?"

She looked around.

"Not yet. But be patient. I'm sure two or three of them will stumble in at some point in the evening."

"I'd appreciate it if one of them comes in looking for me, just point him in the direction of that table over there." I gestured toward one near the far wall.

"Your name? And please don't fucking tell me it's Sal."

I smiled. "Nope. Swann should do it."

"Like the bird?"

"Just like it."

I grabbed a handful of peanuts from a bowl on the bar and carried them and my brew over to the table.

It was a little past nine-thirty when a tall, thin guy wearing a black leather jacket and tight black jeans ambled into the bar. He was maybe in his early fifties, skinny, had jet black hair—obviously a bad dye job—slicked back, and it looked as if he hadn't shaved in at least a couple hours. He looked around, spotted the one thing in the joint that didn't belong—me—and headed my way.

"You Swann?"

"You Sal?"

He didn't answer. He just pulled out a chair and sat across from me.

"Something to drink?" I asked.

He shook his head.

"Sure? On me."

"This ain't no social visit, pal. How you know Nicky?"

"I'm doing a little work for him."

He gave me the skunk eye.

"Nicky works alone," he said, more a challenge than a statement of fact.

"Not that kind of work. I'm trying to help get him sprung."

"Yeah? How you gonna do that?"

"Remains to be seen. I'm hoping you're gonna help."

He shrugged.

"Before we go any further, you got something for me?"

"Like what?"

"Like..." I rubbed my thumb and forefinger together in the universal sign of money.

"I got an envelope here," he said, patting his jacket, "if that's what you mean."

"That's exactly what I mean."

He pulled a manila envelope folded in half out of an inside pocket of his leather jacket. He put it on the table in front of him. I could have reached it, but there was no way I was going to try.

"Nicky says I should give this to you. It's a shitload of dough."

"You waiting for me to sign a receipt?"

He coughed out what was probably meant to be a laugh. "That ain't the way this thing works."

In a scary case of possible déjà vu, I scanned the bar thinking it couldn't be possible but nevertheless checking to see if my partner happened to be here, "keeping an eye" on me. I was on my own, but in this neighborhood, in this bar, talking to this guy, there was a part of me who was disappointed I didn't have some backup.

"You gonna give it to me or not?" I asked, eyeing the envelope.

"Yeah. I'm gonna give it to you. Only I'm gonna give you a message first."

"I'm all ears."

"First off, this ain't the whole thing. It's half."

"I know."

"Nicky ain't the trusting type."

"Does he really think I'd cross him?"

"I don't know what the fuck he thinks, pal. I only know what he says. And he says half now, half when the job is done."

"He knows there are no guarantees, right?"

"I don't know what the fuck he knows, but if I were you, I wouldn't screw around. Whatever it is he's hiring you to do, I'd make sure you get it done. And when you do, you'll get the rest of the dough."

"How do I..."

"Nicky ain't a welsher, pal. I known him a long time I never known him not to pay off on a debt."

I never thought I'd get anywhere near my asking price, so even five grand was a nice payday.

"Okay." I reached for the envelope. He slammed his hand down on it.

"Don't do nothin' stupid, like opening it up in here."

"I was born on a Tuesday, but it wasn't yesterday."

"What's that supposed to mean?"

"Never mind." I took the envelope. It was thick enough to hold five grand. I stuck it in my inside jacket pocket.

"Now what you want to know?" He ran his hand through his thick hair. "I think I will have that drink," he said.

"Sure thing."

He cocked his head toward the bar. "Just tell Jen my regular. And tell her not to slip me that cheap shit they cram into the expensive bottle."

I brought back a scotch on the rocks for Sal and another brew for me.

He picked up the glass, raised it to eye level, sloshed the con-tents around, took a sip, and smiled. "So, Nicky says I should talk to you and maybe help you out, but I'm not so sure."

"Why's that?"

"Maybe it might not be too healthy."

"For me or Nicky?"

"This may take you by surprise, pal, but I ain't that worried about your health."

"You think I should be?"

He shook his head and took another swallow. "Just ask your damn questions, okay? I want to answer 'em, I'll answer 'em. I don't, I won't. You got till I finish this drink." He rattled the ice against the glass, to make his point. I figured I had three or four swallows before time ran out.

"This thing Nicky's in for…"

"Listen, before we go any further, I gotta check to make sure you ain't wired."

I raised my arms. "I'm not wired, pal, but suit yourself."

"Not here, man. In the john." He cocked his head toward the back of the room.

I wasn't sure this was a good idea, alone in the john with a guy named Sal who, unless that bulge in his jacket was a large cell phone… But I didn't have a choice, so I let him lead the way.

The bathroom was small and stank of Lysol. Two urinals with ice in them, one stall, a sink, a towel dispenser, and a cracked mirror smudged and streaked with such a heavy coat of grime I could hardly make out my reflection.

"Hands up against the stall," he ordered.

"Jesus, what is this some B movie? Is this really necessary?"

"You want I should turn the fuck around and get the hell out of here?"

I assumed the position—not the first time in my life—and he patted me down. Expertly. Like he'd had plenty of practice. When he finished, he didn't say anything, he just shoved me to-ward the bathroom exit.

"Now what was that you were saying?" he asked, as we settled back down at the table.

"You know what Nicky's in for, right?"

"Yeah."

"He says he didn't do it."

Sal laughed. He took another sip. I figured he had about an inch and a half left. I wanted him to slow down, but figured making that suggestion would be counterproductive.

"So?"

"He says he was framed."

He shrugged. "It happens."

"You think he's right?"

"How the fuck I know? All's I know is he's the fucking best at what he does and he ain't never been pinched yet. And he ain't shy about taking credit. Chances are, if he says he didn't fucking do it, then he probably didn't. And the fact he got nailed prob'ly means he's telling the truth. Nicky don't mess up. Nicky takes a job, it's as good as done. And he don't leave no calling cards, if you know what I mean. How they say they nailed him?"

"They claim to have physical evidence. Plus someone who's going to testify he heard the murder being planned."

"First off, he don't leave no physical evidence. Second, who the hell's gonna drop a dime on Nicky Diamond? This stinks to high heaven, pal. To high heaven." He took another swig.

"He says his girlfriend can vouch for where he was when the murder took place."

"Which one?"

"Which one?"

"Nicky's a ladies man. He likes to spread it around. I don't know nothing about his private life, but he says he was with someone, he prob'ly was."

"She says he wasn't."

Sal shrugged. "You can't count on skirts."

"You think she's lying? Like maybe she's pissed at Nicky for two-timing her and she's getting back at him?"

He took another sip. At best, I had two more. Three if the ice melted enough.

"Could be. Could be she's telling the truth, too."

"If she's telling the truth and Nicky's telling the truth, well, that presents a bit of a problem, doesn't it?"

"You say so."

"She says she got a warning not to testify for him. That's why she skipped town."

He shrugged and moved his glass back and forth on the table, the moisture leaving a small puddle. I wasn't getting anywhere, so I tried another track.

"If there was someone who wanted to frame Nicky, who do you think it would be?"

"Nicky can be a mean sonuvabitch, so it ain't like he don't got plenty of enemies."

"Like who?"

He smiled. "You want me to name names?"

"It stays here."

"Like I should trust you."

"You'd be doing Nicky a favor and I have a feeling you owe him."

"Why's that?"

"He had you bring me the dough. He's not stupid. He wouldn't have me talk to someone he knew wasn't willing to help him out, someone he couldn't trust."

"You like stories?"

"Love 'em."

"So, here's a story. I ain't saying it's true, meaning I don't swear to it. It's just shit I've picked up."

"Shit you've picked up is fine."

"See, Nicky does a lot of work for the Russian mob and the Armenian mob. Neither one of 'em likes that. They like exclusivity, if you know what I mean. And they don't like each other. You don't fuck with either of them. They're mean sons of bitches.

But if you had your choice, you'd be better off taking your chances with the Russians. The Armenians…" he shook his head. "Shit, they're fuckin' crazy. They do shit we never woulda thought of doing."

"Like what?"

"Let's just say they got a shitload of acid and plenty of bathtubs. They actually enjoy chopping people up. They got these blood feuds, man. You kill one of theirs, not only do you die, but they'll take out your whole fuckin' family. You do not fuck with the Armenians."

"But Nicky did?"

"Nicky ain't the easiest guy to get along with. And he ain't afraid of no one. He don't mind pissing people off."

"Maybe he should?"

"Maybe. Fact is, you don't want to piss off either group, which is why, if you're smart, you work for one or the other. Not both. Nicky, he thinks he's like immortal. Like his skin is fucking bulletproof. Besides, his attitude is, no one's going to fucking tell me what to do or fuck with my living. So, it's possible he was doing a little double dipping. They don't like that and these are not the kind of people you want to piss off."

He took another sip. The sands of time had just about run out on me. I just had to hope he was too much into his story to notice.

"If they were pissed, why not handle the problem permanently? Take a hit out on him."

"That ain't in my pay grade, pal, so you're gonna have to ask them."

"So, what you're saying is that it's possible someone he was working for framed him?"

"Some people say they been abducted by aliens, right? Maybe it happened, maybe it didn't." He winked.

I got his meaning. Anything was possible. Maybe this frame-up, if it was a frame-up, was put together by someone with a sense of humor and a flare for irony. Jana Monroe didn't matter.

She was just a symptom, not the disease. Collateral damage. Focusing on her could be a waste of time. Chances were, if she had been paid off, she didn't know where the dough came from. And if she was legit, and the threat to her was real, then there was no way she'd know who it came from or why. In that case, it was probably the wisest thing for her to do—take herself out of the game.

With Jana out of the equation, it made things easier. What Sal had to say made sense. This was business, pure and simple. There was a good chance Nicky stepped on toes he shouldn't have and now he was going to pay for it, whether he deserved it or not. In the end, it wouldn't be the law that brought him down, but his own kind.

"Who can I get in touch with if I want to pursue this?"

"Why the hell would you want to do that?"

"Because it's my job, and because I want to collect the second half of what's owed me."

He shook his head. "Your funeral, pal."

"I hope not."

"So, you're looking for names?"

"Yep."

He thought for a moment. "You didn't hear it from me, right?"

"I never even met you."

"There's a guy. He hangs out at this joint in Brighton Beach. He might know somethin'. But if he does, it's gonna cost you."

I patted my breast pocket, where I'd slipped the envelope. "That shouldn't be a problem."

"Name's Ivan. Squirrelly little guy. A real punk. He's always got his ear to the ground, playing the angles, always wanting to see what's in it for him. He might be able to give you some answers."

"How do I find him?"

"You don't find him, he finds you."

"How's that?"

"I can get word out to him."

"I'd appreciate it, Sal."

"I ain't in the charity business."

"This is for your friend, Nicky."

"Let me tell you somethin', pal. When it comes to Nicky, he ain't got friends. You don't think he'd take me out in a New York minute he was being paid by someone?"

"Yeah, I've had the honor of meeting Nicky, so we both know the answer to that one. How much?"

"A grand, should do it."

"Easy come, easy go," I said, as I reached into my pocket, removed the envelope, opened it, counted out ten crisp one-hundred-dollar bills and handed it to him."

Without changing his expression, he took them, folded them in half, and stuffed them into the breast pocket of his shirt. "You'll hear from me."

"The clock's ticking, Sal. I hope it won't be long."

"It'll be when it'll be."

Sal brought his glass to his lips, tilted it all the way back, and drained what little was left.

There was no mistaking it. My time was up.

20
JUST ANOTHER FRIENDLY NIGHT IN THE EAST VILLAGE

I was only a handful of blocks from my apartment, so I decided to walk home. Walking equals thinking time. Moving helps me focus my thoughts. Plus, let's face it, other than climbing the stairs to my apartment, it's pretty much the only exercise I get.

With four grand stuffed in my pocket, I walked a little faster than usual. I don't remember ever carrying that much cash. Strike that. I don't remember having that much dough in any form. Even splitting it with Goldblatt, which I actually intended to do—believe me, I was tempted not to, but guilt sometimes sidelines my worst instincts—would still leave me enough to pay off a couple hefty bills hanging over my head. And, if by some chance Nicky was straight with me, I'd get another five grand at the end of the rainbow. Not that I was counting on it. In my line of work, I've learned never to count on anything. Kinda like the suckers whose cars I used to repo when I was eking out a living back in Spanish Harlem. They counted on their dream machine being where they'd parked it the night before, only to have me turn that dream into a nightmare.

If I was any closer to figuring out the situation with Nicky Diamond, and I actually thought I was starting to look in the right direction, it seemed I was further from solving Rachel's problem.

There was something about my meeting with Kate Stephenson,

or whatever her name was, that just didn't sit right. She didn't fit the role of grieving sister. Nor did she seem to feel the least bit responsible for what happened to Rachel. Why was that, I asked myself? The only reason I could come up with was that she was somehow involved. It seemed fishy recommending someone she now claimed she barely knew. And, if it was a setup, she could have been the source of much of the information Susan Finch claimed to have received from the AfterLife.

But there was something Kate said that stuck with me. A slip of the tongue, perhaps. An annoying little voice in my head kept insisting it was more than that. It was one sentence that kept reverberating in my head. "I know him all my life." Not, "I knew him all my life." Present tense, not past, which would have made more sense. Sure, it might have been from habit, after all, he'd only been dead a few months. But was it possible he was still alive? Rachel was only informed of his death two weeks after the fact. It could be true it took that long because Kate had only just found her number. But it also could have been that she just used that as an excuse to keep Rachel from attending a funeral. Otherwise, Rachel certainly would have insisted on being there. If she didn't see the body, how could she, we, anyone, be sure he was dead?

If he was still alive, then the whole thing was a setup, an elaborate grift. Guy meets vulnerable girl. Guy learns she's got money. Guy dates girl awhile, sees she's in a fragile state. See's she's gullible. She's more than a little woo-woo out there. Guy courts girl. Makes her fall in love with him. Then, when he knows she's hooked, he pulls the rug out from under her, knowing she's going to fall apart. Enter his sister, Kate—if, in fact, she really is his sister. She bonds with Rachel. And then, supposedly to help her through this trying period in her life, she introduces her to a woman who can help her: Madame Sofia.

Just because the dots connected didn't make it true. Nevertheless, it was an angle I had to pursue.

I reached Ninth Street and Avenue A, and turned the corner

heading toward my apartment, which was just east of Avenue B. Deep in thought, I didn't notice someone who must have stepped up from behind a stoop of one of the ancient, turn of the last century tenements. By the time I realized there was someone behind me, it was too late. As I started to turn I felt a blow to the back of my head. I staggered but didn't go down. Reflexively, I swung wildly, hoping to connect with my attacker. But all I hit was air and before I could regain my balance there was another blow, this one to my mid-section, followed rapidly by another couple quick, sharp blows to my ribs. I lost my breath and dropped to my knees. I was defenseless. I tried to call out for help. At first, there was nothing. My mouth was open. Air was coming in, but words were not coming out. Finally, after what seemed much longer but was probably only a few seconds, recognizable words began to form. "Help." Weak at first. Then stronger. "Help!"

I don't know what I expected...most New Yorkers resist getting involved. But at this point I was beyond fighting back, so I could only hope that calling for help might rouse someone enough that they'd look out their window and seeing someone getting beaten, would call nine-one-one.

My attacker was now standing directly above me. He was heavyset, wearing a hoodie pulled tight across his face so he was unrecognizable. My first thought was that it might be Sal, but this guy was much shorter and stockier. He could have continued hitting me but for some reason he didn't. Had he worn himself out? Was he thinking about what to do next? Was he going to take my wallet?

I called out again.

"Help! Help! I need help here! Someone! Call the cops!" I yelled, as I tried to hoist myself up.

"Stay the fuck down, motherfucker!"

I don't take orders well. Propping myself up with one arm, while using the other as a shield to my face, I managed to get to my feet. Now we were eye to eye. He was shorter than me and, despite it being the middle of the night, he was wearing sunglasses, which hid his eyes and a good part of his face. Both his hands were balled up into fists. I don't know why he didn't follow up with more blows, but when he didn't, I took a swing at him as I continued to scream. "Someone, please, call the cops!"

"Hey! What's going on?" The voice was coming from across the street. I glanced to my left and I could see a young couple slowly headed toward me. "We're calling the cops!" the man yelled, as the woman pulled a cell phone out of her purse.

My attacker's attention turned toward the couple. I took advantage by swinging at him again. This time I managed to hit the bony part of his shoulder. Not hard enough to cause any real damage, but hard enough to slow him down. He grabbed me around the collar with both hands.

"Listen, motherfucker, mind your own fucking business, understand?"

He kneed me in the groin, and the sharp pain had me gasping for air. He let go of me and started to back away. I didn't know if it was because he was done or because he was afraid the cops were on their way.

He turned and started to slowly walk away, as if nothing had happened. When he got about twenty feet from me, he turned back to me and raised his fist, and faked a quick step back toward me. I couldn't be sure, but I thought I saw him smile.

He spun back around and headed back toward Avenue A, finally disappearing around the corner. Still trying to catch my breath, I staggered toward the closest building and leaned against it. The couple crossed the street.

"Are you okay?" asked the woman, as she put her hand on my shoulder.

"Yeah. I'll be fine in a minute. Soon as I catch my breath."

"I called the cops," said the guy. "They should be here any minute."

"Or maybe an hour," said the woman.

"Listen, guys, thanks. I really appreciate it, but there's no harm done. I'm just a little shaken, is all."

"You should wait here till the cops come," she said. "Maybe you should go to the emergency room."

"No, really. I'm fine. He didn't take anything thanks to you guys. And I live just down the block, so as soon as I get home I'll be fine."

"You're sure?" asked the guy.

"Yeah. I'm sure."

"But someone should be here when the cops come. I mean, you ought to report this, right?" he said.

"No. Really. It's not like they're going to look for him. He's long gone. Why don't you just call nine-one-one and tell them everything's okay. That the guy took off before he could do any real damage."

"Okay. If you say so. But maybe Susie's right. Maybe you ought to go to the emergency room. You know, just in case."

"And you really should report it," she added.

"I'm fine. Just a little embarrassed that I wasn't paying attention. I've lived here long enough to know better."

It took a couple minutes more, but I was finally able to convince them to drop it, and I left them standing there as I limped back to my apartment.

When I got home and looked in the mirror, I could see a big lump on my left cheek. I lifted up my shirt and saw a bruise was already beginning to form on my left side. The guy was a pro. He punched like a boxer, in short, powerful strokes.

He wasn't there to rob me and he wasn't going to kill me. He was delivering a warning to lay off. But lay off what? I was on two cases, Nicky Diamond's and Rachel's. It could have been either of them. But if I had to put money on it, I would have bet on Nicky's. After all, unless Finch or Stephenson were having me followed, they'd have no idea where I'd be at that time of night. But the people who had it in for Nicky certainly could have been tipped off by Sal, or have been aware of our meeting and followed me from the bar. If the latter was true, then I had even more reason to believe that Nicky'd been framed. Unless, of course, that's exactly what they wanted me to think.

21
THE SLAVIC CONNECTION

The next morning I met Goldblatt at a diner on Lexington Avenue, across from the Ninety-second Street Y. When I spoke to him the night before, he was excited to learn I had a task for him. He wasn't quite as excited that morning when I told him what it was.

"You want me to what?"

"I want you to stake out a building for me."

"You mean surveillance?"

"That's a fancy name for it, but yes, surveillance."

"Do you know how boring that is?"

"Yes, I do. I've spent a lifetime watching cars, which is even worse."

"I rescued you from that, you know."

"No. I don't know. If you want to take credit for changing my life, fine. But for the record, I did a lot more than just repo cars before we hooked up."

"Yeah, but you have to admit that once we partnered up the quality of your cases took a definite upswing."

"It depends what you consider an upswing. So, are you up for this or not? It's for Rachel."

"Well, I guess that makes a difference. What's the gig?"

"There's an apartment building up Lex and I want you to take photos of anyone who goes in or out."

"Why?"

"Because I have a hunch."

"What kind of hunch?"

"I'd rather not say right now."

"Why?"

"Because I don't want you to get too excited."

"You think I'm some kind of kid the night before Christmas?"

"No."

"You think this is the first time I surveilled anyone?"

"I have no idea. You don't talk much about your past. Wait. Strike that. You talk way too much about your past, but I have no idea what's true and what isn't."

"Everything that comes out of my mouth has an air of truth to it."

"I have no idea what that means, but it just proves my point. The truth is either the truth or it's a lie. There's no such thing as the 'air of truth.'"

He snorted. "That's how much you know, Swann. There are shades of the truth, and you should know that. And as for my past, let's just say some of it is shrouded in mystery for a good reason."

"Shrouded in mystery? For a good reason? Give me a break."

"Look, there are some things that are confidential, top-secret, for a reason."

"So, you're saying that there are things in your past that are confidential?"

"That's exactly what I'm saying. I've led a very interesting life, and maybe someday I'll make it public…"

"How? By writing a book?"

"You think that's impossible?"

"Nothing's impossible, but there are plenty of things that are improbable."

"Once I get the proper clearance, you'll see what I'm talking about."

"Clearance? From who?"

He made a lip-zipping gesture, running his finger across his lips. "I could tell you, but then I'd have to kill you."

"Well, I certainly wouldn't want to be the cause of you having blood on your hands, so I won't pursue this any further."

"Good."

"So, how about it? You gonna do this for us or not?"

"Yeah, yeah, I'll do it. And by the way, you're getting a real pro for this job, because it ain't my first rodeo."

I didn't have time to keep this ludicrous conversation going. Maybe someday I really would learn more about my erstwhile partner, but today wasn't the day. It was already close to eight o'clock and I wanted him in place by eight-thirty. I gave him Kate Stephan's address and started to tell him how I thought he could pull it off, but he stopped me in my tracks by putting his hand up in a gesture that said, "Stop!"

"I know how to get these jobs done. It's a lot easier now with cell phone cameras. You can be much more inconspicuous. How long you want me on this job?"

"Ideally, all day and into the evening, but I know that's unreasonable, so just do it as long as you can stand it."

"I'm trained in this stuff, Swann. If I have to, I can be there fifteen, sixteen hours. I've even trained myself not to pee for up to six hours."

I was tempted but I didn't ask what exactly that training consisted of. Instead, I just said, "That's very impressive. Obviously, I've chosen the right man for the job."

I gave him the address and told him I was especially interested in any male coming out or going into the building, but that he should photograph females, too.

"And you're not going to tell me why?"

"Not yet. But you'll know as soon as the job's over."

I rushed him through breakfast, which meant only one serving of pancakes with sausages and scrambled eggs on the side. No toast. I guess he was still on that so-called diet.

I headed him in the right direction, told him I'd check in with him every hour or two and, to get some much-needed exercise, started walking west, toward Central Park. It was a nice day and I figured maybe I'd stop by the Met and see if there was an exhibit that interested me, then maybe stroll through the park and see if I could find a softball game to watch on the Great Lawn.

I didn't get far before my phone buzzed. It was Sal.

"You got a pen or something to write this down?"

"I've got a good memory, Sal. What's up?"

"I got that information for you. You know, the name of the guy who might be able to help you, out there in Brooklyn."

"Cool. Shoot."

"His name's Ivan."

"Yes. I remember. How do I find him?"

"Coney Island. Two o'clock. Not ten to two. Not ten after two. Two fucking o'clock. Know how to get out there?"

"I do."

He either didn't hear me or didn't trust me.

"Take the F train. You know where the old Half Moon Hotel is?"

I did. It wasn't called the Half Moon anymore. As I recall, today it was nothing more than a crumbling shell of a building. But back in the early forties, in the heyday of Murder, Inc, Abe Reles, a cold-blooded killer also known as Kid Twist, became a government witness against his boss, Lepke Buchalter, in the murder of a candy store owner Joe Rosen. He also testified against a bunch of other gangsters, all of whom were convicted and executed. His final target was Albert Anastasia, who was the co-chief of Murder, Inc. Reles was put under constant guard by New York City police detectives who stashed him at the Half Moon. Early one morning, with cops guarding the door, Reles fell to his death from his sixth-floor window. It appeared as if he might have been trying to lower himself to the fifth floor using two bedsheets tied together and then to a length of wire that was attached to a valve in his room. The tabloids dubbed him "The Canary Who Could Sing, But Couldn't Fly." The cops who'd been guarding him were demoted and it was widely speculated that he'd been thrown or pushed out of the window while it was made to look as if he was trying to escape. It was the very day he was supposed to testify against Anastasia.

"When you get there, go to Nathan's. Get yourself some lunch."

"Come on, man…"

"You want this to happen, Swann, keep your fucking mouth shut and listen. After you get yourself something, make sure they pack it in a Nathan's bag. Then, head over to the hotel and stand in front of the building holding the bag and eating whatever the fuck you bought. He'll find you."

"Should I buy enough to share?"

"Listen, wise guy, just do the fuck what I tell you."

"How much is this going to cost me? Besides lunch, I mean."

"Five hundred. But if you think the information is worth more, you shouldn't hesitate to sweeten the pot. You're both taking a chance here. You know that, right? These guys do not fuck around. And I'm trusting you to keep your damn mouth shut. We never met. We never talked. Go it?"

"I have no idea who you are. How's that?"

I guess he didn't appreciate my humor, because he just hung up on me.

I had time to kill (before it killed me), so I took that walk through Central Park. It was one of those rare, perfect late spring days. Bright blue skies. A scattering of wispy clouds. The temperature hovering in the mid-seventies. Because it was the middle of the week, I had the park pretty much to myself. I'm a city boy, through and through, and Central Park is my idea of the "country." Yes, there are plenty of trees, exotic animals like pigeons, squirrels, and lately even raccoons and an occasional hawk, and grass, but the park is framed by numerous high-rises, which remind you you're never more than a half a mile from "civilization."

I walked behind the Met and crossed the East Drive. The

softball diamonds on the Great Lawn were empty because it was too early for any ball games. I found a bench near the Delacorte Theatre, facing east, and used the quiet time to try to put some things together.

I'd worked two cases at the same time before—even three—but these two were particularly vexing, though for very different reasons. I felt like I was closing in on a solution to Rachel's case. I was hoping the results of Goldblatt's stakeout would prove my hunch, but even if I was right, I knew the chances of her getting her money back were pretty slim. I'd try, of course, but the only leverage I had—getting the cops involved—was very iffy. I'd put in a call to Rudder to ask his advice. I presented him with a hypothetical close enough to the Susan Finch/Madame Sofia situation and asked him what he thought.

"These cases are very tough to prove, Henry. There has to be intent to defraud. What that means is that if this self-styled fortune teller you're talking about really believes she can do what she says, well then, it's going to be very difficult to prove fraud."

"But Paul, we're talking about talking to dead people."

"Look, Henry, do you know how many people believe in heaven and hell? Or an afterlife? Or ghosts? Or angels? Unless it's ridiculously blatant, the DA has to convince a jury that it would be impossible. What do you think are the chances of that? Especially if this person comes off as being respectable. You and I might know it's all a crock, but you'd have to provide proof that's substantial enough so that twelve men and women believe it's impossible. In my opinion, the chances of that, my friend, are pretty slim.

That wasn't very reassuring, but I've never been one to let steep odds stop me. Besides, even if it would be a steep, uphill battle, it was possible that a bluff might work. It had to work, because it might be all I had.

It would take more than an hour to get out to Coney Island on the subway, so at eleven o'clock I left the park at Seventy-ninth Street and walked downtown till I reached Lexington and Sixty-third, where I caught the F train.

I arrived a little after one, bought myself some lunch at Nathan's: a hot dog, an order of fries, and a large orange drink. I wolfed down the dog and the fries. At one-forty-five, I headed over to the Half Moon, where I leaned up against the building and polished off the fries, washing them down with what was left of the orange drink, making sure the Nathan's bag was visible.

Two o'clock on the dot, a small, scrawny dude dressed in an ill-fitting pinstriped suit and wearing a black fedora with a red feather stuck in it, approached me. He had a thin face, reminding me of a young, skinny version of Sinatra. He looked like something straight out of the forties, a throwback to the Abe Reles era, maybe? Sal was right. He did resemble a squirrel.

When he got a few feet from me he stopped, jerked his head in the direction of the subway, and indicated I should follow him. He had a slight bulge on the left side of his body. It could have been from a cell phone, but I figured that was wishful thinking. I doubted he had a carry permit, but he wasn't worried about attracting the attention of New York's Finest. It was likely they had some kind of understanding.

When we got up the stairs, he headed toward the F track, where a train back to the city was waiting. He walked all the way to the front of the train, then disappeared into it. I followed him. When I entered, I saw him sitting in the two-person seat of that front car. He indicated I should sit next to him, so I did.

"You Sal's friend?" I asked.

"If you mean do I know him, yeah, I do. But we ain't friends." He had a slight accent. Slavic. Russian. Maybe Armenian. Not that I could tell the difference. His teeth were yellow and crooked, like there were too many of them to fit into his mouth.

"You know Nicky Diamond?"

He nodded.

"A friend?"

"Diamond's got friends?"

"You tell me."

"If you know what's good for you, you don't get too close to Nicky. He's toxic. Like Chernobyl."

"I guess you do know him."

A bell dinged. The doors closed. The train started to move. I looked around. We were the only two in the car.

"Where we going?"

He shrugged. "I like trains. I like movies, too. You know *The French Connection?*"

"I do."

"They filmed it out here."

"Live and learn."

He was referring to the subway chase, with Popeye Doyle chasing the assassin who's tried to kill him.

"We got business to conduct, right?"

I removed the envelope with the five one-hundred-dollar bills in it, and handed it to him. He didn't bother opening it before he stuck it in his pocket.

"Aren't you going to make sure it's all there?"

He gave me a hard look that I immediately understood. Why would I want to fuck with him?

"How far we going?"

"I like trains, but I ain't got all day. I hate the fucking city."

I took that to mean we'd be finished before the train headed under the East River.

"Did Sal tell you why I wanted to talk to someone like you?"

"Why don't you tell me."

The train reached the next station. The doors opened. No one got in. I realized the genius of this meet. Because of the time of day, very few people would be hopping the train headed into Manhattan, and since we were in the first car, it would probably remain the emptiest. And if someone did come in, he or she would be in full view of Ivan, which put him pretty much in control of the situation.

I gave him the CliffNotes version of what was going on with

Nicky, but I didn't think I was telling him anything he didn't already know. All the time I was talking he never looked at me once. I don't know what was creepier. That he didn't look at me or if he had.

When I finished, which took two more stops putting us closer to "the border," all he said was, "So?"

"I want to know who might have it in for Nicky, enough to frame him, assuming he didn't do it."

Almost imperceptibly, he shook his head.

"You mean he didn't do it?"

"It means what you want it to mean."

"Did he do it or didn't he?"

He turned to face me for the first time. "You some kind of moron?"

"I just want to be sure I understand you."

"What you do with a picture."

"Frame it."

He nodded. We pulled into another station. An elderly woman, carrying a Pioneer Market shopping bag got on and sat at the other end of the car.

"By who?"

"Why do you need to know that? You ain't no cop, right?"

"Right."

"Then what the fuck do you care who did it?"

"I want to be convinced Nicky didn't."

He turned away from me again. "You got your answer."

"Hypothetically, why would someone want to frame him?"

"Use your fuckin' brain. To get him off the fuckin' streets. To pay him back."

"For what?"

"He pissed someone off, what's the difference who? What's the difference how? What's the difference why?"

"Look, Ivan, I'm working for Nicky's lawyer. He's paying me to find information that can exonerate his client. I have no skin in this game, other than doing my job. All I need is a plausible explanation. One I can take to my employer and one he can use in court. Then I'm off the clock. That's why I'm paying you the five hundred bucks for six subway stops' worth of information."

"You got your money's worth. But in case you want me to spell it out, here goes. Nicky likes to work two sides of the street. He don't care if he pisses someone off. The fuckin' guy thinks he's like invincible. He does it for the money but he also does it because he thinks he can. Someone don't like that. Someone don't like Nicky. Someone thinks he's too fuckin' big for his britches. Someone decides to do something about it."

"Why not just have him killed?"

He laughed. "That'd be too easy. They want him to suffer. What's worse than death for a guy like Nicky is to be played. That's what they're doing. Playing him. You don't think someone's got a hard-on watching him sit in the can, then go on trial and be convicted of something he didn't do after everything he has done? What do they call that?"

"Poetic justice?"

"That's it."

The train slowed down, ready to pull into another station. Ivan stood up. He was done. As far as he was concerned I'd gotten my five hundred bucks' worth.

I grabbed his wrist. "Ivan. One more thing."

He turned to me. "Yeah?"

"The girl. Is she in on it?"

He smiled. "What girl?"

"His girlfriend. Jana."

"I don't know the particulars, man. Even if I did, I wouldn't be spilling them to you. You wanna know the answer to that, you're gonna have to ask her."

The train stopped. The doors opened. Ivan started to leave. I got up and grabbed him by the shoulder.

"Russians or Armenians?" I asked.

He turned around and looked me straight in the eye. "You like borscht?" he asked.

22
THE JIG IS UP

I've learned very little in my life that couldn't be summed up in two statements: "No good deed goes unpunished," a truism uttered by Clare Boothe Luce, and "What goes around comes around," which has been attributed to death row inmate Paul Crump, in his memoir, *Burn, Killer, Burn.* He knew what he was talking about. Crump had been scheduled to die in the electric chair fifteen times, but eventually had his sentence commuted to one hundred ninety-nine years in prison. He was later paroled but returned to prison after being convicted of harassing a family member.

The former has severely limited the favors I've done people, while the latter, if true, and I'm not always so sure it is, provides a certain amount of justice in the world. I felt bad for Paul Rudder, but I assumed he'd get compensated well for his efforts, while also upholding his responsibility to the rule of law. But the idea that Diamond would pay for his crimes, even if it was for a crime he didn't commit, made me feel pretty damn good. It's not the way it's supposed to work, but what's the difference so long as it does work?

The only real victim here might be Jana Monroe, but I had a feeling she'd land on her feet. She was young. She was beautiful. She was probably out of danger. The mob wouldn't care about her, so long as she remained silent, so long as Nicky was out of the way. And Nicky was in no position to hurt her—even if he could I was pretty sure he'd realize there was no sense in it. Hurting her or killing her wouldn't get her to testify on his behalf and besides, he had far more dangerous enemies than Jana Monroe. As for that second five grand I was forfeiting? Well, I didn't have it yesterday and so not having it tomorrow wouldn't matter all that much. Believe me, the gravy train has passed me by before and it'll pass me by again. By this point in my life I was used to riding steerage.

By the time I got back into the city, it was nearly five o'clock. I changed trains to the five and headed up to relieve Goldblatt. I figured if he hadn't gotten what I needed by this time, it wasn't to be gotten.

He wasn't hard to spot. He'd found a small café directly across the street that had an open sight line to the building and he was sitting at a table by the window, nursing a soda.

"How's it going?" I asked, as I pulled out a chair and sat down.

"Time's just flying by," he said. He wasn't smiling.

"Let's see what you got."

"Not exactly Grand Central," he said, as he handed me his cell phone. I whisked through several dozen photos, each one of them perfectly framed, and clear enough so that I could easily make out faces. Maybe he wasn't lying when he claimed to be an old hand at this kind of thing.

"Good enough for you?"

"Are you kidding? These are great. Just what I wanted."

"Now what?"

"Now, you call Rachel and we meet up with her and show her these photos."

"Why?"

"You'll see. Give her a call, okay?"

He got her on the phone and told her we'd be down to see her in an hour.

We met her in Midtown at a small Irish bar on Second Avenue, not far from where she worked. I watched intently as she scrolled through Goldblatt's photos.

"Oh, my God," she said, as her face paled.

"What is it?" Goldblatt asked. "It's like you've seen a ghost."

"She has," I said.

"What do you mean?"

"It's…Michael. He's alive."

"That's what I thought. And that's how Madame Sofia knew so much about you. And him. She got it straight from the source."

"Oh, my God!"

If looks could kill, the look on Goldblatt's face would have turned him into Nicky Diamond.

"Son of a bitch," he hissed.

"Among other things," I said.

"I…I can't believe…it," said Rachel.

"I'm sorry about this, Rachel. But I'm afraid the whole thing was a setup."

"From the beginning?"

The look on her face made it impossible to tell her the truth. No harm would be done if I didn't.

"I don't think so. There's no way they could have known about you beforehand. I think it was a crime of opportunity. I think when he met you out there in San Francisco he really did like you. And probably more than a little. And I'm sure when you guys got back to the city his feelings grew. But at some point, who knows when and who knows why…maybe he needed money…he saw an opportunity and it turned into something else. We could confront him and find out…"

"I don't ever want to see him again," she sputtered.

"Well, I do," said Goldblatt.

"Easy, big fellow. The most important thing is to try to get Rachel's money back."

"What about her self-respect? What about some justice for that little douchebag?"

"She has nothing to be embarrassed about. She had genuine

feelings for him and he took advantage. That's on him, not her."

"So, what are you going to do?" Rachel asked.

"What would you like me to do, Rachel?"

"Yeah, what would you like us to do?" parroted Goldblatt.

"I...I don't know."

"Well, while you think about it, I'm going to see Susan Finch and see what I can do about getting you back your dough. Or, at least some of it."

"That's fine," said Goldblatt, "but that doesn't mean I'm not going to take this further."

"That's up to you, Goldblatt. But before you screw up any opportunity to get the money back, let me deal with it, okay?"

It wasn't easy, but I was finally able to calm him down. As for Rachel, the poor kid was really in a bad way. I could only hope she had some of those anti-depressants left. Eventually, I was sure she'd be okay, sure she'd get through it. But I certainly wouldn't have wanted to be around her for the next few days.

23
WHAT'S A GIRL LIKE YOU DOING WITH A GUY LIKE ME?

It was a Hail Mary kind of thing, but I had nothing to lose.

Let's face it. Goldblatt was mad as hell.

Rachel was embarrassed and depressed.

Nicky Diamond was going down for the count.

Paul Rudder was going to lose a case he probably should have won.

For a change, the only one coming out of this with anything was probably me.

What, you ask? For one thing a few extra bucks in my pocket from the Diamond case. Sure, I wouldn't see anything else, like that extra five grand, but even so, I was way ahead of the game. Even though I'd probably not see a dime from Goldblatt for working his ex-wife's case, I had to have earned at least a few brownie points for helping him out. And it wasn't over yet. Maybe I could get at least part of the dough back from Madame Sofia. The fact that I had proof that Michael was still alive was worth something, even though the chances of getting her on fraud charges were slim. It would have taken me more time and effort to make the connection necessary, to prove Finch knew Michael and the woman who claimed to be his sister which, by the way, I didn't believe for a minute. More likely, she was his girlfriend or maybe even his wife. And that proof would have been necessary for any kind of criminal action to stick. But maybe I could help everyone by turning this into a civil case, like the Goldmans did with O. J. If I could get Rudder to take the case, then everyone would wind up enjoying that sweet smell of success—and I'd make sure that I cut myself in for a piece of the action.

But first, I wanted to meet with Finch to see if I could bluff her into giving back the dough. It was a long shot, but what did I have to lose? Besides, I kind of liked her and wouldn't have minded seeing her again. I considered ambushing her, but I figured it was better just to set up a meeting. So, I gave her a call and turned on the charm.

"Why on earth do you think I'd even consider seeing you again, now that I know what you're up to?"

"Because you're a woman and you're curious why I want to see you."

"And…?"

"You kinda like me."

She laughed. "You do have a set of brass balls, don't you?"

"I have a hard time finding them, so I have no idea what they're made of. So, how about it? I'll come over your way and buy you a drink. Doesn't that sound appealing?"

"I'm going to say yes not because I 'kinda like' you, but because I'm curious as to what you're going to say to me to try and get me to hand over any money."

Me, too, I thought. We arranged to meet at nine o'clock at a little joint on the corner of Seventy-second and Columbus.

She was waiting at the bar when I arrived. Dressed in a pair of stressed blue jeans, black boots, and a black, scoop-neck, short-sleeved blouse, she looked prettier than I'd remembered. That, of course, gave her an advantage. But she was probably well aware of the effect when she chose her outfit.

I slid into the seat next to her.

"I see you've already started," I said, gesturing toward the half empty glass of white wine.

"It's been a tough day. It takes the edge off."

The bartender, a young, muscular stud wearing a pale blue polo shirt, appeared. I ordered a brew. "And another one for the lady, when she's ready."

He nodded and went to work.

"I almost didn't come, you know," she said, as she brought her glass to her lips, polishing off what was left.

"What tipped the scales?"

"Curiosity."

"That all?"

"Maybe."

"You're supposed to be the mind reader, not me."

"I think we all have the ability, we just don't all know how to tap it."

"But you do."

"Yes, I do."

"How long have you had this...gift?"

"Probably all my life, but I didn't realize it till I was a teenager."

"Nice to have a calling."

The bartender appeared with a beer for me and another white wine for Finch.

"Ever hear of Freddie Patton?"

She smiled. I took that as a yes.

"He's a friend."

"I didn't realize he was still alive."

"Yeah. So far."

"And your point is?"

"Just wondering if you were aware of his work."

"I am. He's quite the showman."

"Yeah, he's very entertaining. But he's also got a calling."

"Really?"

"I'm sure you know all about it, Susie."

She arched her eyebrows. "No one calls me Susie."

"Yeah, well, you just kinda look like a Susie to me."

"Is that supposed to be a compliment?"

"Maybe. Sure. I wouldn't bother using a nickname if I didn't like someone."

"So, you like me?"

"Despite what you do for a living, I guess I do."

"You don't approve?"

"Not really."

"I guess that's why you're here. Should we maybe get to the point?"

"Sure. Why not?" I took out my phone and scrolled to the Goldblatt's photo of Michael emerging from the apartment building.

"Am I supposed to know who this is?" she said innocently, although her body language wasn't in synch with her answer. For one thing, she looked away from me and the photo before answering. And then she lowered her eyes and picked up her drink, stared at it a moment, then put it back down without taking a sip.

"Let's pretend for the moment that you don't. You've got this gift, so maybe you can divine who he is and why I'm bothering to show you his photo."

"I don't really have time for these games," she said in that snippy, dismissive tone most women have mastered by their teens, along with the eye roll and the hair flip.

"I don't play games, Susie. We both know who this is; the only question is how far are we going to take this?"

"What do you mean?"

"Let's cut to the chase, and then maybe we can talk about more pleasant things."

"Like?"

"Oh, I can think of a few. But not before we settle this once and for all."

"Meaning Rachel?"

"Bingo."

"There's nothing to settle."

"How about a refund and we'll just forget any of this happened?"

"I don't do refunds. All sales are final."

"Maybe you ought to consider a change in policy."

"That's bad business."

"Funny, I think it's very good business. Especially, if it keeps you out of the clink."

She laughed. "Oh, I don't see that happening."

"Why's that?"

"Because you'd have to prove I intentionally defrauded her, and I just don't think you can do that. The cops have better things to do with their time than to go after little, old me."

"Well, let's just agree to disagree. Let me put it as plain as I can. You either give back the dough, or I go to the DA and have Rachel press charges."

"Do you really think that's the best thing for her?"

"I don't make calls like that, Susie. I'm a hired hand. I'm paid to find you and get the money back. Besides, I have enough trouble figuring out the best thing for me, much less anyone else."

"Well, Henry, I guess you'll just have to do what you have to do."

"That's your final answer?"

She nodded.

I had to smile, only I didn't. Somehow, threats seem to lose a little power when you're smiling while making them.

The final decision was Rachel's, but if she asked my advice, and I doubted she would, I would probably tell her to file the whole nasty matter under Lessons Learned and move on with her life. But if she was going to do anything, I'd urge her to go the civil route. Otherwise, the situation would be spread all over the tabloids. Did she really want to see her face splashed across the front page of the *New York Post*? Knowing what little I knew about Rachel, she was much too fragile for that. Besides, the only one who had any real influence over her was Goldblatt, so I'd just hand the ball over to him and let him figure it out.

I was pretty sure I could provide the evidence and the connections to prove she was defrauded, but the idea of a prolonged criminal investigation and then a trial, was not, I thought, in Rachel's best interest. And in the end, maybe the threat of civil action was more likely to bear fruit, and it might not even have to go to court.

I'd let Goldblatt decide all that. I'd done my job and so for me, it was over.

Right now, all I felt like doing was finishing this drink with Madam Sofia, and then see where things went from there.

24

IN THE LONG RUN, WE ARE ALL DEAD, AREN'T WE?

There is that moment of exhilaration after a case is over. It lasts about fifteen minutes and then reality sets in. That reality, put simply, translates to: what happens now?

Two cases had ended simultaneously. For me, at least. It wasn't over for Nicky Diamond nor was it over for Rachel. But I was no longer part of either of their lives. Nicky would probably spend the rest of his life a guest of the state, while Rachel would, undoubtedly, keep making bad choices. That was their fate, but what about mine?

Therein lies the answer to the question, what happens now? I've faced that question too many times to count, but I've never come up with a satisfactory answer. But maybe the answer was not to even bother asking the question. I mean, what good does it do? As the German cleric Thomas à Kempis once wrote: "Man proposes, God disposes." He was probably right. What's the point of trying to figure out what you're doing next when we really don't know, and even if we did know, we would probably screw it up ourselves or someone else would screw it up for us.

People, including myself, are always looking for answers. That's why they go to the Madame Sofias of the world. If they get themselves to believe that someone more powerful, more knowing than they are, presents them with an answer that answer is right. I couldn't help but wonder if folks like Freddie Patton, who essentially believed it was all a crock of shit, were the ones who really knew the truth. Simply put, there is no truth.

I held my breath when I reported back to Goldblatt my advice that Rachel was pretty much in a no-win situation.

"What about the dough?"

"What about it? You were a lawyer..."

"Still am."

"Weren't you disbarred?"

"Just a technicality. Once a lawyer always a lawyer. I know the law. That's what makes me a lawyer."

"Okay, I'm not going to argue with you. What I was going to say is that you understand the situation. It's not going to be a high priority case for the cops, and even if it was, do you think Rachel's in any condition to go through what she's going to have to endure, if she presses charges?"

He didn't answer, but I knew he agreed. He was probably thinking about how he was going to break it to his ex-wife.

"She could go the civil route, and maybe win the case and get back at least some of the money, but do you think it's worth it? Maybe she should just walk away. I mean, she's got a job. She didn't lose all her money. Maybe this will have a positive effect on how she leads the rest of her life."

"You mean teach her not to trust anyone?"

"Yeah. A lesson you and me probably learned a long time ago."

He shrugged. "I hate giving in, but you're probably right. I can probably make up for some of the dough she lost."

"Excuse me?"

"You know, make restitution for her."

"You're in a position to do that?"

"I don't usually discuss my financial situation with anyone except my money guy."

"You've got a financial situation? You've got a money guy?"

"Doesn't everyone?"

"No. Everyone most definitely does not. And if you're so well off financially, why are we always scrounging around for clients?"

"Man has to have a purpose, Swann. Right?"

"A purpose, huh?" I rolled the words over in my head. "What's mine?"

He smiled and patted me on the shoulder.

"Me," he said. And you know something? I think he meant it.

ACKNOWLEDGMENTS

I'd like to thank all the usual suspects, which means all my friends, students, and former students who keep reading these books, which keeps me writing them. A few names deserve to be repeated because they never complain about using their names and sometimes humiliating them by doing so. Mark Goldblatt (who bears absolutely, positively, definitely no resemblance to *Goldblatt*), Ross Klavan, Mary Jones, and Janet Kirby. And then there's my high school buddy, Elliot Ravetz, who I always go to for guidance and literary advice. The MWA community has always been incredibly supportive, including fellow writers Reed Farrel Coleman, Hank Phillippi Ryan, Michael Sears, David Swinson, Tim O'Mara, SJ Rozan, Suzanne Solomon, Richie Narvaez, R.G. Belsky, Joe Clifford, Rich Zahradnik, Tom Straw, Chris Knopf, and I'll stop there, although I'm sure I've missed so many others.

I'd also like to thank "the girls," Sally Koslow, Mindy Greenstein, and Linda Yellin, my fellow writers who meet once a month for lunch to dish about writing and so many other things. And my good pal, Roy Hoffman, who introduced me to what I now think of as my second home, Fairhope, Alabama, and his wife, Nancy Hoffman, who puts up with my visits and with Roy and me going off on "excursions" when I'm down there. And my Fairhope friends, Mark and Nancy Johnson and Lynn and Corie Jonge, and Susie Bowman, who always make me feel at home when I'm down there.

And then there are the folks at Down & Out Books, who gave Swann a second home when he lost his first. Thanks, Eric Campbell and Lance Wright.

Thanks to Chris Rattigan for his spot-on edits, and to Sharon Gurwitz and her "hawk eyes," for picking up on so many of the small errors before readers do.

And finally, to all my students, present and past, who inspire me with their own work.

CHARLES SALZBERG is the author of the Shamus Award-nominated *Swann's Last Song* as well as the sequels *Swann Dives In*, *Swann's Lake of Despair* and *Swann's Way Out*. He is also author of *Devil in the Hole*, which was chosen as one of the Best Crime Novels of 2013 by *Suspense Magazine*, and *Second Story Man*, winner of the Beverly Hills Book Award. He is one of three of the contributing authors to *Triple Shot* and *Three Strikes*. A member of the board of the Mystery Writers of America-New York, he lives in New York City and teaches writing at the Writer's Voice and the New York Writers Workshop, where he is proud to be a Founding Member.

CharlesSalzberg.com

BOOKS

On the following pages are a few
more great titles from the
Down & Out Books publishing family.

For a complete list of books and to
sign up for our newsletter,
go to DownAndOutBooks.com.

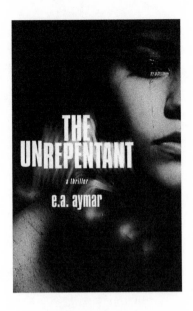

The Unrepentant
E.A. Aymar

Down & Out Books
March 2019
978-1-948235-58-7

Eighteen-year old Charlotte Reyes ran away from an abusive home only to end up tricked, kidnapped, and taken across the country by criminals. Charlotte manages to escape with the help of a reluctant former soldier named Mace Peterson, but she can't seem to shake the gang.

With nowhere to run and nowhere to hide, Charlotte realizes she only has one option.

She has to fight.

Drago Descending
Greg F. Gifune

Down & Out Books
April 2019
978-1-948235-79-2

PI David Drago is a former policeman and Gulf War veteran struggling with his combat experiences, his time spent in a psychological ward, and the darkness of his past. When he is approached by a mysterious client who hires him to locate his missing fiancé, Drago hesitantly takes the case. The problem, she is also Drago's former girlfriend, the love of his life and still an intricate part of the darkness haunting him.

Drago's investigation leads him into a labyrinth of violence, sexual intrigue, black witchcraft and hardcore Satanism. The deeper he digs, the deeper he descends into a dark netherworld haunted by visions that blur the lines between reality and nightmare.

The Hurt Business
Stories by Mike Miner

All Due Respect, an imprint of
Down & Out Books
March 2019
978-1-948235-75-4

"We are such fragile creatures."

The men, women and children in these stories will all be pushed to the breaking point, some beyond. Heroes, villains and victims. The lives Miner examines are haunted by pain and violence. They are all trying to find redemption. A few will succeed, but at a terrible price. All of them will face the consequences of their bad decisions as pipers are paid and chickens come home to roost. The lessons in these pages are learned the very hard way. Throughout, Miner captures the savage beauty of these dark tales with spare poetic prose.

The Furious Way
Aaron Philip Clark

Shotgun Honey, an imprint of
Down & Out Books
May 2019
978-1-64396-003-6

Lucy Ramos is out for blood—she needs to kill a man, but she has no clue how. Lucy calls on the help of aged hit-man, Tito Garza, now in his golden years, living a mundane life in San Pedro.

With a backpack full of cash, Lucy persuades Garza to help her murder her mother's killer, ADA Victor Soto. Together, the forgotten hit-man hungry for a comeback and the girl whose life was shattered as a child, set out to kill the man responsible. But killing Victor Soto may prove to be an impossible task...

CPSIA information can be obtained
at www.ICGtesting.com
Printed in the USA
LVHW111133280519
619152LV00012B/981/P